THE STORY OF MY BALDNESS

THE STORY OF MY BALDNESS

MAREK VAN DER JAGT

translated from the Dutch
by DR. TODD ARMSTRONG

Other Press • New York

This publication has been made possible with financial support from the Foundation for the Production and Translation of Dutch Literature. NLPVF (Nederlands Literair Productie-En Vertalingenfonds)

Production Editor: Robert D. Hack
Text design: Natalya Balnova
This book was set in Janson Text by Alpha Graphics of Pittsfield, NH.

10 9 8 7 6 5 4 3 2 1

Library of Congress Cataloging-in-Publication Data
Jagt, Marek van der, 1967-
    [Geschiedenis van Mijn Kaalheid. English]
    The story of my baldness / by Marek van der Jagt ; translated from the Dutch by Todd Armstrong.
        p. cm.
    ISBN 1-59051-122-0 (hardcover : alk. paper)
    I. Armstrong, Todd.   II. Title.
    PT5881.2.A34G4713 2004
    839.31'37–dc22

                                              2004012956

1

How Old Women Can Get Rich

I went bald early. Early baldness had always been looming out there, but that it would arrive so early, that still came as a surprise to me.

This is the story of that baldness, and after this I have absolutely no intention of putting another word on paper.

Some writers only have one book in them; they write about a war, a gruesome illness, a missing daughter found four years later at the bottom of a well. The story of my baldness pales by comparison, but even pale stories can be important.

Mama was a cool and stately woman who did good things for the poor, but still couldn't bear to go on vacation without her case of diamonds.

She died precisely three weeks after my eighteenth birthday.

Within a year Papa remarried, to Eleonore.

Papa wasn't as stately as Mama. He ate like a pig, even during official dinners, something for which Mama never forgave him. Maybe she suspected that he had married her for her family's reputation, and a bit for her money as well. Papa worked like a madman to dispel this misunderstanding, but Mama said: "Whenever I'm around your father I smell poverty."

Eleonore had already lost two husbands; one in a car crash, the other to cancer. After the death of her second husband she was so overcome by sorrow that she decided to make lots of money. And that's exactly what she did. And about the garnering of all that money she wrote a book, entitled *How Old Women Can Get Rich*.

It was a smash hit. Not only in Germany, Switzerland, and Austria, but in many other countries as well.

About three times a month she'd say: "They've just published another edition. What a success, Marek, what a gigantic success." That was how she reminded me of my own failed ambitions to write.

Papa's friends regarded Eleonore's wealth as proof that he could love only rich women, but the truth is that he himself had put together a tidy nest egg before he even met her.

On the day he married for the second time, Papa waltzed with Eleonore, and whispered in my ear: "The best marriages are marriages of convenience, Marek. Passion is for hysterical women."

Mama did a great deal for poor people and needy artists, but she also had her moments of excess. Countless poor artists had become her lover, though I hasten to add that no connection should be seen between the poverty of the artist in question and my mother's affection. For her, it was not a case of "the poorer the better." Some of her lovers became jealous, and at one point my mother bought herself an elegant little handgun, which she used at our house one evening to shatter a chandelier.

One Sunday afternoon when Papa and Eleonore had taken me along to Eisenstadt, because they knew an absolutely wonderful little restaurant there and because they felt that I, as the youngest, had suffered most under Mama's death, I said: "Eleonore, isn't it about time you wrote a sequel? *How Young Women Can Get Rich*?" But she pretended not to hear, and said: "This restaurant is so romantic, Ferdi."

She was very unlike Mama; she despised needy people, and she had an aversion to handguns too.

Until an unfortunate fall took Mama from this life, I wrote poems in the tradition of Paul Celan. That I stopped writing poetry had nothing to do with that fall; by that time I wasn't writing much anyway. The fall was merely the coup de grace.

But at the age of fourteen, I considered myself as an artist. I organized literary salons in our living room, and if Mama was in a good mood she would come and sing for us. As a young woman, Mama had been an opera singer, and a good one at that, until she had her first child.

Most of the people I invited to my salons were classmates and neighborhood children. Mama had a huge collection of hats. We were all allowed to pick out a hat and wear it. The girls rummaged through her drawers full of cosmetics, and put on makeup at her huge dressing-room mirror. The boys smoked cigars, for my mother had no objections to tobacco. She smoked long, thin cigarettes herself, and occasionally encouraged a child to talk about his or her father. And so I sat there in my salon, with my non-alcoholic cocktails, my pistachio nuts, my velvet gown, my salmon on toast, and my mama in her evening dress, who would sing light opera and, if we begged her, would later read from Rilke as well. By "we," to be honest, I'm referring to myself; the others were more interested in the hats and cigars, although you had a few who pounced on the salmon as if they hadn't eaten for three weeks.

A few of the parents complained to my mama: "Do you really think children that age should be smoking cigars?" But she would always say: "You have your opinions, I have mine. I have nothing against tobacco." That's the way Mama was.

Helmuth, a slightly autistic and backward child with whom no one else wished to associate, was always invited too.

Mama loved Helmuth. In unguarded moments she bought him clothes he never wore, because her taste and that of Helmuth's parents did not coincide.

Papa's colleagues found Mama a bit eccentric, but when you have the kind of money she did, that almost went without saying. No one ever asked her: "Is that really such a good idea?" or "Isn't that a bit extreme?" In fact, no one ever really disagreed with her at all, because she didn't like being disagreed with.

Mama had not conquered much of the world, only a little patch of ground. But over that patch she ruled like an empress. Her name was Constanza. And she hated it when people called her that.

We chased each other around the garden in Mama's hats. Mama would tell the maids to make lots of sorbet and, once the sorbet had been spooned up, the songs sung, and the cigars smoked, she would collect the hats and say: "And now I want you all to leave me alone."

Mama could spend hours staring at her hat collection. Sometimes I would come and stand beside her, and she would put her arm around me and say: "If only these hats could talk."

I have two brothers. Daniel, the oldest, fainted at least twenty times a year. People said he was anemic. Now he's the rather famous director of a symphony orchestra.

Pavel, who's between us in age, is a brilliant economist. He calls me up regularly to say that I should learn to think more practically, and above all to live more practically. He works for the World Bank; on some planes he has his own bedroom.

Six years after I was born, my mother became pregnant for the fourth time. It was to be a girl. But it wasn't a girl, it was a miscarriage.

It fell into the toilet.

"It slipped away from me," she said.

At dinner that evening, Papa said to Mama: "You can't do anything."

Then he turned to us and said: "Your mother can't do anything. Not even have a baby."

Still later that evening, I heard him weeping in the bathroom, and I know for a fact that he wasn't weeping because Mama couldn't do anything, but because his daughter had fallen dead into the toilet.

"It wasn't a person yet, it was a clump of blood," said Mama, who chose to express herself in graphic terms, and who reported even on a miscarriage as though it was a wildlife documentary. "And my stomach hurt, like I'd eaten a rotten mussel."

"Enough is enough!" Papa shouted.

I myself, as already noted, began writing obscure verse at the age of fourteen, much to the chagrin of my mama, who would have liked to see me become a ballet dancer. And to the irritation of my father, for poems had nothing to do with success.

My second book of poems, which, like its predecessor, I stapled together with my own hands, was entitled *Dead Languages*.

I sent that book to every publisher I could find, including twenty-four houses I'd never heard of. No one wanted it. One of them even wrote at the bottom of the rejection slip: "Your language is, indeed, dead."

When the fifteenth rejection slip arrived, I bought a camera, just to be sure. Photography was not poetry, but a lot of people still considered it a creative profession.

In parks I hid among the shrubbery and photographed the human animal.

Everything I did I did to be sure, I lived to be sure. Until I started going bald.

My baldness began with Blondie. With the singer Blondie, and, to be perfectly precise, with her number "Call Me."

I was sitting in a café, one of Vienna's many coffeehouses. In front of me on the table was a ring binder containing summaries of important philosophical works.

Mama had been dead for three years, but I must admit that the demise of my book of poetry affected me more deeply than Mama's had.

The woman across from me, who was nipping at an Irish coffee, suddenly leaned over and said: "Don't you just love this song?"

Strangers often speak to me. I've been blessed with an appearance that people seem to enjoy seeing. I'm of average height, my shoulders are broad, my hair is brown and shiny with a wave to it, and my skin is clear and olive-colored. Many people think I'm Brazilian. As far as I have been able to ascertain, I have no Brazilian blood in me.

I admit that the interest in myself tended to wane when I began talking about *Dead Languages*, but as long as I kept nodding silently I was able to spend entire evenings in the company of the loveliest men and women.

I didn't understand what the woman with the Irish coffee wanted from me. So I smiled. I have no patience with boorishness. There may be those who regard politeness as an empty form, yet even empty forms are preferable to no form at all.

"The music," she said, "nice, isn't it? *Call me*, do you know what that means?"

Despite my good looks, I have never thought of myself as a charmer. On the contrary: people, be they men, women, or children, did not particularly interest me. At least not any more; they had interested me once, it's true, but interest, too, must be a two-way street. I wanted to wake the dead. Charmers must not focus on the dead, but on the smiles of the living.

The lady across the table wore a fur coat, I figured she was in her early fifties. But I'm not good at guessing ladies' ages. Her sunglasses were lying on the table. The name of the designer was clearly embossed on one of the earpieces.

"Don't you like it?"

"I prefer classical music," I said. "That's what I was brought up on."

She took a sip of her Irish coffee and laughed.

"Isn't it about time you started bringing up yourself?"

"I'm studying philosophy," I said.

She pursed her lips, as though to say that she thought my reply was of a dubious nature. But then again, maybe she just wanted to show me her lips.

"And I also do tutoring," I said.

"Who do you tutor?" she asked.

"People."

"Young, old?"

"Primarily young people," I said. "People with. . . ." I searched for the right word and finally chose "learning disabilities." That covered a lot of ground.

The color of her lips reminded me of ski vacations. Papa loved ski vacations. If there was any such thing as happiness, something about which he had grave doubts, if there was such a thing, then for him it was synonymous with going faster and faster down a snowy hillside.

"Learning disabilities," she said mockingly.

"Actually, at this moment I'm tutoring only one boy," I said. "His name is Max. His learning disabilities are rather unique."

"Do learning disabilities interest you?" she asked, and again I heard that mockery.

Not so long before this I had considered myself an artist, and I believed that isolation and artistry went hand in hand. Until I noticed that I was completely alone in that delusion. I started studying philosophy, I earned my money as a tutor, I became a tutor.

Perhaps I had never given in to relations with others simply because I believed that isolation would be good for my poetry. I had given in to relations with dead languages, to paper, to books, to theories about love, to plates of pistachio nuts, to Mama's hats. My naivete, which those around me drew to my attention from time to time, I regarded as a virtue. I still see a certain degree of naivete as a virtue; cynicism is the weapon of the vanquished.

Of course there had been a few brief romances in my life, but of those I remember mostly the relief when the entanglement came to an end, when my flesh parted from the flesh of the other and one could once again speak of separate fleshes. A romance was, I had discovered, above all a speechless thing; it leaves you at a loss for words, in search of that one word that won't destroy everything.

I had deserted and been deserted; one time I was traded in for a brilliant cellist, but none of it felt as though it really had anything to do with me, it felt as though it was about someone else. One was better off not allowing physical love to become an emotional matter.

"Doesn't my choice of studies please you?" I asked, just to be polite. "Had you expected something else? People often mistake me for a music student."

"Philosophy, *ach, ja,*" the lady said. "And do you have a favorite philosopher?"

I wanted to give her a well-considered reply, a reply that would attest to the skill of applying knowledge, the kind of reply that budding philosophers are supposed to give, but she had already stood up and walked away.

Her sunglasses and handbag were still on the table.

I went on reading in my ring binder. I have my mother's elegant bearing, but my father's timidity.

Even at the very first encounter, I agonize at the thought of disappointing the other person. An agony of the sort that usually rules out anything but that first meeting. If I do happen to desire someone, then I do so in silence. And preferably at a thousand kilometers' remove, or twenty-five years later. Or, even better, with the grave between.

Five minutes later she came back. She didn't sit down again.

"In the ladies' room," she said, "under the towels, is a matchbox. If you take that with you, then you'll know where I'll be waiting for you tomorrow at four."

Standing, she took another swig, pouted her lips for the umpteenth time, and put on her sunglasses.

Once again, I was reminded of our skiing holidays, Papa schussing down hill after hill and Mama waiting in the hotel lobby with her coat on. If she talked to anyone, it was always to the personnel. Sometimes she would say to a passing waiter: "Keep me company for a while."

"How do I get into the ladies' room?" I asked.

The question seemed to amuse her.

"Come come," she said, "I'm sure you know how to get into a ladies' room."

She rubbed her hand over her fur coat, the way dog-lovers sometimes rub their dogs.

"Your hair," she said.

"What about it?" I asked.

"Run your hand through it once."

I ran my hand through my hair.

"So," she said, "that's much better."

I looked at that strange woman. Vienna has many strange inhabitants, and many of those strange inhabitants, rich and poor, had been brought home by my mother. She would get in these moods, and then she would bring people home with her.

Once I had, for an extended period, been deeply interested in the phenomenon of *l'amour fou*; had I met this woman at the age of fifteen I would surely have seen in her the personification of the *amour fou*. Matchboxes in the ladies' room beneath a pile of towels, that's how I'd imagined it, that's how I had interpreted the Surrealists, or at least some of them. But then, interpretations tell us most about the interpreter.

At that moment, however, she was just one of many older women who let themselves be taken in by my Brazilian looks.

The woman left without saying goodbye. I took that as a challenge, rather than as a sign of rudeness or pathological timidity.

Blondie was still singing; I could have sworn it was the third time she'd sung that same song.

I wavered, did my best to allow the summary of Kant's *Grunlegung zur Metaphysik der Sitten* to impress itself upon me further, but it wasn't working anymore. I read sentences without understanding them, and by the time I'd arrive at a subordinate clause I had already forgotten the main one.

If Mama hadn't fallen—she was on a mountain holiday at the time—I would never have dreamed of reading matchboxes in ladies' rooms or acting on curious propositions from ladies in fur coats. But suddenly I felt her presence so closely, as though she were a pigeon who had landed on my head and was now picking kernels of corn out of my hair.

Mama, who had, after her own fashion, been a woman unto herself, must have done things like this too. Approached strangers in cafés, and then left messages on matchboxes in the ladies' room. After all, how else could she have met all those needy artists?

Almost all the people who showed up at her funeral were complete strangers to Papa, my brothers, and me. "Who's that," I kept asking Papa, "do you know him?"

Papa said, "We can't turn anyone away."

Mama lived as though the world were hers, and she did all she could to foster that illusion.

At last I went to the ladies' room. That pigeon on my head, it just kept picking.

At the door to the ladies' room, I wavered once more.

I looked around, saw no one, felt ridiculous and uneasy nonetheless, then went into the men's room and washed my hands. A man was standing there, peeing, and I wanted to avoid having him think that I had walked into the men's room for no good reason. The idea that you were always being looked at, even in the toilet, was part and parcel of the way I'd been raised.

Papa's name was Ferdinand, and on more than one occasion he'd said: "Even on the toilet, one is not alone." On good days he called himself "Fernando," and it was Eleonore who had come up with the pet name "Ferdi."

The man came and stood beside me to wash his hands.

He smiled at me in the mirror.

My looks arouse feelings in people, but I have not learned to take advantage of that fact. Perhaps it is the consequences I shy away from. Mama was a pretty woman, and in one of his loquacious moments Papa said that she, with her beauty, submersed people in unhappiness.

I went to the door of the ladies' room for the second time and yanked it open.

I could always say, "Oh, I'm very sorry, excuse me."

The ladies' room was empty.

There was a pile of towels to the left of the washbasin, and I searched through it. I felt like a voyeur, a pervert. At the same time I knew that, had Mama been able to see me, she would have laughed out loud. She liked perverts more than she did pigeons. If the dead could speak, she would have said: "Good, Marek, so you're finally starting to live, at long last." Maybe she would even have loved me, for a brief and fleeting moment. Mama was generous with money, and all that much stingier with her love.

The dead, like hats, are silent by nature.

I did, indeed, find a matchbox. There wasn't much on it. I had hoped for a message written in pen, a matchbox scribbled full of plans for a whole summer and a part of the fall as well, ending with the question: "Will you be there, too?"

It was just a normal little matchbox, the kind the better hotels and restaurants leave lying on the bar. There was a name on it, and the address of an establishment unfamiliar to me. Cocktail Lounge The Four Roses.

I hadn't been to many cocktail lounges. I preferred staying home in the evening.

While Mama was still alive, there was always plenty going on at home in the evening, more than in any cocktail lounge. And lately I had felt a growing need to withdraw, although I didn't know exactly what from.

I went back to the reading table. I had the matchbox in my inside pocket. I saved everything important in my inside pocket, for I was afraid that Papa and Eleonore searched my room when I wasn't home.

Mama had been cremated, at her own request, though the rest of the family would have preferred a burial. She had written a letter to her next of kin, which I had to read out loud. A letter she had written long before her death.

First there was a brief service in a chapel.

A strange man sprinkled shredded rose petals over her coffin.

Rolf Szlapka, Mama's florist, sobbed his heart out.

Papa sat perfectly still in his chair, his hat in his lap.

People came up to shake his hand, but when they saw Papa sitting there with that furious look in his eye, they shied away from him.

The weirdo went on shredding rose petals. Rose after rose he ground fine over Mama's coffin. He was starting to get on my nerves.

Then a gentleman from the funeral home came over and whispered: "It's about time we went."

Papa nodded, and the weirdo went on tearing up rose petals over Mama's coffin. Papa had decided that my brother and I would carry the coffin outside, but suddenly I was afraid the coffin would be too heavy, that I would fall, and that the coffin would slide from my hands and Mama would land on the pavement in her pretty gown. It had been raining all night, there were puddles everywhere.

"Papa," I whispered, "I'm not feeling too well, I'm afraid I can't lift the coffin. Would it be all right if someone else took my place?"

At first Papa said nothing, his hat was still in his lap, then he glanced at it and whispered: "If you can't do it, you mustn't do it, I'll ask someone else."

"I can do it," I said, "that's not it."

"No, Marek," he said, a bit louder now, "you mustn't do anything you can't."

Everyone was looking at me, even Mr. Szlapka stopped sobbing for a moment. Then Papa rose slowly from his chair and said: "Well then, here we go."

The husband of our great-aunt from Feldkirch carried the coffin in my place, I walked behind, my eyes fixed on the shoes I had polished so carefully for this occasion. There was already so much talk about us, we had no desire to feed any more rumors.

The cremation itself took place two days later, and that was when I had to read the letter Mama had written.

"Often, at breakfast, I have looked forward to this moment," she wrote.

Mama was not only a flamboyant woman, she also had her deeply melancholy moments. Sometimes she did nothing but play piano for days at a time. Then she would even forget she had children, and when we would go upstairs to where the piano was, she'd say: "What is it you want from me?"

Daniel, the orchestra director, always blamed Mama for that. I didn't. Mama was a woman who sometimes forgot she had children, but if you took that into account she was a very good mother.

Nasty rumors about my mother had made the rounds more than once, but I am here to deny them all. She sometimes saw things that remained hidden to other people, that's all. In Helmuth, for example, she sensed a great talent, and she called him an "old soul." Most others saw him as a crybaby who would start slobbering at the drop of a hat. But Mama saw in him a great talent and an old soul, and Mama never doubted the truth of her observations.

I leafed through the ring binder again, which contained a gloss of Kant. Most of the philosophers I've read I have read in a gloss.

Then I put on my winter cloak and placed a generous tip on the table. Papa and Eleonore appreciated my being on time for dinner, and although Daniel had advised me often enough to rent an attic room somewhere, I had still not succeeded in leaving Papa and Eleonore. "In Italy," Eleonore said, "the boys only leave home once they are ready for marriage." And from the way she looked at me when she said it I could tell that she felt it would take a good five years before I was ready for marriage.

A waiter, who I'd noticed earlier because of the tic under his left eye, came over to me.

"Are you Marek van der Jagt?"

I nodded.

"Phone for you."

"Are you sure it's for me?"

"Are you Marek van der Jagt or not? Because if you are, there's a call for you."

The waiter pronounced my surname in a comical fashion.

I followed him.

They were playing piano music now. The lights had been turned down. Preparations were being made for the evening.

The waiter handed me the phone.

"And, did you go to the ladies' room?" a woman's voice asked.

"I've been there," I said.

The waiter with the tic under his left eye remained standing next to me, as if he was afraid I'd never get off the phone.

"Will I see you tomorrow afternoon at four?"

I examined my nails. Mama used to send me out for a manicure once a week, but since she'd died I hadn't been to the manicurist even once.

"I've got a teaching session then, actually. But I'll come, if that pleases you."

"You won't be sorry."

"I hope not," I said.

After Mama, nothing could really make me blink.

I was used to people wanting to distort other people's reality, probably because reality undistorted was unbearable to them, or at least not the kind of place where they felt like hanging around.

To Mama, reality was a station hall she had to wend her way through.

"What's your name anyway, if I may ask?"

"Mica," the voice said. "M-I-C-A."

Was that a surname or a first name? It could have been either.

"It's my first name," she replied, before I could even ask.

The waiter with the tic was slowly coming into motion, ready at any moment to take action and tear the phone out of my hand.

"I'll see you tomorrow," I said. On a linen napkin I wrote: "Mica, at 4."

That evening we had pheasant. Eleonore told us that a Chinese publisher was interested in her book, and asked how my studies were coming along. Papa remained silent. The maid had a bad cold and asked whether, as an exception, we would consider fetching dessert from the kitchen ourselves.

Eleonore said: "Of course, Bettina, you crawl into bed with a warm scarf around your neck."

It had come as no surprise to me that Mica knew my name. Thanks to Mama, our name was known throughout Vienna.

The pheasant was wonderful, but I tasted nothing, and I left Eleonore's questions unanswered, because Papa did the same.

At ten-thirty, Eleonore pecked me on the cheek, and Papa said: "There's a nice girl in the credit insurance department I'd like you to meet sometime soon."

I lay in bed and I thought about Blondie, Kant, Mama, and Mica, without knowing that there are matchboxes that can throw you for such a loop that you begin feeling like a stranger in your own life, a visitor, a guest.

I believe Mama felt like a guest in her own life. She always acted as if that life had nothing to do with her, as if it wasn't hers. As if she had stumbled upon it by chance, the way you might walk into a house when you've got the address wrong and then inadvertently keep hanging around in it. Outside it's raining cats and dogs, and you didn't bring your umbrella.

When Papa got fed up with Mama playing music for days on end—in addition to piano, she also regularly turned her attention to the cello—he'd force her to come downstairs and sit at the dinner table. She would keep getting up all the time, between bites. Finally she'd go over to the buffet and vomit in one of the silver chafing dishes, her face turned from us.

We had to act as though nothing was wrong, and simply go on eating. The maid ran to the kitchen with the dish, Papa stirred his soup and said: "I had a good day at the office. Insurance is really booming, it's a growth market."

Mama wiped her lips resolutely, came back to the table and said: "Where's my piano?"

"In Asia, too," Papa said, "they're gradually beginning to understand what life insurance can mean for an entire family."

At a certain point Papa had become convinced that playing all that music would make Mama sick in the head, which is why the room with the piano in it was kept locked. Papa guarded the key like a rare treasure.

"Too much music," he said, "is not good for your dear mother; she's a sensitive woman, and some music can be disastrous for sensitive people."

When I came home from school, Mama would often be standing at the living-room window. When she saw me she'd grab my hand and say: "Marek, where's my piano? What have they done with my piano? And my cello, what's happened to it?"

I had to keep my lip buttoned, I wasn't allowed to say that Papa had hidden the cello and locked up the piano. Too much music was bad for a sensitive person. If Mama listened to too much music, she might start having visions.

We had to hide the newspaper from her as well, because she took suffering to heart in the strangest ways. And on the rare occasions when she would forget about the piano and the cello, the same way she forgot she had children, she would lose herself completely in her charities.

"Joachim Tschudel," she might say, "is wasting his time working at the desk of that stupid magazine. He needs to finish his masterpiece on Mongolia, he let me read a few chapters of it. It's brilliant, frighteningly brilliant. But he doesn't have any money, so he wastes his time at that stupid magazine."

For days she'd talk about nothing but Joachim Tschudel. Sometimes we'd catch a glimpse of Joachim Tschudel, but never more than that. Papa tolerated Mama's artists, but they weren't to enter the living room, they had to stay in the kitchen and the maids' quarters.

Papa would say: "Mama's dining this evening in the kitchen with that man with the beard."

He never wasted more words on it than that.

Yet it would be a mistake to think that my father was not fond of amusement. When he'd had a good day, he'd sometimes say after dinner: "Well, gentlemen, let's dance." He liked dancing around the house. We had a big house, with four stories.

He would put on his dressing gown, and my brothers and I would have to run away from him as he chased us, dancing the whole time. He'd crow with pleasure like a child, because even Papa was happy at times.

And, about once a month, he'd give us a thumping. Not because we had done anything wrong, or because he was drunk, but simply, he said, to prepare us for the thumping life would give us later on.

I never experienced those beatings as something negative. In fact, beside the familial dancing, it was one of the few moments of intimacy between a father and his sons.

During breakfast one Easter morning, Mama asked: "How many children do I have?"

"Three," I said.

Papa stared at the simnel cake and said: "This raisin bread gets better every year."

"No," Mama said, "I have four. Where's the fourth?"

Papa said: "Boys, don't pay any attention to Mama, it's bad for her health. Just pretend she's not here."

Daniel said: "I'm not going to play along with this idiocy anymore." He tossed his napkin on the floor and disappeared. He didn't come home for the next two days, but Papa and Pavel and I remained seated.

That's how we had our Easter breakfast, while pretending Mama wasn't there.

Papa said: "This raisin bread gets better every year, boys, have you noticed that? Let's cut off a few slices for Mr. Edwin."

Papa's chauffeur, Edwin, got food and toys from us on holidays, and sometimes on other days as well.

Did Papa ever dream of anything but life insurance? I can't imagine it. Yet still I know it's true; there were other things he dreamed of, long before I was born.

At eleven-thirty I heard Eleonore shuffling down the hall. Pheasant always gave her indigestion, but even without the pheasant she always found a reason to drink a few glasses of warm milk with tincture of valerian in the middle of the night.

I got up, put on the slippers Papa had given me for my eighteenth birthday, and went to the room where Mama's piano still stood.

I sat down at the piano and thought over my life.

I didn't want to feel like a guest in life anymore, not like Mama, for whom life had been largely a stand-up reception with only a handful of attractive men, all of whom she'd already had.

2

Cocktail Lounge The Four Roses

The next day I arrived exactly on time at Cocktail Lounge The Four Roses.

The bar was in a cellar, I had to walk down five steps to get to it. In a dark corner, someone was playing the accordion.

It was the kind of place I'd always tried to avoid. Too dark, too stuffy, and it smelled too much of wet raincoats that were slowly growing dry.

I didn't see Mica anywhere. I sat down at the bar and, not knowing what to order, asked for a glass of water. There weren't many people there, ten at most. But it was still early, the cocktail hour had not yet arrived.

I waited for fifteen minutes, and was beginning to suspect that she wouldn't show up at all, when the barmaid served me an Irish coffee and said: "This is from the lady over there in the corner."

She pointed to a woman in the corner.

Only then did I recognize her without her fur coat. She was wearing a wig. She had also painted up her face in a different color.

Mica was playing the accordion. When the song was over, she raised a little glass and looked at me. I nodded.

"Go on over," the barmaid said.

I went to her table, the glass of Irish coffee in my trembling hand, and sat down beside her. I waited until she would speak to me. But she didn't say a word. Mica played the accordion and drank vodka as though both activities would soon be barred from her life forever.

After Mica had played another number and a dreary applause had sounded, she laid her accordion on the chair beside her and said: "Marek, you're a man who lives by the clock."

I smiled; if I live by anything, it's the clock.

She had pale skin and inquisitive eyes, and she smelled like a swimming pool, an open-air swimming pool on a hot summer's day.

"Aren't you going to buy me a drink?"

"I thought you already had one," I said.

"The Irish coffee was for you."

I looked at the Irish coffee, then at the little glass on the chair beside her. It was half full.

"It's never a bad idea to offer a lady a drink," she said, "even if she already has one, and let's call each other by our first names. That will make it all a lot easier."

What was there that had to all become a lot easier?

I shook her hand.

"Marek," I said. "Pleased to meet you."

I put on a little smile. One can't avoid a bit of uneasiness if one wants to have the feeling that one is alive.

"Mica," she said. "Could you push that chair a little closer, so I can put my leg up on it? It's stiff. They say it's the dampness."

I slid a chair up closer and Mica put her right leg on it.

I looked at that leg; it was a normal leg, in normal black pantyhose.

"Well, it is rather dampish today."

I hadn't noticed any dampness, but it seemed I was talking to someone who knew about such things.

"Is this your profession?" I said, pointing at the accordion.

She threw her head back and laughed loudly.

"My profession, yes, let's just call it my profession. But we were going to call each other by our first names, weren't we, Marek?"

The first time we met, I hadn't noticed how fat she was. It only struck me now. "Plumpness of person" sounds nicer.

Everyone in my family is thin as a bone.

Mama had a full bosom, but even that bosom couldn't disguise her thinness. Papa once said: "She doesn't have any hips. How she ever had children is a mystery to me."

I find fatness comfy and cozy, especially in women.

"Go get me something," Mica said.

She eyed me from head to toe, and seemed once again to be amused.

That day I was wearing my half boots.

"What would you like to drink?"

"She knows that," Mica said, pointing to the woman behind the bar.

For a moment there I wondered how it had happened that I was letting myself be ordered around by an aging female accordionist with a stiff leg, but then I realized that I shouldn't ask so many questions, that I shouldn't think so much, that I should seize whatever there was to seize.

At the end of her life, Mama had a stiff leg too. Everything about her was stiff. And some of her lovers wanted to go to bed with me. But they were never importune. Mama liked her deviates well-mannered.

"The camel is the ship of the desert," Mama had often said to me, "but my ship is love." That was absolutely untrue. Mama's ship was jealousy. She was capable of making anyone jealous, even the postman, because she could forget from one moment to the next that you existed. While you were still putting out your hand to greet her, she was already disappearing from your life.

The barmaid wore earrings that looked like flies.

"It's for Mica," I said and pointed in her direction, as if I was afraid that not everyone might know her by the name Mica.

My voice was hoarse, the way it had been the time I'd met a publisher from whom I had received a rejection slip two weeks earlier. But he didn't even know about it. He had forgotten it completely. At the end of our conversation, when I reminded him subtly of the fact, he said: "Oh, my dear boy, the fact that a letter has my signature on it means nothing, I don't even get to see those letters anymore." I never met a publisher again after that, not even by accident.

"Another Irish coffee?" the barmaid asked while she was pouring vodka into a little glass. Straight up, no ice.

"Just regular coffee," I said.

"Really? Are you sure you don't want a shot of something in it?"

How peculiar, I thought, that someone should wear earrings that looked like flies, like magnified flies.

"No, nothing in it, just coffee."

"You're new around here." She put a cookie on the saucer.

It wasn't a question, not even a comment, but a judgment; the description of my condition. I'd been new for more than twenty years and it seemed as if my newness would never end. If I didn't watch out, I'd die new.

One evening, not long before she died, Mama said: "Marek, make sure you don't die unused."

"What do you mean, Mama?" I asked her.

"People," she said, "need to be put to use, otherwise they've lived for nothing. They mustn't stand empty, do you understand?"

Refrigerators could stand empty, but could people?

"Am I standing empty?" I asked.

The next morning she and I went on vacation to the mountains, with eight suitcases, and I realized that throughout all those years

Mama had done all she could not to die unused, and that it was now my turn to see to it that I could one day die with the thought: "I've been used, and how."

The first time Papa heard that Mama had a lover, he stayed sitting in his easy chair for a few minutes, completely still, as if pondering some thorny problem with the life-insurance policies. How old was I then? Eleven or twelve? Something like that. Suddenly he said: "And has he seen you in the nude?"

Mama started laughing, we'd never seen her laugh like that; Pavel, Daniel, and I stood there looking at her as though she was giving a concert.

"Has he seen me in the nude?!" she shouted. It must have been one of the brightest moments in Mama's life.

And then Papa yelled: "Upstairs, all of you!" And he chased us upstairs. Even as he ran, he was pulling his belt out of his pants. Papa was extremely adept at that. And he swung his belt around in the air.

One foot in front of the other, I made my way to Mica.

The coffee sloshed over the edge, onto the saucer, and my hands started shaking even worse.

She drank her vodka like a man, I nipped at my coffee. I waited for a word from Mica; impatient, curious, and with the vague premonition that I was no match for her.

When her glass was almost empty, she began tickling me under the chin and said: "No one's going to eat you up."

She shouldn't have said that.

On my nineteenth birthday, Papa gave me a pair of hedge-clippers, a huge pair of hedge-clippers. We have a big garden, but no hedge, and our gardener came twice a week, more often when he needed money. I wanted to ask Papa: "Why did you give me hedge-clippers?" I never asked him that though, because I never would have received an answer. I put the hedge-clippers in my room. Under the desk. If thieves came, at least I'd be armed.

"Mica," I said, once she'd finished the last drop in her glass, "I don't mean to pry, but why did you ask me to come here?"

It's funny how we all think we need someone else to make something out of our lives, and it struck me that Mica had perhaps only asked me to come because she was bored, because she wanted to amuse herself. Some older women were fond of youth.

She started laughing, the way she'd laughed when I'd asked whether playing the accordion was her profession.

She pulled a suitcase out from behind her chair. I thought she was planning to put the accordion in it, but she handed me the suitcase and said: "Here."

It was a brown suitcase, an old-fashioned one. Full of dents and scratches.

Suddenly I was afraid that Papa would come into the cocktail lounge with one of his business acquaintances. He would nod to me, almost unnoticed, then ignore me. Then, three days later, he would suddenly say: "What were you doing in The Four Roses, anyway?"

There's nothing wrong with having two successful brothers, a successful father, and a successful stepmother, the only annoying thing is that every comparison is then to your disadvantage, and in the long term people get the feeling that they need to protect you, the way they protect the terminally ill and are careful not to mention the name of the illness when that person is around.

At family gatherings my name was avoided, which made it seem as though I was one of those deadly illnesses.

According to Papa there was no substitute for success, and Eleonore would say: "I started with a typing diploma, Marek, and look where I am today." And then she'd point to the bookcase with all the translations of *How Old Women Can Get Rich*.

But now I was sitting beside Mica, with a suitcase on my lap.

"You look so innocent," Mica said, "as if you'd just been born."

I put the suitcase down on the floor.

Like I'd just been born, what kind of thing was that to say? Did she think I had a baby face, just because I happened to be blessed with healthy skin and glossy hair?

"I have to go," I said.

Mica lifted her glass to her lips, but there was nothing in it.

A French chanson was playing in the background now, and I tried to remember the name of the singer. Back in French class we'd listened to his chansons and analyzed his lyrics. I went to an international school where everything was analyzed, including chansons.

"Take the suitcase with you," she said. "I didn't drag it down here for my health."

Her voice suddenly sounded harsh, and even though it was dark I could see the pores on her nose quite distinctly. That's how close she'd brought her face up to mine.

I looked at the barmaid, she was leaning on the bar, staring into space, and then I thought about all Papa's money and all Eleonore's money and about people who had died unused.

"I'm sorry," I said, "but I can't accept your presents."

I moved the spoon around in my coffee in useless stirring motions. I didn't take cream or sugar, and the coffee was already lukewarm.

"Don't worry," she said, "these aren't presents."

The door opened, and two men came into the lounge.

"Just take the suitcase," Mica said. "They're not presents, they're your mother's things."

The two men had taken a table. One of them had a pile of papers with him in a file, and I tried to concentrate on the men's socks. They were both wearing socks with patterns on them.

"And order me a drink while you're over there," Mica said.

The lady with flies in her ears had poured a glass of vodka before I could say a thing.

I was going to pick up the glass and walk away, but she laid her hand on mine.

Her hand was strong and warm. Not clammy, the way mine often are. Papa's hands are often clammy too.

"Mica is unbelievable," she said.

"Yes," I said, "unbelievable." I was hoarse.

"You want some more coffee?"

I nodded. Her questions were commands.

She slapped a saucer down forcefully on the bar.

I watched her movements.

The barmaid moved like a woman who knew what she was after.

When I went to pay, she said: "Hot chocolate with rum, have you ever tried that?" And she laughed, as though I would never understand the meaning of what she'd just said.

3

Otto Rents Rooms, Too

When I got back, a man was sitting next to Mica. A little man in a hat. One of those English hats. Nobody in Vienna wears hats like that.

His cheeks were hollow. His mouth was a thin line.

"Marek," Mica said, "this is Otto."

I put the glasses on the table and shook his hand.

He was wearing jewels on his wrist.

He was also wearing jewels around his neck.

I remained standing, but Mica said: "Have a seat, Marek. We don't like looking up to people."

I borrowed a chair from another table.

"Otto makes statues," said Mica.

I nodded.

Otto himself didn't say a word. He was looking at me attentively.

He had a plastic bag with him, full of vegetables.

I would never walk into a cocktail lounge with a plastic bag full of vegetables. Shame was the cork on which my body floated. Mama liked it when men knew no shame, especially when they were poor and artists. Only rich artists were supposed to know shame, because money generates shame.

When I saw the vegetables, I knew it was time for me to go home. Papa and Eleonore would have started dinner already, and

Eleonore would say: "The boy is unhappy, you can see it in everything he does. Doesn't he have a girlfriend yet?"

Papa would say nothing, because he regarded unhappiness as a disease against which no vaccine had yet been discovered. And talking about unhappiness was tantamount to calling the devil's name.

Moving slowly, Otto pulled a pack of cigarettes from his inside pocket.

"Otto rents rooms, too," Mica said.

Again I nodded.

Otto made statues, Otto rented rooms; the sort of information at which one can only nod in response. Every word I said here could be misconstrued.

One of the men whose socks I'd been examining swore loudly a few times, and I looked at the suitcase that wasn't an accordion case.

"I really must be going," I said.

Otto inhaled. I stared at the smoke he blew slowly from his mouth.

He had a brooch on his sweater. A silver airplane with little diamonds at the tail.

"Marriage is a prison," Otto said slowly.

"They're waiting for him with dinner," Mica said.

"What do you do," Otto asked, "with your life?"

"I go to school," I said, "and I'm a tutor."

Otto smiled. The word "tutor" seemed to please him.

He had jewels in his ears as well, I noticed then. His lips were so thin that it almost looked as if he didn't have any. He was looking at me expectantly. Mica said: "Otto, don't scare the boy."

I got up and was about to walk to the bar, but Otto said: "Don't pay, Marek, let me do that."

He had a slight accent, one I couldn't pinpoint. His voice was hoarse. Talking seemed to cost him effort.

I slid my chair up to the table, a habit, the vestige of an upbringing. The bag full of vegetables fell over. The next moment I was squatting down, busy picking lemons, pears, plums, and green onions off the floor.

Mica laughed.

The patrons of The Four Roses were looking at me.

Even the man who had sworn so loudly was quiet.

"I'm sorry," I said. "I'm sorry."

"It doesn't matter," Mica said. "Otto washes everything very carefully."

A couple of plums had rolled to the other end of the cocktail lounge, and were badly damaged. I offered to pay for the damage, and Mica said: "Aren't you an extremely genteel young man!"

"So tell me, what's in the suitcase?" I asked after I had put everything back in Otto's bag.

Otto hadn't lifted a finger to help. Mica hadn't either. But then they were old, and maybe they both had stiff legs.

"Clothes," she said.

I smiled, the answer was as obvious as that. Suitcases contained clothes, with only few exceptions. Some suitcases had skeletons in them.

"Neatly washed and ironed," Mica said.

I heard myself say: "How thoughtful of you to have ironed them, ma'am."

I try not to ask questions, out of fear for their answers and to avoid being impolite. Maybe Mama had left half her wardrobe with one of her needy artists, who had decided after a few years to give it all back. Or was it an artist who never cleaned the house and had found the clothes only now?

"We had agreed to call each other by our first names, Marek. Every time you say 'ma'am' I feel so old. If you like, I could sell them for you."

"What?"

"The clothes."

"No," I said, "no, that won't be necessary."

A phone rang, the barmaid answered it. I heard her snarling at the caller. In her profession, you did a lot of snarling. Maybe a profession like that was something for me, Pavel always said I should learn to snarl at people and stand up for myself.

"Otto was very keen to meet you," Mica said. "And now he's met you."

First I shook Mica's hand, then Otto's. Then I picked up the suitcase and left The Four Roses.

4

Inge from Innsbruck

The tomato soup had already been served.

We ate tomato soup three times a week, because Papa liked tomato soup.

In the hall I ran into the maid.

She had a basket of bread in her hand and she was smiling.

Someone had once taught her to smile and she'd never stopped. As soon as she saw people, she started smiling.

"Tell them I'll be there in a minute," I said.

"Do you need me to help with anything?"

"No," I said.

I trotted upstairs with the suitcase, tried to push it into one of my cupboards; when that didn't work, I slid it under the bed.

I glanced at myself in the mirror and calmly went downstairs.

Papa looked at me in irritation, but I ignored him and quickly ate my soup.

"Someone should tell her to put less paprika in it next time," Eleonore said.

Papa spooned the last bit of soup from his bowl, almost without a sound, and said: "I don't taste anything."

"Tomato soup is not supposed to have paprika in it," Eleonore said firmly.

The maid gathered our plates and said: "Doesn't Mr. Marek look handsome today?"

I thought about the suitcase under my bed, the way criminals think about hastily covered evidence.

I smiled. And Eleonore said: "Yes, much better than yesterday."

The maid was a font of cheerfulness, tolerated by Papa and Eleonore because she never crossed certain boundaries.

She noticed everything, the maid did, the tiniest spot on a pair of trousers or a crumb on a couch, but in her world cause and effect did not exist. And even if they did, she wasn't interested.

She succeeded in skirting Papa's law that there was no substitute for success, or maybe that was because Papa defined success differently when it came to maids.

Papa who pushed all those around him to give it their all, Papa who said: "Don't count on a reward in the next world; anyone who wants a reward has to go in right now and claim it," Papa who always insisted that you keep climbing, never stop trying, let the maid alone. She didn't have to do anything, she was allowed to remain who she was, where she was.

She'd been with us for almost twenty-five years, had no children and no husband, but she got a raise each year and a generous Christmas bonus. She seemed content.

On her days off she was occasionally seen with men in certain cafés, but she was even more discreet about her own life than she was about ours, if such a thing was possible.

Once, when I was still a child, it seems something happened to her that was referred to in our home as "that tragic affair." No one ever talked about it, and I never asked, because that would have detracted from her—in my eyes—almost divine status.

Papa and the maid would sometimes exchange no more than six words in the course of a given day, yet still a remarkable rapport had developed between them. When she handed him his jacket in the morning, or said: "Not so fast, Mr. van der Jagt, hot coffee burns the gullet," she reminded me somehow of a mother, a mother like the ones in books and movies.

Lamb was served.

"Would you like to carve it, or shall I?" the maid asked.

Papa said: "I'll do it."

"Lovely, lamb," Eleonore said.

She looked at me happily, perhaps in the hope that I would agree with her that, as far as I too was concerned, this lamb was the crown on a perfect day.

Papa carved slowly while I looked at the big portrait of Mama that had been painted just before her twenty-fourth birthday. I had already suggested removing it from the dining room. "We don't have to look at it while we're eating, do we?" I'd said.

For Papa, the subject was closed to discussion.

"As a work of art, it's unaesthetic," I said.

"That's not a work of art," Papa replied, "that's your mother."

Eleonore too thought it would be rather disrespectful to take down the picture. "It doesn't bother me at all," she said. "I think it's a nice painting. Looking at it doesn't remind me of your mother at all."

And then she suddenly fell silent, as though she'd shocked herself by being so honest.

"One slice," I said, "is enough for me."

Papa glanced up, then looked back down at the meat he was holding between fork and ladle and seemed to give just the slightest of shrugs, as if he didn't find it worth arguing about.

A lack of appetite was anathema to him.

Eleonore and Papa took two slices.

"Eleonore's book," Papa said, "was sold to Romania today, it's unbelievable. And then to think that at first all those publishers were skeptical."

I bowed my head. Eleonore beamed. "I've struck a chord," she said, "without even knowing it, it just happened."

I thought about old women all over the world who were now making desperate attempts to get rich, with Eleonore's book as the bible on their nightstands.

Eleonore swallowed, wiped her lips and said: "And then to think that a couple of years ago I didn't even know I could write."

I bowed my head even farther, Papa poured us some more sparkling water.

"The managing director of the publishing house," she went on enthusiastically, "said to me: 'Eleonore, you write better than all those so-called literary authors, your grammar is impeccable.'"

I couldn't bow my head any farther. "Eleonore," I said, as I examined my meat, "literature isn't a matter of grammar, is it?"

Eleonore wiped her lips with the napkin, then looked at the napkin as if trying to home in on the spots she'd left behind.

"I'm only repeating what the managing director said to me, and I'm quite sure he knows what he's talking about. I am, he said, a mouthpiece for a forgotten generation."

Papa got up and turned on the music. Mozart's "Requiem." In Papa's world, Mozart was success incarnate, the redeemer for those whose religion was succeeding where others had failed.

"Fer, how do you like that?" Eleonore asked. "A mouthpiece for a forgotten generation!"

Papa didn't reply. Papa had his eyes closed.

"A mouthpiece for which generation?" I asked without lifting my head, although I knew Papa hated it when I did that. At least five times an evening he'd say: "Don't let your head hang, Marek, it's not a sack of potatoes. Look at people boldly when you speak to them."

"A mouthpiece for older, single women," Eleonore said, and looked at Papa. But he still had his eyes shut tight. He was listening to the music. Papa didn't like discussions. At least, he didn't like senseless discussions, which he considered a particularly abject form of senseless violence, especially when held within the family circle.

"But you're not single," I said.

"When I began writing I was single, older, and I was a woman; society treated me like a Negro. You should read the letters I get, women who write to say: thanks to you I've regained my self-confidence."

Papa opened his eyes and closed them again. He didn't like words like that, words like society, self-confidence, Negro. Eleonore's plate was empty now. No one said a thing, so she started talking again. "The managing director says, Eleonore, you're at your best when your writing is personal."

Another slap in the face. The managing director was Eleonore's idol. A man in cowboy boots who made money on books like the ones Eleonore wrote, and who occasionally published something that was reviewed quite favorably in the book sections of the major dailies but barely sold a copy. He claimed to have discovered Eleonore.

"That's right," Eleonore said, "the managing director said: try writing a story, Eleonore."

The way some people play tennis against a wall, that's the way Eleonore carried on conversations against a wall. No real response was needed, the sound of her own words bouncing back at her was more than enough.

Once everything in this house had reminded me of Mama, but now I couldn't take a step without being confronted with *How Old Women Can Get Rich*. And that book would definitely not be the last. God only knew what other books Eleonore might secrete if no one stopped her.

The maid came in.

"Mr. Marek," she said, "sorry to disturb you, but there's someone on the phone."

Papa opened his eyes. The telephone call had disturbed his fragile harmony.

Papa hated phone calls in general, and phone calls after six he considered barbaric.

If everyone is a book, then Papa was a set of directions in at least seven volumes.

"Please excuse me," I said.

I went into the next room, which I regretted later on. I should have gone into the kitchen; the sliding doors between the two rooms were open, and Papa and Eleonore's conversation was not lively enough to keep them from hearing me.

"Marek van der Jagt," I said.

"I hope I'm not disturbing you at dinner?"

"Not really."

"I completely forgot to say that I'd like to have the suitcase back."

I was stunned for a moment.

"You want it all back?"

"Only the suitcase. There's no hurry," Mica went on.

"Fine," I said, "that seems like no problem to me."

"Maybe you could bring it by The Four Roses this week. What about tomorrow, at four?"

"I'll bring the book tomorrow," I said. "I should have my notes finished by then."

"So you're not alone?" Mica asked.

"No," I said, "it doesn't seem like a difficult topic to me, either."

"Then I'll see you tomorrow."

"Okay, till tomorrow."

I went back to the table and rearranged the napkin on my lap.

No one asked me about the call.

Papa wiped his mouth carefully and said: "That girl I told you about, the one from credit insurance, is coming by at nine for a cup of coffee. I'd appreciate it if you were present. Her name is Inge."

"A lovely name," Eleonore said. "Such a soft ring to it."

I glanced at the painting. Mama looked like a courtesan.

There were all kinds of feathers painted all around her.

The maid served pineapple.

"And so intelligent," Eleonore said.

"What?" I asked.

"Inge," Eleonore said. "Some names sound so much more intelligent than others."

Papa raised his eyebrows. He cracked his knuckles, which he often did when trying to control himself. Mama had hated it.

"That's ridiculous, Eleonore. Names aren't intelligent. People, perhaps, but only by rare exception." Papa laughed his peculiar laugh. A laugh that sounded a lot like a cough, like someone choking.

I remembered that I had an appointment with Max the next day at four. Max was sixteen. For a modest fee, I went to his house three times a week, sometimes more.

I never mixed up my appointments, I was extremely conscientious about that. A tutor has to be conscientious. Little mistakes could sow great panic. I couldn't leave Max in the lurch. Max and his mother were counting on me, they were perhaps the only people left who still counted on me. At first I had seen being counted on, being needed, as something that could give me a blind and instinctive confidence in life. Until that being needed, which was such a pleasant feeling at first, became pressure, a burden, a promise you had never made out loud but had apparently made anyway, and which slowly corrupted you.

Professor Hirschfeld had spoken of the need to have a blind and instinctive confidence in life, and of what could happen when that confidence disappeared. Professor Hirschfeld and I often talked about criminals and philosophy.

"A penny for your thoughts, Marek," Eleonore said.

I couldn't leave Mica in the lurch either; anyone who had saved my mother's clothes in a suitcase deserved to get that suitcase back.

Papa stood up, the meal was over, and we followed him out of the room. It wasn't nine o'clock yet, but he was already going to seat himself in the salon.

He liked to take his time preparing for visitors. Eleonore sat beside him, meditating or saying nothing, which may ultimately be a form of meditation too.

Papa had already introduced me to many women, about eight in total. Almost all of them worked at the insurance company. Papa viewed life as something that had proven to be a defective invention for which both invention and inventor were to be punished with silence. Everything that came after that life, however, would probably prove a great deal more defective. And so, strangely enough, haste was the order of the day. Once you had been forced to take part in the defective invention known as life, there was no going back.

"I'm going to freshen up a little," I said.

First I went to the toilet, then I washed my hands and combed my hair, and after that went upstairs and took the suitcase out from under the bed.

There were stickers stuck to it, with illegible texts on them.

I heard the maid coming up the stairs, on her way to prepare the bedrooms for the night.

The suitcase was dirty, as though it had stood out in the rain for a long time on a sandy road.

For a moment I considered the possibility that it didn't contain Mama's clothes at all. That an error had been made; a willful error, in light of my experiences with Mica so far.

It had three locks.

Someone knocked at the door.

"Marek," the maid said.

"Not now," I said, "I'm naked."

She went away without a word.

All three of the locks were equally easy to open.

The dress on top was an evening gown which had, indeed, belonged to Mama. I recognized the material.

There weren't many people who wore dresses like that.

Most of the other dresses were familiar to me as well. They were neatly folded and ironed, just as Mica had promised.

I sniffed at the dresses, but could smell nothing. No matter how deeply I buried my nose in the fabric, nothing, only something faintly chemical, but that could also have been my imagination.

I thought briefly about taking the dresses out of the suitcase, but then realized that I could never fold them up so neatly again. As though there was something crucial about the state of those dresses.

The doorbell rang, and I ran downstairs. I had to be in the salon in time to welcome Inge.

Inge was big. She wore shoes that made her even bigger. And no one would ever have accused her of leanness.

The four of us sat in the salon, and Inge talked a lot.

She had blonde hair, but she'd mixed something red through it and now parts of her hair looked pink and others purple.

Her face was ruddy, but not unattractive.

"I haven't been in Vienna very long," Inge said. "I'm originally from Innsbruck."

"Innsbruck, we've been there often," Eleonore said.

Papa held up a plate of bonbons and said: "Take, Inge, these are the best bonbons in all of Vienna. Maybe even in all of Austria."

She took a bonbon, placed it on a napkin and said: "And you, I hear you're studying philosophy?"

She crossed her legs. I admired anyone who would walk on heels as high as hers.

Eleonore answered for me. "He's brilliant, we've all read what he's written about Schopenhauer."

"It was Hegel," I said. "A gloss of a gloss of his *Einleitung zur Phänomenologie des Geistes*, nothing special really."

Somewhere in the house a clock chimed.

Papa bent over to lift his cup of coffee from the salon table.

"Eleonore writes too," he said with a grimace, as though this announcement caused him pain. But then, all other announcements probably caused him even more pain.

I concentrated on Inge's heels, and suddenly I saw her using the hedge-clippers Papa had given me. She was pruning rose bushes. And she sang a song as she pruned.

"Do you sing sometimes?" I asked suddenly.

She giggled a little.

Papa cleared his throat.

"Only in church," Inge said, "but not very often there either."

"We don't sing very often either," Eleonore said. And Papa said: "We're also not real churchgoers."

My father had a grudge against the church.

Inge bent over. She looked at me. I felt as though I were being inspected.

Then I imagined that we would walk down the street together and that she'd wobble and grab hold of me and drag me down in her fall, until we were lying on the ground in a Vienna suburb. The neighborhood was new to me. And she giggled a little, the way she'd giggled when I'd asked if she ever sang. She pressed her lips to mine, and I was breathless.

"Does he look more like his mother, or more like you?" Inge asked.

Everyone stared at me.

A search was being made for a resemblance between me and my parents, but my father and my stepmother said nothing. Eleonore in particular looked at me with an intensity which was, by her standards, striking. "Marek," she said suddenly, "you don't trim your eyebrows, do you?"

How deep must a person bow his head to become invisible?

"Marek?"

"A little," I whispered.

"But don't you know that only makes them grow faster, all that clipping makes them proliferate."

I'm sure that, in the silence that fell and rested for at least a minute, everyone was thinking about eyebrows, and more specifically, about my eyebrows.

"I'd say more like your wife," Inge said, "although of course I never knew her. She had pretty hair like that too."

I watched the way she looked at Papa, and in her eyes I saw that she liked Papa a lot more than she did me. It had happened before, girls he brought home to meet me were more drawn to him. They were probably attracted to a world where there was no substitute for success. A world like that must be teeming with eroticism.

"I suffer from insomnia," Inge said. And, after a brief pause: "So I think I'd better be going."

But she didn't get up. She just crossed her legs in the other direction. And the remains of the Van der Jagt family stared at her, full of amazement at this sudden outburst between bonbons number three and four.

She not only suffered from insomnia, she also suffered from an affliction that kept her from sitting still.

Eleonore looked around, and seeing as the silence seemed to be weighing on all of us, I said: "I like your shoes."

Legs crossed and uncrossed again.

"Oh, I just bought them," she said.

She arched her back, which made her breasts stick out, and she suddenly reminded me of a statue in an ornamental garden, an overrun, ornamental garden. There was moss growing on the statues, and some of them were covered in bird shit.

"So you write," Inge said. For a moment there I thought she was talking to me.

Eleonore perked up. "That's right."

"What, if you don't mind my asking?"

"*How Old Women Can Get Rich.* I'll get you a copy. You can take it with you. Your parents will like that. Fer, I'm allowed to say that, aren't I?"

"You're allowed to do anything, Eleonore," Papa said.

Without pursuing that thought any further, Eleonore strode out of the room.

"My parents don't read much," Inge said.

"No," said Papa.

"My mother has migraines."

"Lots of rest," Papa said, "and dark rooms."

"So you know about it."

Papa laughed. Or coughed. Or both at the same time. He made parrying motions with his hands, which could have meant: "Don't slap me on the back," but also: "Tell me about it, there's nothing I don't know about migraines."

If reincarnation existed, Papa would come back as a deaf-mute.

Eleonore returned, in her hand a copy of *How Old Women Can Get Rich.*

"Here," she said to Inge, "give it to your parents, I already signed it." For the first time I noticed the determination in Eleonore's face, the determination of someone who was rich and old and who had no intention of letting anyone take away either her life or her riches. For the first time I saw the man in Eleonore. It wasn't a nice man.

Inge leafed through it. Eleonore waited, Papa stared at Inge, and in the doorframe appeared the maid with another plate of bonbons.

When Papa saw that, he motioned with his hand and she disappeared discreetly. And came back a little later with Inge's coat.

We all stood up.

Again I thought about the suitcase with Mama's ironed clothes in it, and about Mica and the double appointment I had made in atypical fashion. I would have to cancel my meeting with Mica, but how? How could I reach her?

Suddenly Inge was standing before me, her hand held out.

"Goodbye, Marek," she said, "it was very nice meeting you. I hope we'll see each other again soon. In any case, we have the same taste in footwear."

Automatically, I looked down. They were up close, her shoes.

"There's more to the world than shoes," Papa said.

Then Papa coughed three times, and the maid knew that she was to show Inge to the door with all due speed.

5

An Interesting Man

Max's mother opened the door.

I was five minutes early, as usual. She took me into the kitchen and made tea.

"I have to leave a little earlier today," I said.

Her face clouded over.

"But I can come one time extra next week."

A kitchen cupboard swung open forcibly. The scent of cinnamon filled the air.

"Gratis, of course." I smiled.

"He hasn't been doing well lately," said Max's mother, who I was never to call Mrs. Blumenthal, even though that was her name.

I was supposed to call her Trude.

But I didn't call her Trude.

"Lately," I said pensively, "I actually think we're making a lot of progress."

I looked out the window at a bare tree.

Lots of kitchens are gloomy, but Max's mother's kitchen was the gloomiest I'd ever seen. When it wasn't smelling like cinnamon, it smelled like frankfurters.

"I don't know," she said, "I just don't know. Lately, he hasn't been doing well."

That afternoon she was wearing her hair down.

On off days, her hair smelled like frankfurters.

Today was not an off day.

It was Thursday, and on Wednesdays she went to the hairdresser's. So Thursday was never an off day. Tuesday was an off day.

"Go see for yourself," she said.

I'd found Mrs. Blumenthal through an ad on the faculty bulletin board.

The piece of paper that was hanging there had read: "Wanted: kind and patient tutor for difficult but intelligent young man."

Kind and patient, that's what I hoped to be. And it seemed wise to me to start earning a bit of money myself, even if only to have the feeling that I could do that, earn money myself. Perhaps money generated not only shame, but also self-respect. First self-respect, then shame, that was probably the way it went.

According to Mrs. Blumenthal, at least twenty people had applied, but she'd known right away that I was the one, because of my eyes.

From other students who'd replied to the same ad I heard that they'd thought about it, then withdrew their application.

Mrs. Blumenthal's husband worked as a hotel doorman. I'd seen him once, in his doorman's uniform.

He had looked at me with dull eyes, and his wife had to repeat it three times: "This is the tutor, Marek van der Jagt."

Then he shook my hand, without really seeing me. He looked right past me.

"He was screaming again last night," Max's mother said.

She poured me some tea.

"We all do that sometimes," I said, and laid a hand on her shoulder.

Before I met Max I'd met all kinds of victims, but never a traffic victim.

His mother had told me there was something wrong with him,

but I'd been thinking more along the lines of a depression associated with early puberty.

After the second meeting, she'd said: "Let's just try it together for a couple of months." And then: "Now the time has come to introduce you to Max." Because, until then, I hadn't been allowed to meet my pupil.

We went to Max's room. She walked out in front, I walked behind.

The woman I was supposed to call Trude had fat calves.

The room was dark.

At the desk sat a boy in a wheelchair. He was staring at a wall with a birthday calendar hanging on it. To the left of him was a computer. There were fish swimming around on the screen.

"Max," his mother said, "here's the gentleman who's going to tutor you."

The boy had whitish blond hair, and he wore a green sweater.

But he didn't move, and the wheelchair didn't either.

I concentrated on the fish swimming around the screen.

"Max," his mother said again, "this is Marek van der Jagt, the man I told you about."

"The silence of God," someone once told me, "is an answer as well." This silence didn't seem like an answer to me, though, this silence was a question.

"Max!" his mother shouted.

I tried to remember my own puberty. A series of ejaculations and poems passed my mind's eye, and my mother telling the future, her cigarette plugged, for a change, into a black holder.

Mama dressed like a gypsy.

Mama putting one of her hats on my head.

And finally, then, Mama shooting the chandelier.

Now that my puberty had become part of a carefully cordoned past, I had seen that I had overestimated the beauty of my poems, and underestimated the beauty of my ejaculations. The poems had become increasingly better—not good enough, but better in any case—while the ejaculations became less.

I had confused emotion with sperm, and that had occasionally led to beauty, and sometimes even to happiness. But much more often to misery.

"Max!" his mother yelled. "I'm only going to say this one more time!"

Who was yelling at who here, I wondered. And what was that "one more time" all about?

"Max!" shrieked the woman I was supposed to call Trude.

Slowly, the wheelchair came into motion.

It was a wheelchair with an electric motor.

The wheelchair turned halfway around. I listened intently to the humming of the motor, and stared at the linoleum floor and my shoes, until I heard his mother shout: "Max, turn off the motor, stand still!"

I looked up.

Max's face looked like it had been pulled apart and then put together again by some miscreant who had finally been given the chance to create someone in his own image.

"Introduce yourself," his mother said.

It seemed better for me to take the initiative.

I walked over to my pupil.

Once I was standing in front of him, his left arm moved slowly in my direction.

The hand didn't open completely anymore, the way that is with some old men, too.

The other arm lay lifeless on a wooden hand rest.

I wormed three fingers into Max's left hand. For a moment, he held onto them.

Because I was afraid my eyes would betray something, fear or disgust perhaps, in any case something I didn't want to see myself and which should therefore remain unseen by my pupil as well, I stared over his head at the birthday calendar.

Then I pulled my three fingers back and walked to the door.

There I said: "Hello, Max. Nice to meet you, I think we'll get along well."

The only reply came from the wheelchair, which pivoted ninety degrees again.

Max was now sitting exactly as we'd found him, staring at the flowery birthday calendar, but maybe he wasn't seeing the calendar at all, maybe he saw completely different things, the way I in my puberty had seen things that weren't there, that were based on misunderstandings, and the way Mama had seen things all her life that didn't exist.

"Well," Max's mother said, "that's enough for one day."

When I looked back again, it was as though there was no life at all in that room. Of course, with a bit of goodwill, the fish on the screen could have counted as life.

Trude closed the door carefully. Then she whispered: "Mentally, there's nothing wrong with him."

"No, no, of course," I said. "That goes without saying."

"I bet you could use a drink."

"Yes, please."

She took a bottle of white wine from the refrigerator.

"Fog on a mountain road," she murmured while pulling the cork. "He was in the car with his friend's parents. Not wearing belts, of course. The others are in much worse shape."

Then the cork popped.

In much worse shape. What would that look like? Not like much of anything anymore. Maybe somewhere in the vicinity of a genetically manipulated earthworm, but then magnified ten thousand times.

Two glasses were filled.

"Of course, there's still some plastic surgery to be done, but that wasn't our main priority. Let's go to the living room."

When we got there, Max's mother said "Cheers," and she smiled.

"Cheers," I said. "But then, matters of aesthetics are rarely of crucial importance."

She moved closer, I felt her breath, and she whispered in my ear: "The insurance is being difficult about the plastic surgery. They don't want to pay for it all. They say it doesn't really look that bad. They say men used to flaunt their scars."

She ticked her glass against mine, and her breath smelled of old wine.

"Come, sit down," she said, "I don't get to meet very many interesting people, especially not since the accident."

We sat down.

Apparently I was an interesting man.

There were a lot of plants in the room. She saw me looking, and the woman I was supposed to call Trude said: "I have a green thumb."

The silence that followed this remark didn't last long, because from Max's room came a screaming that contained no words, only noises.

We both listened tensely.

It wasn't the drawn-out scream of a baby, it lasted no more than thirty seconds, maybe less. But because it contained no words, there was something tedious about it.

When it stopped, we continued our conversation.

"The doctor says to let him scream, that it will stop by itself. That it's part of the healing process."

"Yes, of course," I said. And then I spoke the sentence I would speak so often in this household. "It happens to all of us at times."

"When would you like to start?"

"Mrs. Blumenthal," I said, and swallowed some saliva.

I wasn't completely sure I wanted to start at all, in fact it seemed better not to.

There are some things you shouldn't start, not even for money.

She sprang to her feet.

"Trude Trude Trude Trude Trude Trude," she shouted, and stamped her right foot like a little girl who isn't getting her way. "How many times do I have to tell you!?"

This family had a unique, almost playful way of dealing with emotions.

The son screamed, the mother stamped, and the father was a doorman. He preferred night shifts.

She dropped back down on the couch again. "When would you like to start?"

I thought about posing the rhetorical question: Can I handle this? But instead I said: "Next week."

If anyone had asked me why I was starting when I didn't feel like starting, I would have told them: "Because she stamped her foot."

I was being led to the front door.

"God bless you," she said, and again the smell of old wine came from her mouth.

Since that day, God and Mrs. Blumenthal's breath have been inseparable.

I had been working as Max's tutor for ten months.

I came two times a week, sometimes three. For someone in his condition, he was a diligent pupil.

He could talk, but he didn't do it very often.

One afternoon I heard him say: "I feel like eating everything in the medicine cabinet."

I jotted down his remarks in the same notebook I used to keep track of his progress.

His mother, on the other hand, talked all the time.

Wine was her font of language.

After three months of working with Max, there I was sitting on the couch with his mother, amid the houseplants. As usual, after the tutoring was over.

She paid me once every two weeks, and she always made me sign a receipt on which she had neatly written: "Paid in full by Trude Blumenthal, honorarium for six lessons for Max."

The money was always in an envelope, as though it was something we had to be ashamed of.

I had just signed the receipt. A few times already I had told her that, as far as I was concerned, no receipt was necessary. She didn't listen, she was used to working with receipts.

She took the receipt from me and said: "I don't have a life."

Then, without waiting for a reply, she laid her head in my lap.

When people in an airplane think they're going to crash, it seems they embrace each other in strange ways as well.

I kissed her gingerly. On her hairdo.

That was how, for the first time, I noticed that her hair retained the smell of frankfurters.

If her life was a crashing plane, then it was taking a hell of a long time to hit the ground.

Max's mother cried in my lap, and I sat there with an envelope full of money in my hand and said: "It'll be all right, it'll be all right. It happens to all of us at times."

Providing hollow comfort is one of my strong points. I don't do it maliciously, though.

The way you have people who don't like curried chicken, I don't like emotions. Even after Mama's body had cooled and stiffened, I kept saying to myself: "It'll be all right, it'll be all right."

Mrs. Blumenthal's hands felt as though they'd been in dishwater for twenty years straight, they were big and rough and still feminine, and I felt myself growing sleepy as her hands caressed my arm.

"You have pleasant hands," I said.

Mrs. Blumenthal's teary face looked up at me expectantly, and she said: "I went to school to become a physiotherapist, but I never finished it."

Then Max began screaming again and his mother remembered that she was his mother.

She stood up, arranged her hair, clumsily because she had no mirror, and put away the signed receipt.

She walked me outside.

A föhn wind was blowing. I was dressed too warmly.

"Sorry that I let myself go like that."

Back when I was still working on my book of poetry, *Dead Languages*, I had thought up and discovered a love that was different from pity. I had been an inventor, but the only thing I'd invented was love that didn't work, the way other inventors invent airplanes that don't fly and pest-control agents that don't control pests.

Very nice, but not very practical.

"It doesn't matter," I said. "I let myself go too at times."

Some people mistook my bumbling replies for wisdom, while in fact they were born of nothing but timidity. But even more than timidity, out of social clumsiness, and actually even more than clumsiness, out of powerlessness.

From that day on, the day of the föhn wind, the day she said "Sorry that I let myself go like that," Max's mother let herself go with a certain regularity. After our tutoring sessions she pushed her head in my lap at least once a week, almost always preceded by the statement: "I don't have a life." Later she started skipping that statement as well. She had discovered that she was allowed to put her head in my lap even without that excuse.

"What is my son good at?" she sometimes asked me.

Her son wasn't good at anything, at least not anymore. But I didn't want to say that. So instead I said: "Mathematics, he's awfully good at mathematics."

At first I'd kept his mother up to date on the weensy bit of progress he made, but after a while I sensed that that wasn't what it was all about.

If I gave her a little kiss on her hairdo when she put her head in my lap, that was more than enough.

One time Max asked: "What do you think of my mother?"

It took him a long time, a minute or two, to ask a simple question like that, and I had gradually learned to understand him quite well. Still, the question took me by surprise.

I picked up a pencil sharpener. And then an eraser.

"Your mother loves you a great deal," I said.

I smiled.

It was the kind of statement that needed to be accompanied by a smile.

The hum of the electric wheelchair filled the room.

Max drove over to his cupboard.

He yanked on a drawer.

"What are you looking for, Max?" I asked.

I waited in vain for a reply, the way I'd once, long ago, waited for a phone call from Mama. She had gone on vacation with some man, an artist, to an island.

I don't remember which island, I was too young. Crete, Sicily, Malta, Rhodes, Sardinia, one of those.

We waited for Mama's return, but she didn't come back, because she was happy.

Thank God Mama's happiness never lasted long, not even on romantic islands.

Postcards arrived. From Mama, with drawings by the artist. During dinner Papa passed the cards around the table without a word.

The drawer fell to the floor.

Max's mother came bursting in. "What's going on here?" she asked.

As if I'd thrown myself on her son like some kind of pederast.

He was looking for something, I wanted to say. But it wasn't necessary anymore.

Max's mother picked up his fallen sweaters and Max himself looked at her, the way people at an aquarium look at the dolphins. Full of amazement and a slight suspicion, as though he knew he was being deceived.

"Well, Max," I said, "let's get on with it."

He shook his head.

I walked over to him, carefully picked a piece of loose skin from his cheek. His skin was rather dry.

At first I would have asked his permission to pinch off pieces of loose, dry skin. Now I did it without asking.

"It's about time we rubbed you with lotion again," his mother said.

When she said "we," she was referring to herself.

Max was sometimes rubbed with lotion from head to toe, because his skin was dry everywhere. It happened even while I was there. If I closed my eyes a little, he became a huge clump of dough being kneaded by Mrs. Blumenthal.

Before long, she'd slide Max into the oven and we would be alone at last.

One afternoon, our lesson had taken a bit longer than usual, Max's mother said: "Would you like a piece of homemade pie?" This was about four weeks after she'd first put her head in my lap.

It's easier to refuse pie from the corner bakery than it is to refuse homemade pie.

She had made pear pie.

It was still warm.

She cut off a big piece for me, and put a blob of whipped cream on it.

I ate it standing in her kitchen.

Mrs. Blumenthal rubbed salve on her hands, to make her hands softer. It didn't help much, but she did it twice a day.

"Marek," she said while smearing the salve evenly over her hands and wrists. I smelled her breath, I smelled the hand salve, and waited for what was coming.

"Marek," she said again, "did you know that the first smooch is the best?"

I put my plate down on the counter.

"You mean in general?"

"No," she said, "I'm talking about my own first smooch."

My thoughts became bogged down by the word "smooch." I usually talked about a kiss, smooch had something overbearing about it, kiss on the other hand something old-fashioned, something from long ago, something quaint.

She picked up the jar of salve again; no end had yet come to the smearing.

"Funny," I said, "a lot of times you hear the complete opposite, that the first kiss is so gooey, and such a disappointment."

She examined her hands, which had deep lines running through them.

"Gooey, no. The first one was the best."

Although I'm not accustomed to washing dishes myself or even carrying things to the kitchen, I rinsed my plate under the faucet.

"I was fourteen," Mrs. Blumenthal said.

I put the plate in the dish rack.

"The first one, and the best one, too."

"Oh," I said, as noncommittally as possible.

I tried to imagine her as a fourteen-year-old in the midst of a soul kiss, but I couldn't.

"After that it was nice sometimes too, but never again as intense."

"Oh," I said, drying my hands.

She yanked the dishrag out of my hands and folded it neatly.

"You don't want to smooch with me, do you, Marek?"

I looked at Mrs. Blumenthal. It hadn't even entered my mind, but now that she started talking about it, worlds were opened to me. "Me, with you, Mrs., uh, Trude?"

I shook my head.

"Didn't you just think about smooching with me? Be truthful now, Marek."

There was mild mockery in her voice.

She advanced on me like a giant war machine. Her mouth kept getting bigger.

"I come here for Max," I said. "You know that. And for the money, of course."

I kept my eyes fixed on her bra straps, which were visible beneath her blouse. Come to think of it, she still dressed like a fourteen-year-old.

I cleared my throat.

"It's good to sublimate feelings of lust," I said. "It's a matter of mental hygiene."

During my first year at college, a professor had once brought up the subject of mental hygiene. In fact, he never dropped the subject again.

Physical hygiene was a wonderful enough invention in my view, but mental hygiene seemed even better. Even though no one had been able to explain to me exactly what it was.

She was standing right in front of me. I lowered my eyes.

"You're very special," she said. "Someday other people will realize that, too."

Someday, when I was already dead; a lot of good that would do me.

Back when I'd studied *l'amour fou* as though there was nothing else to study, I'd read in a book that some cases of *amour fou* could result in death. Professor Hirschfeld shook his head when I said that, and as I went out the door one afternoon he told me: "I'm giving up my quest for knowledge. From now on, I want to sleep in a lot and spend my evenings in front of the TV."

"Believe me, you're special," I heard Max's mother saying. And I heard myself reply: "So are you."

In the distance I heard the hum of the electric wheelchair.

"I'll walk you to the door," she said.

We stopped by Max's room. I gave his shoulder a little squeeze.

"Bye, Trude," I said. "Thanks for everything."

"Thank you, Marek," she said, "thank you."

How many days went by between Trude Blumenthal's confession that her first kiss had been the best and the moment she began pressing her mouth to mine when we said goodbye? One single day. Twenty-four hours, no more than that.

She didn't even say: "I don't have a life." She said nothing. She locked lips with me like her life depended on it.

After she'd extricated herself, she said: "I wish I could leave him behind, I can't take it anymore, I wish I could leave him in a hospital or a shelter."

And then, before I could reply, she pressed her mouth against mine again.

The movements of her tongue were stronger than words, and in a certain sense the proof of everything she had claimed.

"Stay," she said, after she'd pulled her mouth off mine.

I said: "I have an exam tomorrow."

"Stay," she said, "I'm begging you."

She grabbed my hand. I let her pull me along into the kitchen, which we had left only a few minutes earlier, after I had stood at the rickety kitchen table and signed her receipt. Now I sat down at that same table. And Max's mother poured us pear liqueur. "I keep this for very special occasions," she said.

She drank quickly. The pear liqueur burned in my mouth, but Mrs. Blumenthal had emptied her glass before I knew it, then she stuffed her tongue in my mouth again right away and it burned even more.

When she walked out of the kitchen, I followed her like a child, half reluctant, half curious.

The door to Max's room was open a crack, but this time we didn't stop in.

The bedroom smelled of wet clothes. A doorman's uniform was hanging against the cupboard.

"Where's your husband?" I asked.

"He changed shifts," she said. "This week he's working days."

Mrs. Blumenthal was suddenly in a hurry. She unbuttoned her blouse, while I rubbed the material of the doorman's uniform between my fingers. "Very nice," I said.

She sobbed and took off her shoes. "I'm going to drop him off at a shelter," she shouted.

"Who?"

"My child, my husband."

"It happens to all of us at times," I said with the voice of a corrupt priest, which may be exactly the same voice as that of a tutor whose only interest is a passing grade.

"A shelter is for animals," I said. "Max is not an animal, Trude. Max is a person. And he's making progress."

Then she pounced on me. There's no other way to put it. Her eagerness made her prettier than she had ever been before that.

When all I had on was a pair of underpants and a sweater, I said: "I'm the tutor, I don't know if this is such a good idea. We should think of Max. And your husband."

"All I've thought about in the last couple of years is Max," she said, "only Max, I can't take it anymore," and peeled off my underpants like a poacher skinning a rabbit. She said nothing about my body. She only looked at my crotch and sighed.

Pleasure came to me in the form of Mrs. Blumenthal, who I was to call Trude. Pleasure smelled of wet clothes and maybe a little of mothballs too. But I'd be lying if I said that I was deaf and blind to that pleasure, even though I'd imagined that it would smell different, even though the decor was not all it could have been. No, I had no choice but to fall to my knees and humbly accept the pittance life had in store for me.

Max's mother's sex tasted like pear liqueur. Or would everything taste of pear liqueur from now on?

She grabbed my hair and pulled me to my feet.

"Talk," she said.

I gulped.

"Talk to me," she said.

It was an order. But I didn't know what to say.

"Doesn't your husband talk to you?"

"He has to talk to hotel guests all day. By the time he gets home, he's done enough talking."

She moved up against me. My body was cold, compared to hers.

"Talk to me like a whore," she said.

I scratched at my two-day beard. Beard was maybe a bit of an exaggeration, it was stubble. Her crumpled blouse lay on the bed.

"Mrs. Blumenthal."

"Talk to me like a whore."

"Trude," I said, "I'm the tutor, we should think of Max."

I tried to pull away.

"Talk to me like a whore, I'm begging you."

"Can't your husband do that?" I asked quietly.

She started sobbing again. "All my husband thinks about is the hotel," she said.

"I don't know how to talk to whores," I shouted.

She sobbed even harder, and no matter how I pulled, she wouldn't let go.

"I'm trying to lead an ethically principled life, how can I talk to you like a whore!"

She looked at me. My ethically principled life had come like a slap in the face. It looked like she was about to throw herself at me. Not the way a woman throws herself at a man, but the way a prisoner throws himself at the guard who's been torturing him for years.

"A philosopher," I said, "is a servant of the truth. And you are Max's mother, my employer; you're not a whore, so I don't want to talk to you that way."

"What do you know about me?!" she shrieked.

"Nothing," I whispered, "almost nothing."

"Tell me what to do," Max's mother said.

"I don't know," I said. "I'm the tutor."

I didn't want this pittance, I despised this pittance, I didn't want any pittance that smelled of wet clothes.

"Maybe," I said, "you should look for another tutor, maybe we're not good for each other."

The scream that came out of her mouth then had nothing human about it anymore.

She started yanking me around by my sweater. "You're all I have," she said. "Because of you I still feel like a woman."

I pulled myself free. Wool tore. "I don't want to hear about it," I said. "It doesn't interest me. There's no point to it. It doesn't make any difference."

"Talk, Marek," Mrs. Blumenthal said, "talk to me. Tell me how to lie, tell me what to do."

I looked at her teary but still-expectant eyes, I looked at my legs and then at the door, and finally at the doorman's uniform.

"Kiss my feet," I said.

It was a brainstorm.

Max's mother kissed my feet with an abandonment I would never have expected from her, and I remembered the first time I'd walked into this house, dry lips, résumé in hand.

She kissed and licked my shins, and then Max began scream-ing. The way he always screamed, but this time it sounded more like he was being tortured, as though someone was working on him with a hot poker.

"The walls are thin," Max's mother said, and she moved her tongue in a way that reminded me of a lizard, "they're old working-class houses. Do you know anything about the property market in Vienna?"

"Nothing," I said, "nothing, go on."

"Everything goes to the asylum-seekers, there's nothing left for us."

I pressed my hands to my ears in order not to hear Max, not to hear her, and especially not to hear myself, but it didn't help.

I dressed hastily. Max's mother was sitting on the floor.

"Don't forget this," she said.

She handed me the envelope with money, which had fallen out of my pocket when she'd thrown herself on me like there was no tomorrow.

"Goodbye, then," I said. "See you next time."

She grabbed my hand and pulled me down. "We're going to do this again, aren't we? We'll do this again, right?"

"Whenever you feel like it," I replied, "whenever you feel like it." Which sounded different from "it happens to all of us at times," but meant exactly the same thing in the long run.

"This was almost as wonderful as my first smooch," she whispered.

I freed myself, closed the bedroom door quietly behind me.

Max was still screaming.

I ran out of the house, as though even houses could come after me. It was raining gently, a warm, almost pleasant rain.

In front of a drugstore I stopped and looked at myself in a mirror.

I didn't see anything, nothing different from what you always saw.

6

Amour fou

My first kiss, unlike Trude Blumenthal's, was a nightmare; a nightmare that is, after a certain fashion, still in progress. There are nightmares you get used to, and those are the most dangerous ones, because they are addictive. At a given point you can't get along without them, you start thinking that life without that nightmare doesn't amount to anything.

As I walked through the warm rain to Cocktail Lounge The Four Roses, Mica's empty suitcase in my right hand, I wasn't thinking about Mica, or about Mama's wardrobe, or about Mrs. Blumenthal or an ethically principled life. I was thinking about that nightmare again, the way I'd thought about it so often. Austria's nightmare came from Braunau am Inn; my father's nightmares came from my mother's womb; my nightmare came from Luxembourg.

I was fourteen when I first read about *l'amour fou*.

A few weeks later, I'd made up my mind: *l'amour fou* was the chief end of man.

I wasn't sure exactly what it involved: *l'amour fou* didn't come with a starters' manual.

From older people in my surroundings who I suspected of a certain wisdom and experience in life, I tried to pry information. Especially as that wisdom and experience related to actual practice.

That didn't get me much of anywhere either. A couple of people said: "What your mother does, that's *l'amour fou*."

But I couldn't have agreed less.

What my mama did was perhaps mad, but in my eyes it had nothing to do with love.

I devoured everything I could find about *l'amour fou*. In translation and in the original French, with the help of dictionaries. A great deal of what had been written about it turned out to be awfully dry and boring. I found that unbelievable.

When, four months after my decision concerning the chief end of man, nothing drastic had happened yet, I decided to seduce our maid.

To sneak out of the house one morning with the maid and take a bus to an unknown destination came awfully close to *l'amour fou*.

Not that I felt particularly attracted to the maid, she was extremely tall and gangly and had two warts on her right knee, but when it came to Great Causes, one could not let anything as banal as attraction get in the way.

A mésalliance seemed to me a particularly strong foundation for my *amour fou*.

One evening, right before dessert, I made my first attempt to kiss the maid wildly in the kitchen.

Four peach-halves tumbled to the floor, and I took a blow that was intended for my left ear but landed on the back of my head instead. Later she explained to me that she had hit me because of the peaches, and not because of the kiss.

"I understand completely," she said, "but you have to promise never to do it again."

I looked at her, speechless. How could I keep a promise like that without betraying myself and my principles? And hadn't I read somewhere that the definition of a man is someone who doesn't betray his principles?

"I won't tell your parents," she said. "You'll grow out of it."

"Life is what you grow out of!" I shouted angrily.

Then I slammed the kitchen door behind me and went into the dining room.

This was to be the first day of my new life.

My family was sitting silently at the table, and everyone was looking at me.

"Bettina may not be much of a cook," I said, "but she's a great kisser."

My brothers looked bored, with an air of "there-goes-Marek-again," my mother began laughing loudly, and my father sprang up as though he'd been stung by some gruesome insect and chased me to my room.

After I'd received a few blows to the head, I locked myself in and began weeping passionately.

I couldn't kiss passionately, or make love passionately, play sports passionately or speak passionately when other people were around, but I could weep passionately.

L'amour fou became an obsession.

I started wearing a hat with a feather in it, but the international school considered that a violation of the dress code and kindly requested that I wear the hat only outside school hours.

The management of the international school began seeing me as a problem child. They said: "Your brothers were never a problem." But had my brothers ever read about the amour fou, had my brothers ever understood the chief end of man?

I turned fifteen, and my condition was showing no progress whatsoever.

What I was looking for, I had decided, was impossible to find with an Austrian woman, and so I crisscrossed Vienna in search of foreigners.

In parks and public gardens I now wept passionately as well, until I realized that red eyes and teary cheeks would not help in my attempts to meet foreigners.

And so I wandered back and forth through town, my hands behind my back like a skater's, and I believed that the aficionado, the initiated, would recognize me immediately as a man of *l'amour fou*.

One afternoon in an ice-cream parlor, after weeks of crisscrossing town without much to show for it, I finally made contact.

Two young women asked me to take a picture of them. There could be no doubt about it, these were foreign tourists.

A slight panic overcame me, for I knew that it would have to happen now. Now or never.

I was holding in my hand a cone, with one scoop of lemon.

"Wait," one of them said, "I'll hold that for you."

She spoke a strange kind of German.

I took their picture.

Too bad ice cream melted, for otherwise I could have taken that scoop of lemon home with me as a relic and saved it in a wooden box.

I could, of course, put the cone in a wooden box.

"My name is Marek van der Jagt," I said solemnly.

Their names were Milena and Andrea, and they both said: "Hello, Marek van der Jagt."

Andrea was the prettiest, it was Andrea who had held my ice cream for me, and it was Andrea who said: "It's too cold to be eating ice cream."

Here begins the nightmare of my first kiss, a nightmare that survived my first kiss, countless ejaculations, copulations, letters, gifts, holidays in the snow, and finally even my baldness.

I may have started thinking at a certain moment that my life was intended to be a nightmare, and that all I needed to find peace was to surrender to that intention. Hadn't I been told that happiness was the acceptance of one's self? Perhaps happiness was also the acceptance of the nightmare others had cooked up for you.

Milena and Andrea were from Luxembourg.

I had never met anyone from Luxembourg.

I hadn't even realized that people spoke German there, but then it *was* a particularly bizarre kind of German. Sometimes they descended into dialect, and then I couldn't understand them at all anymore.

What brought people from Luxembourg to Vienna?

"Vacation," Andrea said. "We've been working hard."

"I've always wanted to go to Luxembourg," I said.

It was an obvious lie; after all, who the hell wants to go to Luxembourg?

"Why would you want to do that? Did you lose something there?" Andrea said, not without a certain aggressiveness in her tone.

She had a diamond stuck in the side of her nose.

Milena said: "Luxembourg is dead." And then they both started writing postcards.

They were seventeen, they said. Two years older than me. But I seemed older, because I didn't say much. Even the kindergarten teacher had mistaken my reticence for wisdom. That's why I thought they'd believe me if I said I was seventeen, too.

My ice cream was leaking. I threw it away, but saved the cone for my wooden box.

"Do you have time for me to show you around town?" I asked.

"We're going home on Wednesday, on the night train," Andrea said.

Today was Saturday.

A lot could happen in four-and-a-half days.

"What would you two like to see?" I asked.

Andrea looked up from her postcard.

"We don't want to see anything right now," she said. "We'd rather eat something."

"We've seen so much already," Milena said.

"And we almost haven't eaten," Andrea said, "we're dying of hunger."

Food. That could be arranged.

"Would you like to try something typically Viennese?" I asked.

"Listen," Andrea said, "we've haven't had a decent meal in ages. We don't care what we eat, even if we go out for Chinese. You understand?"

I did understand. Every day I had a decent meal, and on many occasions, even at the most unexpected moments, people had said to me: "You're a decent fellow." As though I could no longer wring the decency, or rather the veneer of decency, out of my skin; even the mud I'd been dragged through other people saw as decency.

"Wait here," I shouted, "I'll be right back. Just wait for me. Don't go away. I'll be back in a minute. We're going for a decent meal. We'll get you a decent meal."

Then I ran home, faster than I'd ever run before. With the cone in my hand.

If in twenty years' time no one would remember a thing of this *amour fou*, it would all have been for naught. I wanted biographers, entering my room with gloves on, to be able to say: "This is where Marek van der Jagt lived, don't touch anything, anything you find here could be a remnant of his *amour fou*."

"Mama," I screamed as I ran up the stairs, "Mama, Mama, Mama."

I threw open the bedroom door.

Sitting in the rocking chair in front of the balcony was a man I'd never seen before. He was wearing a bathrobe.

And he was reading the paper.

"Mama!" I screamed.

"Your mother is out shopping," the man in the rocking chair said. "Are you the youngest?"

It was none of his business who I was, the youngest, the eldest, the one in the middle, it had nothing to do with him. Had I asked *him* who *he* was? He wasn't old, in any event, and for a change this specimen was clean-shaven. My mother had left the era of the needy artists a bit behind her now.

On her nightstand, I saw one of Mama's handbags.

She had at least thirty of them.

But there was no purse in it.

"What are you looking for, young man?" the visitor asked.

I ignored him.

I yanked open the dressoir and searched through the plastic bag where my mother kept all those presents she found ugly or gaudy. Or that had been given to her by men she had gradually come to despise.

I took out two brooches and a little necklace.

Then I put back the rest.

"Tell my mother I said hello," I said, and was gone.

I ran to my room and put the cone on my desk.

"Goodbye, little cone," I said. "Just stay there. No one's allowed to eat you, and you're not allowed to get dusty. You brought *l'amour fou* into my life, and you must be preserved forever."

Clutching the two brooches and the necklace, I ran back to the ice-cream parlor.

They were still sitting there. Milena and Andrea. Still working on their postcards.

"Don't go away," I said, "I'll be right back."

They looked at each other. They were puzzled, that much was clear, but then I still had to explain it all and there was no time for that yet. Later on they would understand everything.

"Just give me twenty minutes," I said.

Milena looked at her watch. "Twenty minutes, okay, but not a minute longer."

"If you're lucky, we'll still be here," Andrea said.

That made me run even faster. I wanted to be lucky.

In front of the door of a jeweler's, where I had often come with Mama, I stopped.

You had to ring the bell before they'd let you in. I rang the bell hard, and when they didn't open up right away, I rang it again.

A young woman I'd never seen before opened the door.

The shop was full. A couple of Japanese tourists, a husband and wife, a man and a girl with a basket.

I wormed my way through all the people until I was at the counter.

The owner of the jewelry shop was named Mr. Hobmeier. A fat man with a creepy smile and a moustache.

I didn't see Mr. Hobmeier anywhere, but his son was there.

Mr. Hobmeier's son looked exactly like his father, but then without the moustache. And without the creepy smile.

Both father and son groveled so badly in front of my mother that it made you sick.

As soon as I spotted Mr. Hobmeier's son, I started waving my arms as though I were about to faint and I yelled: "Emergency, an emergency!"

Since leaving the ice-cream parlor, at least six minutes had gone by; I had fourteen left.

Just to be sure, I yelled again, but now really loudly: "Emergency! This is an emergency!"

Then old Mr. Hobmeier appeared at last. With a magnifying glass in his hand.

Since he'd stopped smoking, he always walked around with a magnifying glass in his hand.

I fell into his arms.

"Mr. Hobmeier," I cried, "Mr. Hobmeier, an emergency!"

All transactions and conversations in the jeweler's came to a halt. Everyone was looking at me and my emergency.

"Ah, young Mr. Van der Jagt," Mr. Hobmeier said, fingering my haircut.

Mama had told me that Mr. Hobmeier liked little boys, and although I had less talent for cynicism then than I do now, I decided the moment had come to make use of his weakness.

"Talent is a matter of willpower," Papa once told me. I'd never believed him, but at that point I hoped it was true, because my willpower was truly enormous, my willpower had never been so huge.

"Mr. Hobmeier," I said, pressing the two brooches and the necklace into his big, warm hand. "I need to sell these, and I'm in a hurry. My life is at stake."

Mr. Hobmeier glanced at what I'd put in his hand. Then he sighed deeply and said: "Well, all right, let's go to the back."

There was a Mrs. Hobmeier, too.

Mrs. Hobmeier was as skinny as a rail. She never went into the store to help customers, because she hated customers.

Mrs. Hobmeier opened the mail.

Most of it she tore up afterwards.

I nodded to her briefly, but she didn't noticed, or didn't want to notice.

"These two," Mr. Hobmeier said, showing me the two brooches, "are worth nothing, or virtually nothing. While this," and he held the necklace up before my eyes, "is worth absolutely nothing."

"The bastards," I said.

"What?" Mr. Hobmeier asked.

"Nothing," I said.

They had given Mama worthless presents. I'd get back at them for that. Traveling at her expense to Sardinia and Crete and Malta and who knows how much farther afield, but a halfway decent necklace was apparently too much to ask.

"Hansi," Mr. Hobmeier said, "look who's honored us with a visit, it's young mister Van der Jagt."

Mrs. Hobmeier was Hansi to insiders.

But Mrs. Hobmeier didn't even look up. She tore a big envelope into four equal pieces. Perhaps she knew about her husband's predilection for boys.

"I'm in a hurry," I said, "how much will you give me for them?"

Mr. Hobmeier was leaning back against the wall. He seemed distraught.

"I can't do it," he said. "I don't sell junk like this. I'll never get rid of it."

"I'll buy it back from you within six months."

He sighed even more deeply now.

"Two thousand," he whispered.

That seemed a little on the low side to me.

I walked up and stood as close to him as I could.

I don't have much talent for selling, and even less for selling myself, but this was an emergency.

I pressed my lower body against his. Because of the difference in our heights, my lower body bumped against his sturdy thigh.

We both remained standing like that.

Then, his voice cracking, Mr. Hobmeier cried: "Hansi, look who's honored us with a visit."

He threw himself away from the wall and took a few steps towards the glass door that separated the shop from the office. The glass was painted, so no one could look through it.

Mrs. Hobmeier didn't like busybodies.

Mr. Hobmeier began laughing creepily. Although I must admit, this time his laugh sounded more desperate than creepy.

Hansi didn't even look up.

Mr. Hobmeier was sweating.

He walked back to the wall and whispered: "Four thousand, that's all I can give you. Out of my own pocket."

Didn't everything here come from Mr. Hobmeier's own pocket?

Reaching into his inside pocket, he pulled out four thousand-schilling notes and discreetly pressed them into my hand, as though I was the doorman at a nightclub and this was how he hoped to be admitted to the floor show.

He held my hand a few seconds longer than necessary.

I saw drops of sweat on his forehead, and crumbs in his moustache.

"Give my regards to your mama," he whispered. "My best customer. My very best customer."

Mrs. Hobmeier looked up for the first time and said: "You're forgetting the Hungarian."

Mrs. Hobmeier's voice cut through the room. Her voice was like a knife, one that needed sharpening.

"No, no," Mr. Hobmeier said quietly, "the Hungarian is a good customer too, but different, very different. From Mrs. Van der Jagt."

I walked to the door.

"Mrs. Hobmeier," I said, "Mr. Hobmeier. Adieu."

In those days I peppered my German with French phrases, appropriate or not.

Then I made a slight bow, the way Mama had taught me.

She had taught me that back when she still hoped I'd become a ballet dancer. She wanted me to thrill the world with my dance steps.

"The Hungarian cannot be compared with your mama," I heard Mr. Hobmeier mumble. "Tell her to come by again soon."

In the shop I said a quick goodbye to young Mr. Hobmeier, and then I was out on the street.

I had four thousands schillings, seven minutes to go, and I couldn't recall ever being so happy.

7

The Mozart among Florists

Mama's florist was named Rolf Szlapka. He adored women and flowers, and had come to the conclusion that he could best do justice to both these pursuits by opening a florist's. This to the chagrin of his father, who was a BMW dealer and would have been pleased to see his son take over the business.

But the love of cars skipped a generation in this family, and Rolf Szlapka became a florist.

Mama liked BMWs and flowers, especially white roses, and when she went in one day to trade her old BMW for a new one, Mr. Szlapka, Sr. said: "Mrs. Van der Jagt, my son Rolf just opened a little flower shop, maybe you should stop by there sometime. In fact, maybe you'd like to attend the opening?"

"Maybe I would," Mama said.

The festive opening of Rolf Szlapka's flower shop was particularly festive for Mama, for that afternoon she hooked up with no less than two lovers. One of them was Rolf Szlapka himself.

Favorable conditions were established for all. Mama received a standing discount at Rolf Szlapka, Jr.'s, in exchange for stolen kisses. And unless I am mistaken, they once even made love at the back of the shop, where all the funeral wreaths and bridal bouquets were assembled.

Old Szlapka began giving her considerable discounts on his cars as well, and Mama convinced her entire circle of acquaintances to buy a BMW from the best BMW dealer in Austria, Szlapka, Sr.

But as for Rolf, with time the arrangement began to take on more painful facets.

Mama's ship of state had come sailing into his shop, and refused to leave.

He couldn't understand how she could love him one moment and lie in his arms, and the next moment be with someone else and forget that Rolf Szlapka even existed.

Perhaps no one can understand that, perhaps it's not human to understand that.

And then, when he'd call, she would say: "Never call me at home, I know how to find you."

Each time he had once again decided to forget all about Mama, she would come strolling into his shop with a gleam in her eye and a present in her hand, and her first question would always be: "Where have you been all this time? Why didn't you get in touch with me? You've been neglecting me. What beautiful roses! I'd like forty of them."

Rolf Szlapka didn't dare to say: "You're the one who said I shouldn't call. Where have *you* been?"

He was simply pleased to receive her kisses. My mama dealt out pittances of gold and silk, and paraded through life as though it were a play undeserving of her acting talent.

As I was standing in front of the jewelry store with Mr. Hobmeier's four thousand shillings in my hand, the happiest moment in my life till then, I suddenly decided to pop by Szlapka's flower shop. I had a little less than seven minutes, which would be just enough.

I had my doubts about whether flowers were suitable for *l'amour fou*, but one always had to work one's way up from the bottom.

Besides, it seemed to me that it would do no harm to walk in on the girls from Luxembourg with an armful of flowers. "Everyone likes flowers," Papa used to say, whenever Mama would ask: "What on earth can we give them?"

I ran to Rolf Szlapka's and, with happiness now within reach, I ran faster and faster without growing tired, without feeling the pain in my side, without asking myself what the people in the jewelry store must have thought and were thinking about me now, or what Rolf Szlapka would think of me when I came bursting into his shop.

The shop was empty.

"Mr. Szlapka," I yelled, "Mr. Szlapka!"

I ran to the back. I'd been here so often with Mama, I knew the way.

Mama always walked on through to the back as well. Even when the shop was full and Mr. Szlapka was still helping a customer.

Rolf was working on a funeral wreath. He abandoned it as soon as he saw me.

He walked over and slapped me on the shoulder. His father always did that, too.

"Marek," he said, "how's your mother?"

"Good," I said, "very good, at least I think so. I need two bunches of red roses, fast. Long-stemmed."

That's what Mama always said: "Long-stemmed, Rolf, you can't make those stems too long for me."

Whenever Mama had been with Rolf Szlapka, she always came home with white, long-stemmed roses.

"Make it two bunches of eight."

Why eight, I had no idea, but it seemed like a nice number.

He went to the front of the shop and calmly began picking out the prettiest roses. So calmly that it gave me the jitters.

"I'm in a hurry," I said, "please."

He started pulling roses out of the bucket more quickly, faster and faster, and I saw myself rushing into the ice-cream parlor with

Rolf Szlapka's flowers. "Rolf Szlapka is the Mozart among florists," Mama had said once. Probably to annoy Papa, and it worked, because he'd shouted right back: "How can you compare a florist to Mozart?"

"It's been such a long time since I've seen your mother," Szlapka, Jr. said. "How is she doing?" And then, in a whisper: "I've put aside some beautiful white roses for her, be sure to tell her that."

If you didn't know better, you'd think that Mama's goal in life was to be promiscuous. But she was not a slave to her lust, nor was she prompted by financial cares.

All she was looking for was something that can't be found in this world.

In the end, everyone was a stranger to her, that is why she could never stay too long in one place, that is why she had to keep going.

Other people must have seen in her an unguided missile hovering over Vienna, unpredictable and dangerous to anyone who came too close, simply because unguided missiles are always unpredictable. And dangerous. But who wouldn't like, at least once in their life, to be struck by an unguided missile, who wouldn't like to succeed where others fail, who wouldn't like to conquer where others remain defeated for all time?

Rolf Szlapka had made me two bunches of eight long-stemmed roses.

"I'll put it on the bill," he said.

Szlapka thought he had to win me over in order to win my mother's love. If only everyone thought that.

He held the door open for me.

"I'll tell Mama that you've put aside those white roses for her," I said. "If I see her, that is. She's sort of been on the move lately."

His face clouded over. He must have thought I was a nasty young man, even though I was only trying to be honest.

Honesty is a nasty business, but I only discovered that later.

I had three minutes left.

Wearing my black ankle boots and clutching two bunches of roses, I ran to the ice-cream parlor where, all things being equal, two young ladies from Luxembourg were waiting for at least a decent meal.

I dropped the roses twice, but that didn't matter, I was running headlong towards happiness.

And while I ran through Vienna with Szlapka's flowers, I thought: if only Mama could see me now, then she'd finally see in me the ballet dancer she'd always wanted me to be. And if I was now the ballet dancer I was meant to be, then this was my ballet, a ballet for my mama.

They were sitting at the window, on stools, and an older man was sitting between them.

Andrea was talking to that older man.

Milena was staring out the window, slightly bored.

"Here I am," I said.

My voice cracked.

Milena looked at her watch.

Andrea was looking at the old man as he spoke. She had no time for me right then.

I sat down.

The old man smelled of hard liquor, and he had spots on his shirt. His head glistened with sweat. I had seen him before, on the street.

"Clack click clack say the horses' hooves," I heard him say, "and when you hear that—clack click clack—then you know you're still alive."

Andrea laughed.

I shook the old man's hand and said: "Marek van der Jagt, pleased to meet you."

He held onto my hand for a second, but couldn't summon up much more attention than that for me.

"Clack click clack say the horses' hooves," he said. "Wait a minute, I want to draw your soul."

"He wants to draw her soul," I told Milena.

Milena didn't say anything.

I had put down the flowers, as though I just happened to have them with me, as though I'd picked them up on an errand for my mother.

"Does she do that often?" I asked Milena, "Let people draw her soul?"

Milena had long brown hair and brown eyes and a stern mouth. The first time you saw her you thought she looked like she didn't approve, but when you got to know her better you realized that she really didn't approve. The world did not meet with her approval.

Later she told me that her mother had come from Algeria and her father was Norwegian, and that they'd ended up in Luxembourg by accident.

Milena looked at the flowers, then glanced over at Andrea, who was following the old man's movements. He was drawing on a crumpled scratch pad.

"She's very open," Milena said.

I heard in the way she said it that she would have liked to be that open too, that maybe she was waiting for someone to open her, like a can of sardines. Isn't that what we're all waiting for? To be opened and devoured, for then we've proved our usefulness. According to Papa, a useful life was a happy life. And even though Mama would never have put it that way, and even though she would definitely have had other associations with the word "useful," wasn't that exactly how she felt about it as well?

Useful summed up everything I had no desire to be.

A young man wiped down our table with a damp cloth. Ashtrays were being emptied. He was wearing a little paper hat. Someone had once told me they were hygienic hats, to keep dirt from falling from his hair onto the customers' ice cream.

Papa always said: "All kinds of garbage falls out of people's hair, which is why you should never touch your hair while you're eating."

I couldn't believe that garbage fell out of Andrea's hair. And as far as I could tell there wasn't any garbage falling out of Milena's hair either.

"Before very long, we should probably go and eat a decent meal," I said. "You two were starving, right?"

No one responded.

I was afraid the drunk was going to go with us and that, by the end of the evening, I'd be left behind with him and that he'd still be making the sound of horses' hooves.

Mama would have thought that was wonderful, she would have wanted me to take him home with me.

He was finished with his drawing.

We admired Andrea's soul, which according to the drunk looked a lot like Jesus on the cross.

"Hey, sorry I haven't been talking to you," Andrea said, "but I'm busy with something else right now."

"That's fine," I said. "Have you known him for a long time?"

"He came in here and sat down beside us and started talking."

That's how simple life was. Sit down beside someone and talk. Is that the way Mama did it? No, Mama didn't sit down, Mama remained standing, and she usually let the other people talk, then interrupted them and said: "I need something at the stationer's. Can we go and buy that?"

Meaning she wanted you to buy it for her.

I shoved aside the flowers Rolf Szlapka had wrapped so carefully. Maybe he'd thought the flowers were for Mama, maybe that was why he'd wrapped them so lovingly. He had caressed the paper, it seemed, while I had stamped my feet in impatience.

"I'd like to marry you," I heard the old man say. "In my head, of course, not for real. Shall I give you my post office box?"

Andrea laughed.

It was perverse of her to laugh so sweetly at such propositions. Of course I was aware that perversity and *l'amour fou* did not rule each other out, but *l'amour fou* could never be something along the lines of: comrade Stalin says it's good, so it's good. *L'amour fou* wasn't Stalinism.

The drunk's stubbles were white in some spots, gray in others.

"How many bottles of wine have you had?" Andrea asked in a loud and cheerful voice, as if the question was the start of a good joke.

The man thought about it a little, then said: "Where do you want me to start counting?"

His hand touched Andrea's hair.

"Start counting from this morning," I said, because I wanted to add to the conversation, and because I wanted Andrea to look at me and to understand that none of this was about anything but *l'amour fou*. Not about small talk in an ice-cream parlor, followed by a Chinese dinner.

But my own voice sounded unpleasant in my ears, and I realized immediately that one did not make comments like that to older people who were half-drunk.

"I think I'll start at the first of the month," the old man said. "What day is it today?"

For a moment, no one spoke.

"Saturday," I said.

He counted.

His hand toyed loosely with Andrea's hair.

His hand was the color of cement.

Andrea was looking at him as though she'd just met her personal savior.

An Italian hit came on in the background. The ice-cream parlor was run by Italians from Trieste, who had been in Austria for more than twenty years.

Mama had been in Trieste once too, with a lover, but I don't remember which one. She didn't like Trieste much, it was too close to home. "It was like staying in Austria," she said.

Szlapka's flowers were still lying on the table, like the leftovers from a stand-up reception that had broken up half an hour before time.

Mama had wanted me to beguile the world with my dance steps, but it suddenly seemed distinctly possible to me that not only would my dance steps not beguile the world, but my *amour fou* wouldn't either, and neither would my homemade salmon on toast. That I, Marek van der Jagt, would leave the world unbeguiled.

I had to revolt. There was no other choice. Without revolting, I would end up in life insurance.

As from that afternoon at two, I was a man in revolt. If I were destined not to beguile the world, then I wouldn't let that happen without a fight.

I slammed my hand down hard on the table and hurt myself.

But the old man didn't even look up, and Andrea paid no attention to my pounding either.

Milena lit a cigarette.

"My father was a Viking," she said.

"I brought you flowers," I shouted.

"Two days before I was born, he ran away," Milena said, "and we never saw him again."

I tore the paper off the flowers and began passing out roses.

"Here, this is for you," I said, and shoved a couple in Milena's hand, "and for you," and laid a few roses in the drunkard's lap, and the rest I pressed against Andrea's breasts. "Throw them away," I said, "if they bother you. It was only the thought."

The girls from Luxembourg stared at me, but the old man ignored me and my flowers.

He was busy counting.

When he finally opened his mouth, however, it was no number that came out, it was not even a rough estimate.

"Clack click clack say the horses' hooves," he said, "and when you hear that you know you're still alive."

He was still holding on to Andrea's hair, and she said: "Shall I give you my address? Then we can write to each other."

8

Peking Duck

In the phone book I found a Chinese restaurant, and reserved a table for three.

"You don't meet people like him in Luxembourg," Andrea said, once we'd finally left the ice-cream parlor.

"Come on," I said, "you run into people like that in every big city."

"But Luxembourg isn't a big city," Andrea said, and Milena shrugged.

Once we were in the taxi, she asked me: "So, and what's it like to be an Austrian?"

The restaurant wasn't far, we could have walked just as easily, but I wasn't taking any chances. I figured: if we walk, they'll stop in front of shops, then they'll want to go in to look at a blouse or a plastic necklace, and before you know it I'll have lost them in the crowd.

"Fine," I said. "What's it like to be a Luxembourger?"

The remains of Rolf Szlapka's roses were lying in Milena's lap.

It was starting off awfully tame for an *amour fou*, but maybe it always went that way.

Maybe it always started off tame and then suddenly went wild.

I looked at the diamond in Andrea's nose.

"I'm admiring your diamond," I said.

"Oh, that," she said. "I've had it since I was fourteen."

"She's got a lot more sticking in her," Milena said, and rolled down the window.

No one in the restaurant recognized the name Van der Jagt, no one knew anything about a reservation.

"I reserved a table," I said for the umpteenth time, "for three. I'm absolutely sure."

The restaurant wasn't exactly what you'd call crowded.

There were eight people sitting at a long table. They were celebrating something. It looked like a copper wedding anniversary.

There were red tablecloths everywhere.

The restaurant people flipped through a big book, searching for my name.

But the name was nowhere to be found.

"Why don't we just sit down?" Andrea said.

They showed us to a table by the window. I didn't like that very much. I was afraid Papa would come by, wearing his hat and carrying his briefcase, and that he would stop in front of the window and look in and see me.

He wouldn't show that he'd recognized me. He would just stand there for a few seconds, as though he was waiting for something else to happen. To have me run outside and say hello and ask: "Come in and have something to eat, Papa." And when that didn't happen, he would walk on in silence.

Andrea and Milena sat beside each other on one side of the table, I sat across from them. I had a view of the street, they had a view of the restaurant.

They were looking at the menu.

My happiness was already starting to evaporate, but I still had four thousand schillings in my pocket and the day was still young. A lot could happen.

Perhaps there had been secret signs I had missed, or interpreted wrongly.

Andrea had a little nose, and she wore a shirt that looked like it had been washed too hot, too often. Maybe that was just the fashion.

Whatever it was, it only made her prettier.

"What do you do?" she asked. And she closed the menu, on which a yellow dragon had been drawn with a great lack of skill.

"I'm still at school," I said. "What about you two?"

"We're almost finished," Andrea said. "That's why we're here."

"To celebrate having worked so hard," Milena added.

The white wine I'd ordered was brought to the table.

"Is it Chinese?" Andrea asked. She seemed to think that was an awfully funny question, because she started laughing loudly, and just to be sure I laughed along.

Both of them were sitting there as though they might get up and walk away any moment, without even saying goodbye.

"What's your name?" Andrea asked the waiter.

He mumbled an unintelligible name.

Then he mumbled another unintelligible name, and then another, and then we realized that he was summing up the day's specialties.

No one wanted a specialty of the day.

"Nice to meet you," Andrea said to the waiter. "You have pretty eyes."

A smiled appeared on his face, but it was a pained smile. A smile that looked like it hurt.

He wrote down our orders and left. We had ordered duck. The three of us were going to share a Peking duck.

"That's festive," I said. "Peking duck."

Papa always talked about festive salmon, festive steak, a festive slice of *foie gras*, and now I was doing the same thing.

L'amour fou and Peking duck, it was a strange combination, but not one that ruled out all chances of success.

"We've never had Peking duck," Milena said.

"No," Andrea said, "we had to come all the way to Vienna to discover Peking duck." And then she plucked something out of her nose.

"Sorry," she said, "there was something in the way. You don't mind, do you? Ordinarily I don't do that when other people are around, but you're so nice, and it really *was* bothering me."

I shook my head. The kind of shake that could mean anything. That I didn't mind, that I did mind, that there were all kinds of things in my nose too that needed to be removed.

They hadn't thanked me for the flowers. Of course it was awfully traditional, maybe a little too traditional, to thank someone for flowers, even if they were long-stemmed roses from Rolf Szlapka.

Amour fou came without thank-yous.

"We're not embarrassing you, are we?" Andrea asked.

Again, I shook my head.

How could they be embarrassing me? If I was embarrassed by anything, it would have to be myself and my having said "festive," the way Papa always did.

Andrea was slender, but she ate half of what was on Milena's plate and at least three-quarters of mine. Peking duck is fairly greasy, at least this Peking duck was awfully greasy.

When she shivered, I gave her my sports coat.

Andrea looked at herself in the mirror with my sports coat on.

Mama always picked out my sports coats for me.

"Where are you two staying?" I asked.

Our conversation was dotted with ominous silences.

Andrea had already said a few times: "If you don't know what to say, then just sing for us."

I told them I couldn't sing, that my mama had once sung for money, but that she'd stopped doing that after she had her first baby.

"And what does she do now?" Milena asked. "Your mama?"

I tore some skin off the duck that was on my plate, and Andrea lit a cigarette.

What did my mama do, what did she do now? What could I say? My mama breaks hearts? Could you say that about your own mother?

Papa never raised a finger to stop her, he tolerated her lovers as long as certain unwritten laws were not violated.

Sometimes I had the feeling that she blamed him for that. That she somehow regretted the fact that he never yanked her by the hair and said: "Now it's over, no more lovers, now you're going to behave yourself."

She would never have said as much to Papa, of course, but then she didn't say much to Papa anyway. There were days, however, when it seemed she was trying to provoke him, hoping he would say: "Where are you going at this hour?" Or: "I don't want you going out like that, put something else on." But Papa never said anything. Papa was silent.

"My mother," I said, "has a busy social life."

"And what about you?" Milena asked.

"I'm a man in revolt."

"Is that fairly demanding?" Milena wanted to know.

"How long have you been doing that?" Andrea asked.

"Since this afternoon," I said.

Andrea squinted like she was looking into the sun, and said, "When we met you, when you said you wanted to show us around town, we thought you were a rapist."

"That's right," Milena said. "We've already met three rapists in Vienna."

"But you haven't been raped, have you?"

"No, not yet," Andrea said, sniffing loudly.

"But how did you know they were rapists?"

"You sense that kind of thing," Milena said.

Andrea dropped some cigarette ash on my sports coat.

I couldn't tell whether it was an accident, or whether she did it on purpose.

"Please don't burn a hole in it," I wanted to say, but fortunately I heard how sappy that sounded even before I could open my mouth. *L' amour fou* could survive a few holes.

Andrea was still cold. She kept getting colder all the time, it seemed.

"Do you guys feel like leaving?" I asked.

"We feel like having a cup of coffee," Andrea said. "Otherwise we'll fall asleep. We didn't sleep much last night."

"Or the night before, either," Milena said.

That lack of sleep sounded like a good sign to me. From what I'd understood, the thing I was after was accompanied by a lack of sleep.

The copper wedding anniversary party was slowly getting up from the table.

It looked like the food had been too much for them. Or maybe it was the copper anniversary.

The coffee arrived. Milena got up and went to the toilet. She wasn't thin at all.

"Did she tell you that her father is Norwegian, a Viking?" Andrea asked.

"Yes," I said.

"Don't believe everything she says. Her father's really only Danish."

"Only Danish," I echoed.

"But don't tell her I said that."

"No, of course not."

Andrea looked at the roses, which were pretty much bedraggled by then.

She sighed.

"I don't really like roses much," she said. "At least not red ones."

"I don't either," I said. "Shall we throw them away?"

Milena came back from the toilet.

"We're staying with a friend of my stepbrother's, isn't that what you wanted to know?"

I'd asked that about half an hour ago.

"Yes," I said. "That's what I meant. Nice place?"

Both of them shrugged at the same time.

"It's a place," Andrea said, and Milena whispered: "A pretty cold place."

Some Chinese desserts arrived, but they did as little for Andrea as had the roses.

The Chinese waiter laid the bill on the table and disappeared quickly, no doubt afraid of more unsolicited compliments.

"We like men more than we like flowers," Milena said.

I picked up the bill from the little plate where it lay with a few wrapped peppermints, and studied it, until I realized that was far too traditional as well.

I looked at the total. In the future I would look only at the total.

"Watch out," Andrea said. "Her mother's from Algeria, she's very warm-blooded."

"My father's a Viking," Milena said.

"An Algerian Jewess," Andrea went on, "extremely warm-blooded."

"Algerian Jewesses are especially warm-blooded," Milena said, "and also very fat. But fortunately I also have Viking blood in me."

"Do you feel like having a drink before we go?" I asked.

"What time is it?" Andrea asked. And then, without waiting for a reply. "We'll have to call, her stepbrother's friend will be waiting for us. Do you have any change?"

I searched in my pants pocket, then laid a handful of coins in Andrea's elegant little hand.

Minutes went by. If this had been Mama's ballet, she'd now be shaking her head, disgruntled and impatient. She was basically an impatient person. Almost everything went too slowly and took too long for her.

I adopted the pose of a man in thought. The waiter brought the change, and I kept pretending to be deep in thought.

Milena was chewing gum. "Do I look Algerian?" she wanted to know.

I examined her face.

"No, not Algerian," I said. "But exotic." Right away I regretted that reply as well.

"She's a blabbermouth," Milena said. "But that's because she's so unsure of herself."

She wrapped her chewing gum in an empty cigarette pack.

"Every morning she takes a bath with my stepbrother's friend, and she talks a mile a minute."

"In the tub?"

"Yeah, where else? She sits in the tub with him for hours, it drives me nuts."

"Aha," I said. "So they sit in the bathtub and talk. Is your stepbrother's friend a Viking too?"

"No, Algerian. A half-blood, just like me."

Andrea came back, but she didn't sit down.

"It's all arranged," she said. "Let's go."

The door of the Chinese restaurant was already locked from the inside.

The waiter with the pretty eyes let us out with a bow. And the roses I'd planned to throw away, because Andrea was less than delighted with them, Andrea now held in her hand.

She saw me looking.

"It would be a waste, wouldn't it?"

It was a "wouldn't it" with one of those long, drawn-out question marks.

I had no idea where to take them. Andrea was still wearing my sports coat, I was cold, but I had sworn to God and to Mama that I wouldn't let my teeth chatter. And the Peking duck had made a sizeable dent in my bankroll. I'd always thought Chinese food was cheap.

"I don't care what we go and do," Andrea said. "I just don't want to hang around here."

9

We Don't Seem to Excite You Much

Catty-corner to the Jewish Museum was an American bar where I'd never been before, but into which I now walked as though I went in there every day.

An American bar in a cellar, that seemed the right thing for young women from Luxembourg.

There were four barstools. And a few tables with little candles burning on them.

Instead of chairs, the bar had sawed-off tree trunks.

Andrea looked around.

"I'm not going to sit on a sawed-off tree trunk," she said.

"No," Milena said, "we've got those at home."

The barkeeper wasn't American either. The barkeeper was from Tyrol.

"This is my first night here," he said, "so you people will have to help me a little. If you want anything complicated to drink."

"We don't want to drink anything complicated," Andrea said.

And Milena said: "We just want to drink something, so make whatever you can."

"I actually feel like a cup of coffee," I said, "do you have coffee?"

The man from Tyrol looked around the bar and said: "I think so."

It was my turn now to prepare myself for a wakeful night.

"Don't you have any friends?" Andrea asked.

She was playing with the candle wax.

"I have two brothers," I said.

"Ah," said Milena. "Now the cat's out of the bag." And she giggled.

How do nightmares begin? I've asked myself that many times. Stories begin, lives begin, the sea begins somewhere and ends somewhere else, but nightmares don't begin. In nightmares you get lost, and only when you're in the middle of them do you realize it's a nightmare, and then you ask yourself: "Why didn't I see this coming? Why didn't anyone warn me? How could I be so blind?"

The coffee arrived. It was lukewarm. I didn't dare to say anything about it. So what if the coffee was lukewarm? So what if they washed their hands in the coffee?

"Can't your brothers come down here?" Andrea asked. "Or are were going to be stuck with you all night? Hey, I didn't mean that to sound nasty, but there are two of us and you're all alone."

I looked at the ceiling. It seemed to be made of tree trunks too.

"My brothers are older than I am, and they're always busy," I said.

"We figured you were probably the youngest," Milena said.

"You did?"

"You can sense these things," Milena said. "I'm the youngest too."

"At first we thought you were a rapist, when you wanted to show us around town before you even knew us. We looked at each other and thought: here we go again, another rapist."

I wiped my hand on my trousers. My hand was clammy, clammy the way the woods can be clammy in autumn.

"I'm not a rapist," I said. "I just thought you two might want to see the town."

"We've seen most of it already," Andrea said. "Maybe tomorrow we can go to a good museum."

A man had just come in, and I heard the barkeeper from Tyrol say to him: "This is my first night. If you want anything complicated, you'll have to help me out a bit."

"A palace would be okay too," Milena said. "An old palace."

Mama liked palaces, and I thought about her wardrobe and remembered that one evening not so long ago she had gone out in hot pants. Red leather hot pants. Papa had shaken his head, but even the hot pants couldn't lure him into surrendering his silence. Mama had the figure of a young girl, her eyes were the only thing that showed you she was older and that life had eaten away at her. Mama wanted to glitter, and to elicit desire. But anything that went further than desire she fended off. It would only erode her glitter, it would ultimately destroy her glitter. It hurt Mama when she didn't glitter, the littlest imperfection tormented her, she had driven countless hairdressers to despair. Those who only want to glitter don't exist when no one else is looking.

"Call your brothers," Andrea said. "Maybe they feel like going to an American bar."

I searched my pockets for any change I might still have.

"Is there a phone in here?" I asked.

"Back by the toilets," the barkeeper said.

"I don't think they'll want to, but I'll try," I told Andrea.

The diamond in her nose glittered in the candlelight.

"Just try it," she said. "I know you can do it."

The maid picked up the phone.

"Marek," she said, "where are you? You didn't show up for dinner."

"No," I said, "I couldn't make it."

I asked to speak to Pavel. Then I heard her calling his name, and I thought about Milena and Andrea and about Pavel's career, which he had taken so seriously even when he was nine.

"Yeah, what is it?"

His voice always sounded like he needed a cold remedy. He rubbed his hands a few times a day with costly ointment, because he had costly hands with which he planned to play costly instruments on international podia. Until a few years later, that is, when he discovered economics and decided from one day to the next to become a brilliant economist. I think it didn't really matter to him much what he became, as long as he could pass for brilliant.

Ever since I'd known him he'd been waiting for the world to applaud. It must have been a disease that ran in the family.

Some people wait all their lives for the world to applaud, and discover only right before they die that they've been playing to an empty auditorium.

Maybe that's what failure is, the failure my brothers and I had learned to combat by hankering after success and recognition. It depends on your definition of failure. Most people would say I have already failed, because the world doesn't applaud for many philosophers. But then, I don't really want to be a philosopher, my study is an excuse, an alternative punishment.

I explained to Pavel where I was, and with whom.

Of course I didn't say anything about *l'amour fou*, or about Mr. Hobmeier and the jewels Mama got from her lovers that turned out to be worth less than we'd supposed. We never talked about important things, Pavel and I, we never really talked about our parents. The most we ever said were things like: "Isn't that just like Mama?," or "Papa's gone to Frankfurt for two days."

Pavel sounded enthusiastic. That was unusual.

He said he knew the bar and that he would stop by, and I could tell from the way he said it that he would come by as the older brother, the gifted older brother who touched costly instruments and been allowed to play them, and who rubbed his hands several times a day with costly ointments.

The thought of it made me smile, because I couldn't image Andrea and Milena being all too impressed by him and his stories.

"I'll be there right away," he said. "But I don't think I'll stay long. I just want to see these two teenyboppers."

"Well, teenyboppers," I said. "Girls from Luxembourg."

"Knowing you, they'll be teenyboppers."

Some women remain teenyboppers all their lives. Their voices stay a little too high, they swing their handbags a little too wildly, they keep giggling at the wrong moments and, once there's nothing else coquette about them, they still go on making movements with their head and hands that in some remote past had once passed for coquette. I think Pavel liked that, because he married a woman who is still a teenybopper and will remain a teenybopper until the day she dies. She doesn't like me. As though she senses that I look right through her and see the naked teenybopper she never grew beyond.

I went back up to the lounge. "Pavel's coming," I said. "I'm sure you'll like him."

"Does he look like you?" Andrea asked.

He didn't look like me, he didn't look like anyone in the family, maybe a little bit like Papa, because he was tall, too. "He's taller than me," I said. And I felt like saying more, but it seemed like a better idea to me to let them find out for themselves. There were still a few crumpled roses in torn paper on the table beside Andrea.

Sometimes Mama couldn't remember a lover's name, and she'd say to me: "That man, over there beside the piano, I'm sure I know him, what's his name again?"

Some men didn't mind having to refresh Mama's memory all the time, even when it came to something as seemingly simple as their own name. Others refused to put up with it, and said: "If you can't even remember my name, maybe we should stop seeing each other."

Mama would look at me then and say: "Some people are so demanding."

Mama's love needed no names. Mama said: "I remember the important things. A name isn't important, in fact, an address isn't either."

What the essentials were, if names and addresses were so unimportant, I never got around to asking.

She was drinking coffee now too, Andrea, as though readying herself for yet another wakeful night.

"You don't look very excited," Milena said suddenly.

She was staring at my crotch.

Andrea was looking now too.

"No," she said. "We don't seem to excite you much."

"No, I just ate," I said.

"Oh," Andrea said. "So you never get excited after eating. If I were you, I'd start eating less."

And Milena said: "Well, I mean 'just'; we ate at least two hours ago."

It was time for me to do something, but I didn't know what.

I was paralyzed. When Mama died I was paralyzed too, like being frozen. Everyone talked to me and tried to comfort me, and all I could think was: should I keep living with Papa, or find a place of my own? As if the thoughts running through my brain didn't belong there, but I couldn't stop them, either.

Later, I thought: I hope they put a pretty dress on Mama and not some hand-me-down, just because they think it's a waste to bury her in an Emmanuel Ungaro.

Mama loved Emmanuel Ungaro, she even claimed to have met him once. If life is a room, then Mama hung streamers all over that room, and streamers aren't the same as lies. But other people tore those streamers down off the walls and ceiling.

Maybe Mama's streamers weren't pretty enough, or maybe she'd hung them in the wrong place, or at the wrong moment.

One day she grew tired of climbing the stepladder and hanging up streamers all the time, and decided to live in a bare room.

"I don't digest that quickly," I said.

Andrea brushed the back of her hand across my cheek.

"What is it you want from us, besides sex?"

I did my best to look noncommittal.

And then I also did my best to smile.

Gasping for breath was for fish, not for humans.

Now I knew how *l'amour fou* began.

Andrea's touch smoldered on my cheek, like someone had held a couple of burning cigars against it.

Papa smoked cigars, and he had ruined two of Mama's dresses by accidentally bumping against them with a Montecristo. Whoops, there went another hole in the dress.

Mama said: "Your father is one of the clumsiest men I've ever known, I must have been blind when I met him." But Papa said: "That's what she gets for buying dresses that fall apart as soon as you put them on."

"I want to show you the town, I already told you that."

They both laughed so eagerly that they almost seemed cheerful.

A few minutes after that, Pavel came in. He'd dressed for the occasion. He had put on his best suit and his hair gleamed with pomade. Or maybe he rubbed that hand ointment on his hair, too.

"This is Pavel," I said, "my brother. This is Andrea, and this is Milena."

I looked at Pavel's hands. He has very small hands. Some people fell in love with his hands, that's how uniquely elegant and well-tended they were.

He laid his hands on the bar. Everyone has some part of their body they use to show off.

"We missed you at dinner," Pavel said, "but then I realize that ladies come first."

Pavel liked to use words and expressions that made him seem older. Now that he's older, he uses the same words and expressions, but without the same effect.

Andrea sighed deeply.

"Pavel," Andrea said, "tell us, what's it like being Austrian?"

We were standing next to each other in the men's room, pissing.

I couldn't piss well with other people standing next to me, but Pavel didn't have much trouble with it.

While I was still busy pressing fluid out of my bladder, Pavel looked at himself in the mirror. He plucked something from between his teeth and tossed it on the floor. Pavel was very particular about minor flaws and blemishes. He was the first one in our family to start trimming his eyebrows. Our eyebrows are the greatest thing we have in common.

Pavel didn't like to fight, but he had told me on occasion: "When it comes right down to it, go for the eyes and push as hard as you can."

"Aren't you finished yet?" he asked.

Pavel had made Andrea laugh loudly with his story about how I had tried to kiss the maid in the kitchen, and how the peach halves fell on the floor. That was rather amazing, because he didn't usually make people laugh. But Andrea laughed a lot that evening.

I buttoned my fly, held my hands under the tap for two seconds, and said: "Yes."

"Yes, what?"

"Yes," I said, "we can go."

When it turned out that I would not become a ballet dancer, not even an obscure one, Mama turned her hopes to Pavel and his costly instruments.

It was spring, but the nights were still cold, and when we went back out onto the street I saw Andrea and Milena shivering. Pavel took off his sports coat and put it around Milena's shoulders, even though she said that wasn't necessary. You could see the goose bumps on her arms even from a distance.

I had to learn to forget everything I had learned. That, I reckoned, was the essence of *l'amour fou*, at least in the beginning.

And maybe that's what keeps you busy for the rest of your life, forgetting what you've learned, tuning out the voices that tell you there's no substitute for success. And that you'll never be successful if your sports coat is covered with spots.

Mama didn't care about spots. She said: "We'll buy you a new one."

But Mama had farmed out our upbringing to others.

At the international school, they had asked me once: "Who does the upbringing at your house?"

A peculiar question, as though doing the upbringing was something like doing the dishes. The maid does the dishes, and the upbringing we don't do at all.

I had looked at the guidance counselor when he asked me that.

"I think it's my father," I said. "Because Mama tends not to be there."

"Does her work keep her busy?" he asked interestedly. "She does a lot of charity work, doesn't she?"

"That's right," I said rather glumly. I was still bothered by the question of who did the upbringing at our house.

The guidance counselor took my hand. "It's people like your mother," he said, "who make the world go 'round."

I smiled.

Pavel paid for all of us. The man from Tyrol thanked us, and I saw him looking at Andrea and Milena with a look I would see so often after that. Pavel led the way, his costly hands waving in the air, and we followed him.

It had started raining, and Milena said: "I haven't had a shower for a while."

"Her father's a Viking," I said, and I was sorry that I'd phoned Pavel. I should have said I didn't have any brothers, any friends either, and that they'd have to make do with me that evening, and that if they didn't like it they could go back to that stepbrother's friend.

Pavel tried to flag down a taxi, but they were all taken, because it was raining.

I put my arm around Milena. Pavel already had his arm around Andrea. The choice was limited.

"Let's go to our house," he said. "Everyone there's asleep already, and Mama has other things to worry about."

That last part was true, but it didn't mean she wouldn't worry about whoever we took home with us.

"All we want is a little coffee," Andrea said. "We don't want to drink anymore."

"I'd like some tea," Milena said.

Then Pavel succeeded in hailing a cab.

He sat beside the driver, and I sat in the back between Andrea and Milena.

They had stopped talking, so I asked Milena why she hadn't taken a shower for so long.

"Because that sweet thing over there spends two hours in the tub every morning," she said.

10

My Father Is a Viking

"Better take off your shoes," Pavel said, once we were in the hall. "Our father's a light sleeper, he's always lying in wait for burglars."

There was a gun in Papa's nightstand. And before long there would be a gun in Mama's nightstand too.

Sometimes Papa put cotton in his ears, because he was driven crazy by the sounds Mama made walking around the house at night in search of some lost object. But how can you lie in wait for burglars with cotton in your ears?

Andrea and Milena took off their shoes.

We went upstairs, to Pavel's room, with its many costly instruments on the floor and walls.

He played piano and the violin. People said he was better at the piano, but I couldn't hear the difference.

"I'll make some tea," Pavel said, and ran downstairs.

It was unlike him to be so attentive.

Milena and Andrea walked around the room and looked at the instruments, and at the big poster for an opera by Alban Berg that Pavel had hanging on the wall, maybe because he hoped to one day get that far in the world himself.

"You guys have a nice house," Milena said.

"Are you rich?" Andrea asked.

"Well, rich," I said.

I closed the curtains. Not that anyone could look in, but it was the thought that counted.

At some point everyone must think they're the loneliest person in the world. I thought that for a long time, about once every hour. Later you meet other people, and one day you meet someone who's even lonelier than you. And you think you share a certain sarcasm, or a love of walking in the woods, or of a book, or of tiny little seedless grapes, you think there must be a reason why you spend your time with that person and not with someone else entirely, until you discover that it's the loneliness that attracts others, and repels them too.

"Is your brother a musician?" Andrea asked.

"Pretty much," I said.

I was sitting in Pavel's office chair.

I didn't sit there often. I didn't come into his room very often. To be precise, I wasn't allowed to enter Pavel's room, upon pain of a boxed ear.

"Is your brother famous?" Andrea asked. Now it was my turn to laugh. "No," I said, "not yet, but I'm sure it will happen." Upstairs, in my room, was a sugar cone, and I was suddenly reminded of Rolf Szlapka, Jr. "I can't forget you," I'd heard him say. "I keep trying, but I can't." And I heard Mama saying: "Poor baby! If at first you don't succeed. . . ."

I heard footsteps and thought it was Pavel with the tea, and maybe some chips he'd pilfered from the pantry.

But it was Mama. In her peignoir, but she still hadn't forgotten to put on lipstick and arrange her hair. The mules she had on went wonderfully well with the peignoir. They were pink mules.

Everyone was silent again.

She stood there and looked at us, as if the curtain had just risen and she was wondering whether this night at the opera would be well spent.

"This is my mother," I said, and was about to introduce Andrea and Milena to her, but Mama was having none of it.

She walked resolutely towards Andrea and Milena, then walked right on past them to the curtains, which she opened with a yank.

"It's so horribly stuffy in here," she said. "This is no way to receive guests, Marek. What would you like to eat?"

"Mama, this is Andrea, and this is Milena," I said, "and they just ate."

Mama gave me a look that said "Who's asking you?"

"Well, a little something, that would be very nice, ma'am," Andrea said.

Mama led us down to the salon, where she passed out cookies. It was something of a miracle that she'd known where they were.

She asked no questions, she just watched as Andrea and Milena ate.

Pavel came in with coffee and tea. He had to share the stage with Mama now. "Did you all have a nice evening?" Mama asked while Pavel was pouring Milena's tea.

"Yes, very nice," Andrea said. "We had Peking duck. Your son was very sweet to us."

Mama nodded, and in my head began a parade with marionettes and drums and people carrying a banner on which *l'amour fou* was proclaimed and its praises sung.

"Your son was very sweet to us." That counted for something, that was not your dime-a-dozen assessment. That meant, your son was very sweet to me, and that meant, I think your son's sweet, and from there to, I love your son, was only a hop, skip, and a jump. It wasn't far away now, it would start any minute, it was so close I could smell it.

Later I learned and understood that we attribute meaning to words, and not the other way around. The sounds themselves are innocent. A language you don't understand at all rarely causes pain, which is perhaps where people came up with the strange idea that a foreign language can best be learned in bed. We can, if we choose, attribute more meaning to the sound of someone clearing their throat than to one of Shakespeare's sonnets. I had learned that, and now I had to teach that to others, to freshmen who had little interest in meaning, and who could blame them?

These days I think that my efforts were perhaps directed towards having someone attribute meaning to the sound of me clearing my throat, that someone would discover in my throat-clearing something I would never have recognized myself, no matter how I tried.

The room fell quiet.

There was the sound of spoons stirring coffee and tea.

"You're a pretty girl," Mama said suddenly, looking at Milena. "What does your father do?"

I stood up.

The chair slid across the parquet and the parquet cracked.

"Mama," I shouted, "what difference does it make what her father does?"

But Milena said very calmly: "My father is a Viking who ran away two days before I was born, because he felt hemmed in."

Mama leaned over. Her peignoir fell open a bit, but this time it really was by accident.

"A Viking?" she asked.

"Yes," said Milena.

And Mama repeated: "A Viking," in a voice that sounded as though she were ordering an ounce of caviar on a crepe with sour cream.

I was still standing, and Pavel was quietly drinking his coffee. He thought it was a sign of maturity to never let yourself be thrown off balance.

"A Norwegian," Milena said. "Very big and blond, the exact opposite of my mother."

"And he ran away?" Mama asked.

Something about that Viking seemed to fascinate her.

"In an overwrought state," Milena said, "he left the house, and we never saw him again."

Mama leaned back and plucked at her peignoir. Maybe she was thinking about leaving the house in an overwrought state herself, right then. She liked doing that. Of course, there were times when she left the house in a normal state, but I believe she found that rather boring. Boring: it wouldn't surprise me to find out that that was her chief objection to life, the fact that it was boring, with not enough blood to it. That's probably why she was so fond of operas, particularly bloody operas.

A clock was ticking.

No one was saying anything.

The terrible thing was that Mama had no intention of going to bed. It was a quarter past one already, but Mama was enjoying herself.

"He almost never brings girls home," she said suddenly.

She looked at me.

"And he doesn't either," she said, nodding towards Pavel, "but that's different. He's occupied with his music."

She sounded hoarse, from smoking, or maybe it was the booze.

She had taken up smoking after she had her first child. She sometimes said: "Before I had children, I never smoked. But with kids, you can't really get by without cigarettes."

"Oh, no?" Andrea asked. "You really mean they never bring anyone home?" Her impudence wasn't faked, it wasn't playacting, it wasn't something she'd seen others do and was now imitating: her impudence was completely genuine, and never again have I witnessed such lovely impudence.

Mama nodded absentmindedly. She was already somewhere else.

"More tea?" Pavel asked.

Milena shook her head.

If they had stood up right then and said, "Well, we'd better be going," all would have been lost. All would have been for naught, my trip to Mr. Hobmeier, the Chinese restaurant, the flowers, the American bar, all useless, because it had not led to *l'amour fou*.

"Mama," I said, "we're going up to Pavel's room to play a game."

She rose from her chair.

Other people got up, but she rose.

"A game. What kind of game?"

"Monopoly," I said. It was the first thing that popped into my mind.

"Is that a game?" Mama asked.

I saw Andrea and Milena glance at each other. Pavel just sat there grinning.

Mama sat back down.

"Perhaps you were planning to go to bed?" I said circumspectly.

Mama didn't like it when other people told her what to do, not even when it sounded like a question.

She shook her head, as though flies were pestering her.

"And you," she said to Andrea. "What does your father do for a living?"

I slid my chair loudly again over the parquet.

Everyone looked at me, except for Mama.

What did it matter what Andrea's father did, even if he was in prison and would never get out again, even if he'd strangled three women in the woods with his bare hands, then I still would have felt like throwing myself at Andrea's feet and begging her: "Please, take me with you, don't let this go on any longer."

But I didn't throw myself at anyone's feet. Between what I did and what I felt like doing lay a desert, littered with the corpses of people who hadn't survived the crossing, dead of dehydration or driven barmy by the sun.

"Mama," I said, "stop asking questions like that. Pavel, say something."

But Pavel remained silent, and Andrea said: "My father didn't run away, he's very well-behaved."

At the word "well-behaved," a smiled appeared on Andrea's face, and on Mama's face a smile appeared as well. There was music playing in her head now, I just didn't know which music it was.

"Well-behaved," Mama said. "Most men are well-behaved."

"I went by Rolf Szlapka's today," I said, trying to create a diversion. "He says those white roses are in again, he's put some aside for you."

But Mama kept smiling. The thoughts forming in her head would have been better off not forming there. You could tell from the look in her eye, from the way she stubbed out her cigarette, from the way she looked around.

She got up.

With other people you more or less knew where they were going, but not with Mama. Maybe it was because she didn't know herself, she sometimes couldn't find her way around her own house. One time she'd said to me: "When you're standing in a darkened corner of the room, Marek, you can't expect to be able to draw a map of the city." I didn't know whether she was referring to herself or to me, and besides, who wanted to draw a map of the city? And who was standing in a darkened corner of the room?

Other mothers went to bed or to the bathroom to remove their lipstick when they got up from a chair in the salon at one in the morning. When Mama rose, she might leave the house in an overwrought state, or she might stay at home in an overwrought state. With Mama, you could never tell.

She walked over to me.

I looked at her pink mules.

Does anyone else's mother walk around in the middle of the night in pink mules?

I had to keep talking now, to distract her. I turned to Andrea and Milena like an accomplished entertainer.

"Mama's florist is named Rolf Szlapka," I held forth, "he always puts aside white roses for her; his father is a BMW dealer, a very famous BMW dealer, or at least very famous in Vienna. Anyone who's anyone at all buys their BMWs from Szlapka, Sr. My mother is very fond of BMWs and of white roses, which is why she happens to know the Szlapka family so well."

Pavel laughed, sort of the same way Papa might laugh. "Especially a certain member of the Szlapka family," Pavel said dryly.

All Vienna knew about Mama's men, her love lay in the street for all to see, but she didn't care, as long as she wasn't lying in the street herself, as long as she could hover high above the city and extract love from the male portion of the Viennese population.

I watched Mama from the corner of my eye. Milena and Andrea had not reacted to my speech. Milena stood up, as if she too were getting ready to leave the house in an overwrought state.

Mama was standing behind me now, and she threw her arms around me the way lovers did in old movies.

I stopped talking. It was no use anymore. There was no diverting Mama's thoughts.

Once she had an idea, she was like a tiger creeping through the jungle. She had to jump, even if it meant jumping to her death, because somewhere in her head she'd heard a voice that said: "Jump."

"This one needs a lot of love," Mama said.

I yanked myself free.

"Mama," I shouted, "stop it! Just stop it now, would you!"

I didn't care whether I woke Papa. Maybe he was sleeping with cotton in his ears, he had enough on his mind to keep him overwrought, and the life insurance business certainly offered enough overwrought things to deal with. Profit accruement, after all, is really nothing more than one huge overwrought state, and according to Papa, shareholders who demanded profit accruement were worse than a hundred Mamas.

"Pavel, now I want you to play something for us," Mama said. And right after that, to Milena she said: "Your posture's all wrong, you hang in your pelvis like a sixty-year-old man. If you don't do something about that, you'll have back problems in ten years' time."

"So what!" I shouted. "So what if she has back problems in ten years' time? What about it? You think she cares? Do you think she cares at all, do you think she loses even a minute of sleep over that, over back pain that may or may not show up in ten years' time?"

Andrea giggled, Milena stared at me as though I was a wild animal.

Then I picked up the first object I saw.

It was a vase.

A lover's gift, something Mama tolerated in the salon only by great exception.

I lifted the vase above my head. I looked at Mama and at Andrea and at Milena, only Pavel was nowhere to be found.

Then I realized that Mama didn't care whether that vase shattered in a million pieces, she wouldn't even care if every vase in the house shattered in a million pieces. She'd step over the shards and say: "Now I want Pavel to play something for us."

I set the vase down carefully on the table.

"That was a present," Mama said. "A present from Rolf Szlapka."

11

A Girl Can't Feel Anything with This

Pavel played his violin. It kept getting later and later.

Andrea and Milena were slouched down on the couch. Maybe they were sleeping with their eyes open, some people can do that.

Mama was on the edge of her chair. She shivered. That had nothing to do with the temperature. Sometimes she'd shiver when it was 35 degrees out, and in the middle of winter she'd say: "I don't think it's cold at all, what's wrong with these people?"

When Pavel was finally finished playing, we clapped. Mama clapped the loudest.

She kissed Pavel and me goodnight, and shook hands with Milena and Andrea. She stopped when she got to Milena.

"So your father's a Viking?" she asked.

Milena nodded.

"Interesting," Mama said, "that's very interesting. But you shouldn't hang in your pelvis like that."

Then Mama went to her room.

We stood around in the salon like partygoers who've realized too late that the party's over. Even the host had already gone to bed.

"Shall we go upstairs?" I suggested.

When you're trying to buy time, the only thing that matters is the time you buy and not the way in which. Every minute was of vital importance. In *l'amour fou*, there are no important and less-important minutes, all minutes are of equal importance, all minutes should be equally intense.

Pavel put away his violin. His graceful hands moved in the air as though he were directing an entire orchestra.

"Just for a little while," Andrea said. "The streetcars have probably stopped running anyway."

"That's right," Pavel said, "the streetcars stopped a long time ago. But if you wait a little while, they'll start again."

"You play nicely," Milena said.

"Yes," Andrea said, "you play very nicely. Are you a genius or something?"

Pavel snapped the violin case shut.

His hands, I thought, if I could chop off one of his hands, maybe then I'd be happy. I had read somewhere that *l'amour fou* shouldn't shy away from a little blood.

"Well, a genius," Pavel said. "It's still a little early for that."

"That's not really something you can say about yourself," I said, "that you're a genius."

But my comment was ignored, my comment vanished as though I was the only one who'd heard it.

We climbed the stairs, a little less carefully this time, a little less afraid of making noise.

If Papa hadn't woken up by now, he wouldn't be waking up at all.

When we were back upstairs, and I was sitting at Pavel's desk again, where I was never allowed to sit otherwise upon pain of a boxed ear and a flood of curses, then it was as though the time we had spent in the salon had never existed. As though Mama had never opened the door to Pavel's room and said: "What would you like to eat?"

"I have this horrible taste in my mouth from the coffee," Andrea said. "Don't you have something sweet and strong?"

Something sweet and strong, we had to have that. We had everything.

Pavel and Andrea went downstairs in search of something sweet and strong, and I stayed in the room with Milena.

"I don't want you to touch me," Milena said.

I looked up.

She was leaning against the Alban Berg poster.

In her face and in her body I tried to find some trace of the Viking who had run away two days before she was born, but I didn't see him anywhere.

"But I don't even want to touch you."

A derisive laugh was her reply.

And then: "I probably can't smoke here, can I?"

"Pavel wouldn't like it," I said.

In a few hours it would be light.

"They've been gone for a long time," I said.

"Maybe they're not coming back."

Milena rubbed her eyes.

According to Camus, whether to live or not to live was the only philosophical question that mattered. That was one of the reasons, of course a very naive reason, why I later studied philosophy. Of course I could also have studied chemistry to find an answer to that question. Raiding a bread factory would have been an equally good option.

"I have a headache," Milena said. "Do you have any aspirin?"

"No," I said, "not here."

That answer seemed to satisfy her, because she didn't ask again.

Way off in the distance I heard giggling, but maybe that was my imagination.

"So your father went back to Scandinavia?" I asked, and I looked at one of Alban Berg's ears, the one that was showing behind Milena's back.

"He went to Greenland," she said. "He found a job there."

"Cold," I said. "Are you still in contact with him?"

"No, but the South Pole is colder, don't you know that?"

"I'm not very good at geography. It doesn't really interest me."

"Me neither," said Milena. "But everyone knows that."

The giggling was not my imagination. The giggling came up the stairs and stopped in front of the door to Pavel's bedroom.

"There they are," Milena said, as though it was the subway we'd been waiting for.

"Yes," I said, "there they are."

The door opened. They came in. They were happy, from the looks of it.

They had a bottle of pistachio liqueur.

It must have been a gift from one of Mama's lovers as well. Mama got more gifts than she knew what to do with.

They sat down on the bed. The bed creaked.

Milena closed the door.

I thought: I have to remember all of this, because if I remember everything I'll know what *l'amour fou* is, and once I know that I can apply it later on. It was like driving a car; you need a couple of weeks between the theory and the driving exam itself, it's safer that way.

Pavel was holding Andrea, and Milena said to me, still standing by the door: "I have no culture."

"What do you mean?"

"Well," she said, pointing to Pavel's instruments, "your family has culture."

I looked at the instruments and I looked at Pavel, who was rarely happy; the fear of not being or not remaining the best blocked his view of almost every form of happiness.

Was this culture?

THE STORY OF MY BALDNESS

"Ah," I said, "I don't know."

I could have asked Mama what culture was, but maybe she wouldn't have told me; to her, the definition of a word like that was probably like an address, something you didn't need anyway.

"So what *do* you have?" I asked, pleased with any form of conversation, even if it was about culture.

"No culture," Milena said resolutely.

"Marek," Pavel yelled. "Stop this nonsense." When I turned around I saw that his mouth was glued to Andrea's. Or maybe it was the other way around. It was all going so fast that the details were escaping me.

"What *is* culture?" I asked.

Then I looked at the bed again, to see how Andrea and Pavel were coming along, and I saw that one of her breasts was no longer completely covered. Once it gets started, it all races along like a roller coaster. I'd thought it would go slower than that. More deliberately, step by step, with long intermissions in which you could go downstairs to the buffet to buy a cup of coffee and discuss the quality of the performance with your colleagues.

I also realized that Andrea's half-naked breast shocked me less than I had thought it would, but then of course there were a few yards between me and that breast. With regard to veins or nipple color, I could draw no meaningful conclusions. Perhaps such conclusions are best left to doctors and nurses, medical people who bring you your test results with an earnest look, and conclude by saying: "With a little luck, you could live another ten years."

"What's your definition of culture?" I asked. The silence was becoming unbearable.

"Are we going to talk about that now?" Milena said, and she stood at the door with her hands on her hips, like a mother waiting for her child to come inside.

It wouldn't have surprised me if Milena had clapped loudly, but she didn't.

I walked over to her. I stood beside her.

All I could think of was: I'm standing beside the daughter of a Viking.

Andrea was now half-naked.

"They're taking off each other's clothes," I said, feeling like a reporter at a billiards match. I was afraid that, were I to undress someone or if someone were to undress me, I would always imagine that there was a reporter in the room commenting in a whisper on the veins and the color of the nipples.

"Yes," Milena said, "they're taking off each other's clothes. That does happen."

"Oh," I said, "then it's okay."

I brushed the back of my hand across Milena's cheek, the way you might touch a crocodile the keeper says isn't dangerous because all its teeth are rotten.

She pushed my hand away.

"You can fuck me," she said. "But I don't want you to touch me."

L'amour fou was a little like the flames of purgatory: you had to be consumed in order to emerge purified, better prepared for what was to come.

"Right," I said, and I thought about Pavel's hands, about Milena's father, the Viking, and about a movie I'd seen where a woman hid her fiancé from the police and then ran after the squad car when they finally arrested him anyway.

If they arrested Papa, Mama wouldn't even notice. She'd probably help the policemen make the arrest.

"You still have to take your shoes off," Andrea said.

"Can't I just keep them on?" Pavel asked.

"No," Andrea said, "I'd like it more if you take them off."

Pavel always wore shoes with laces that went on forever. He didn't like boots with zippers on them.

We watched as Pavel struggled with his shoes, as Andrea tried to help and tore at his laces like a madwoman. We didn't help them. That would probably have been unseemly. It was up to them whether the shoes got taken off or not.

"The lace has a knot in it," I said, when it started becoming too painful to watch.

I took a pair of scissors from Pavel's desk, and he used them to cut his shoelace. Then I went back over to Milena and started unbuttoning my shirt. Touching may have been taboo, but it seemed to me that nakedness was becoming more or less obligatory.

Sometimes lovers would call my mama and say: "I just wanted to hear the sound of your voice."

To which Mama would reply: "Well you're hearing it now, aren't you?"

I wondered whether Mama ever longed to hear someone's voice, and if so, what kind of voice that would be, and what it would say.

If you've been longing to hear someone's voice for a very long time, does it matter what that voice says? Or is "You're hearing my voice now, aren't you? Is there anything else I can do for you?" good enough?

Mama sometimes told us at the dinner table about men who wanted to hear her voice, and she always sounded as though she pitied such foolishness. Papa couldn't laugh about it.

Papa said: "Your mother attracts poor men. She's like socialism."

I threw my shirt on the floor.

I didn't have any hair on my upper body at the time; hair growth started late with me.

Milena looked at me.

Then she pulled her blouse up over her head. In one single movement. So casually that it seemed as if she hadn't taken off anything at all.

I looked at her, the way I'd looked at other children when we'd all been standing around half-naked, waiting for the pediatrician to arrive. The way I'd sat in the sandbox and the nanny had said "Play, Marek, play with the other children." I didn't know how to do it, I just sat there beside the nanny and watched. Not long after that, the nanny got fired. She believed in God, and Papa felt that was no way to raise children.

Milena took off her bra. It was a white one. With lace trim.

"Yes," I said, "culture. What is that anyway?"

"Not now," Milena said.

I could have told you everything about her breasts, not a single detail would have escaped me if I had only looked.

Andrea's underpants had little animals on them. I couldn't tell what kind of animals. Monkeys, donkeys, maybe horses, it could have been anything.

We looked at passion, Milena and I did, leaning bare-chested against the bedroom door.

I'd never seen passion in real life.

I looked at hands sliding down backs and over buttocks, into underpants. I wondered whether that was pleasant.

Milena was wearing things that reminded me of bath slippers. Her feet played with the slippers, and I said: "That Peking duck was really nice."

She sighed.

"Algerians have no culture," she said. "Have you ever heard of a famous Algerian? In fact, Jews don't either."

A famous Algerian: I had to think about that one.

"I don't know that many Algerians," I said quietly, "I've never been there, either."

"That's what I mean," Milena said.

"I think my mother's been there, though. She's roamed all over the Mediterranean."

Then Andrea's underpants went off. They landed on the floor. There were bears on them, I could see that clearly now, and I felt nauseous.

The Peking duck whose praises I'd just been singing suddenly rose eight inches.

It wasn't because I was so startled by Andrea's nakedness, I'd seen Mama naked before, and I'd looked at a number of photographs of naked people, and it wasn't because Andrea's nakedness was so shocking. Her body was taut and young, and she had a diamond in her navel, just like the one in her nose. Her naked body was more general than specific.

It seemed there truly was a nakedness that could cause pain, that could make a Peking duck rise up eight inches. That is the nakedness that lingers before your eyes as you walk down the street on your way to a newsstand; the way someone laughs, the way underpants with bears on them are taken off, the way hands not your own grab hold of a leg. And later, while giving a lecture to freshmen who can't help it either, and to whom you have just assigned an essay you barely believe in yourself, you suddenly see the nakedness you thought you'd long forgotten. You see it in the look of a woman you think belongs with you, a look she's wearing at a party that turns out to be pretty much a dud, and you're not even completely certain for whom that look is meant. You don't know who saw that look, and you tell yourself you don't know what's going on, because you don't want to know. And a few days later you see that same nakedness as you pace back and forth in a deserted railway car in the train between Linz and Vienna, and you ask yourself: "Who else?" Even though that question can't be answered at all, or at least not to your satisfaction.

Then you think about Mama roaming around the Mediterranean and sending postcards with drawings by men whose names and addresses she can't remember, because names and addresses are unimportant. And finally you see the nakedness that hurts every-where. In every shop, on every mountain, in every station.

"A famous Algerian," I said. "Well, I'd have to think about that."

Then Andrea and Pavel climbed under the covers and most of it disappeared from sight.

L'amour fou was no undivided pleasure.

Mr. Georgi, my French teacher, had once told us: "Literature, *mes amis*, is packed with unpleasant truths."

"Do something," Milena said.

Her voice had an edge to it.

More talk had been ruled out, the time for action had come.

I took off my half boots and wondered whether there would be animals on Milena's underpants too, and if so, what kind of animals they might be.

There was nothing on my underpants. My underpants were olive green, that was all.

Milena was still playing with her slippers.

I took my socks off as well.

There was heavy breathing going on in the room. It sounded like the noise that came from Papa's antique prewar radio.

Love really did have something prewar to it, and here I'm speaking of physical love, something prehistoric. Milena took off her skirt.

I remembered that I wasn't allowed to touch her; the rest, okay, but no touching.

Papa wasn't big on touching either. A good trouncing now and then, that was something else. But a trouncing is also a form of touching, and there can be tenderness in a good trouncing too, although I only realized that later. By then it was already too late.

Her underpants were black, pitch-black. Fortunately, without animals. I was afraid the animals would start dancing before my eyes if I had to pull off her underpants.

The wallpaper in my nursery had had animals on it.

Mama almost never took off her own underpants, she had them taken off for her, or so I'm told. Which is how I know that the removal of underpants is a real man's job.

"Yes," I said.

Then Pavel began breathing even more heavily, and the Peking duck that was already almost in my lap jumped up a bit further. The Peking duck, I thought, was like a film being played backwards.

Right after that I pressed my lips to Milena's and kissed her.

I kissed the way I cried. Endlessly, in deepest sorrow and with long heaves.

Milena pushed me away and said: "Take those things off."

She was pointing at my olive-colored underpants.

The maid was the one who bought our underpants, and she liked cheerful colors.

"Did you?" I heard Andrea ask.

The same way the maid always asked: "Have you finished eating? Can I take your plate?"

Pavel didn't answer. At least not audibly.

I took off my underpants. And smiled.

Smiling is never a bad idea.

At the international school I smiled a great deal, even when I was walking around in my green hat with a feather in it, because the traditional attire of *l'amour fou* was still unknown territory to me.

Milena took off her underpants too, but without smiling.

Then we leaned against the door again and looked at the blanket under which things were gradually calming down.

I wondered what kind of contraceptive Pavel had used, and whether they'd used any contraceptive at all.

Milena was staring at my crotch.

My smile kept getting broader.

As though I'd received a present I didn't like, but for which I still wanted to appear very grateful.

Then I had to sneeze. Three times.

"Excuse me," I said.

"Gesundheit," Andrea said from beneath the blanket.

Then she said: "You're a star."

And Pavel said: "I'm going to be a star; I've given myself two years."

"You already are one," Andrea said, but Pavel said: "Just give me two years."

On Pavel's desk was the box of tissues he used to wipe the excess ointment off his hands.

Pavel and his hands. He rubbed them in before dinner, he rubbed them in after dinner, when he got up, when he went to bed, he thought a splinter in his ring finger would ruin his two-year plan.

I blew my nose into a tissue, went back and stood by the door and asked: "Have you ever seen a belly dancer?"

"I didn't want to say anything at first," Milena said, "but are you ill?"

No one had ever asked me that before.

I looked healthy. As far as I could tell. A little pale around the edges perhaps, but that didn't necessarily make one unhealthy.

Milena had beautiful brown eyes. When she asked whether I was ill those eyes became even more beautiful, and my thoughts turned more than ever to Algerian culture.

"No," I said. "Not that I know of. Why?" I had read somewhere that extreme passion could be seen as an illness, but it was still a bit too early for that.

"Are you excited?" Milena asked.

"Oh yes, extremely," I said.

And I went on working on my smile. As though that smile was to be my masterpiece, as though everything would finally culminate in a naked smile.

"Andrea," Milena said, "come look at this."

"No," I said, "that's not necessary."

Spectators were unnecessary. No one needed to look.

In history class we had learned that some believers consider the body to be a punishment from God. So you could tell from the body whether God had wanted to punish you very severely, or only a little bit.

"Shall we get dressed again?" I suggested.

A little nudity helped liven up the evening, but it was not a good idea to overdo it.

Milena had her arms folded across her chest.

"No," she said. "It's too late for that now."

Andrea climbed out of bed while one of Pavel's hands slid down her back and over her buttocks. She walked up to me; her nakedness didn't get in her way, her nakedness fit her like a glove.

It's too bad some people have been given bodies it would take ten good tailors a month to repair, but in that, too, one can probably see God's hand.

She stopped in front of me.

I looked at her and smiled, and she and Milena stared at my crotch.

"Egyptian culture," I said, "is one of the oldest on earth, and Egypt isn't too far from Algeria."

"Doesn't it get any bigger than that?" Andrea asked.

I looked down.

"No," I said, "it doesn't get any bigger than that, that's as big as it gets."

I coughed, because my throat had gone dry.

"At least I think so," I mumbled then. "I don't really keep track."

Andrea was squatting down, kneeling before my crotch.

Embarrassment seemed foreign to her. Just as it did to Mama. Mama knew no embarrassment, because she knew that everything she did was right. Papa saw Mama primarily as a natural catastrophe. Something that had overcome him and that he had to undergo patiently, until it blew over. What saved him was largely life insurance, because the natural catastrophe he called his wife was not allowed to enter the head office.

"You have the penis of a dwarf," Andrea said.

She pronounced her verdict as she squatted.

It was a verdict that did not even require standing up.

I tried to think about the work of the French Surrealists, but Andrea's verdict seemed to carry infinitely more weight than the work of the French Surrealists.

Then I tried to think about Mr. Hobmeier's shop, and about how happy I'd felt when I left the shop with four thousand schillings in my hand, but there was nothing left of that happiness, and the harder I tried to get it back the less of it remained, the more it seemed as if it had never been there, as if all this time it had been just my imagination, a feverish dream wallpapered with animals that started spinning around whenever you looked at them.

"No offense," Milena said. "But this is real shit."

"You're doing it on purpose, right?" Andrea said. "It gets bigger than this, right? You're doing it on purpose."

"No, really," I said. "I'm sorry. I've never seen it get any bigger than this."

"Goddammit," Milena screeched, "you can't leave me like this. Always the same old story. I get the rejects. Well, I'm not doing it anymore!"

"Take it easy," I said. "We'll find a solution."

There may have been something surrealistic about a dwarf, but that was no comfort now. Too little comfort, in any case.

"Have you ever seen Pavel's weenie?" Andrea asked.

"Never," I said, "it's a big house and we have our own bathrooms and, well, we sort of live in separate worlds anyway."

I picked up my underpants.

Living in separate worlds seemed to me like one of life's necessities. Distance was there to be kept; intimacy was more for the family plot.

"Pavel, come here and show him," Andrea called.

"Brace yourself," Pavel said.

He was sitting on his bed like a little pasha.

"Goddammit," Milena said. And Andrea started giggling. She wasn't squatting down anymore.

"There's no hurry," I said. "I don't really need to see my brother naked, we can see each other naked every day if we want, and the street cars will be running soon anyway."

"They already are," Pavel said.

He climbed out of bed. My musical brother, who now has his own bedroom on some planes.

He was wearing a condom, which he tore off, and for the umpteenth time that night I thought that I should remember all of this, as if remembering was all there was to it. As if everything happened in order to tell about it, to be able to report on it. Later, in some other life.

Milena was still standing beside me, leaning against the door.

And in front of me was Andrea, naked. As if it was meant to be. As if nakedness was the only state that could do justice to her, that could let her blossom.

My brother came and stood beside Andrea.

"See the difference?" Andrea asked.

"We're built differently," I said without looking.

Don't look, I thought, don't look.

My smile didn't leave me. It was still right there. It would never go away again. A relic of *l'amour fou*, perhaps the only relic besides the sugar cone.

Then my curiosity won out, and I tossed a glance at Pavel's thing. It was like holding up a twenty-volume encyclopedia beside a piece of toilet paper. They're both paper, that's right, but that's where the similarity ends.

"Two years from now I'll be a star," Pavel said. "In two years I'll be the greatest violinist in the world."

"A girl can't feel anything with this," Milena said.

"And that's not right," Andrea said.

"No, I realize that," I said. "You do have to feel something."

Now Andrea was smiling too, and she said: "You're sweet."

Sweet. So I was sweet. Who would ever have thought?

"Maybe you should see a doctor," Milena said. "The way it is now, it's no more than an inch, less than half my pinkie."

Less than half a pinkie, that was very little indeed. It had always seemed like a lot more to me, but perhaps that was an optical illusion.

"Did something go wrong when you were born?" Andrea asked interestedly, almost worriedly.

"Not that I know of," I said. "Nothing that I know of."

Pavel's thing was gigantic, a carnivorous plant reaching for the sun. My thing was more like a dandelion broken in the bud, ready for the grave.

Pavel said: "It's genetically determined. That's how it goes."

"Doctors can do something about it," Andrea went on. "Just like with woman who don't have breasts. These days they just screw in a couple of bags of water and sew it closed and you can't even see it."

"No, no," I said. "I know that. It's a relatively minor procedure."

It was the first time I'd ever fantasized about castrating myself.

It was a little operation with a big pair of scissors, and I felt no fear, more like pride, even though the sinews were tougher than I'd expected. But when I'd finally cut through the last fiber and my penis fell to the ground, it was as though a young fir tree had been felled to liven up the living room at Christmas. Andrea put her hand on my shoulder.

"It doesn't matter," she said, "maybe it's just temporary. I was really late getting breasts, and look at me now. Maybe it'll grow some more."

"Cow," Milena said.

I looked at Milena's black underpants, and then I watched as Andrea walked over to Pavel's desk, took a tissue and wiped herself between the legs.

She turned around.

"It just keeps dripping," she said. "Nothing went wrong, did it?"

"No," Pavel said. "I've never had it go wrong."

She took another tissue. "Some men keep going after they come, because they're ashamed of coming so fast, but that's risky. Some sperm is so aggressive that you feel it in you all night, like you've turned into an anthill."

"Really, nothing went wrong," Pavel said.

She crumpled the tissue. "At home I've got a fuck cloth," she said.

We said goodbye in the hall.

Pavel was wearing his bathrobe. I'd put all my clothes back on. I didn't like bathrobes much.

I've never seen him so happy since then. On the day he married the woman who would remain an eternal teenybopper, he whispered, just before we went into the church: "Remember those two girls from Luxembourg?"

The streetcars had been running for a while already, but Pavel insisted on calling them a taxi.

"Thanks for a wonderful evening," Milena said.

"Yes," I said, "it was my pleasure."

"Things like that happen," she said.

"Yes," I said, "that happens sometimes."

Then Milena whispered in my ear: "She's such an egotistical cow. I always get the rejects, and I fall for it every time."

I had wrapped up Rolf Szlapka's flowers all neatly again.

"Here," I said to Andrea, "don't forget these."

Rolf Szlapka was now sleeping in his lonely bed, dreaming perhaps of Mama. It wasn't completely unthinkable that she had promised him that she would leave all the other men in her life, just for him. That he had only to be patient, even though she'd been telling him this for the last two years. But to someone with so little regard for names and addresses, time was of course only a relative concept, and a promise nothing more than a ditty, a little background music, the accompaniment for a love that lay in the street for all to see.

Mama could make promises without speaking them; a caress could be a promise, a nod, the way she shook your hand and looked at you longer than necessary.

Andrea took the flowers.

We had to wait for the taxi. Pavel had said it could take ten minutes.

"It was a lot of fun," Andrea said, "thank you."

We kissed each other on the cheek, three times. Like they do in France, she said. Smiling happily, it seemed.

We'd agreed to meet that afternoon.

We were going to do something fun. The four of us.

"Your brother is nice," Andrea said, "but you're nice too."

I took the compliment with a smile, with the smile that would accompany me the rest of my days, slightly aloof, but friendly still. Frozen. The kind of smile you wouldn't notice, a smile that could offend no one.

"Your mother is also very nice," Andrea said. "I just wish I had a mother like her."

Then the taxi arrived.

Pavel walked outside in his bare feet.

I stood in the doorway and waved.

When he came back and closed the door, I asked him: "Do you really think I'm ill?"

"No," he said, "not ill. Merely handicapped."

"Aha," I said.

If life is a job, I wanted to resign.

But I couldn't find the office where they took resignations.

12

A Bavarian Lump

For three days, the format of the male sex organ pursued me morning, noon, and night. Even in my sleep I was pursued by male sex organs.

Whoever I saw, and wherever I saw them, I saw only the possible formats of the male member. When I saw men I examined their crotches, when I saw women I tried to imagine the various formats they had felt in them. And what they might interpret as the minimum length.

My physics teacher, Mr. Kiepe, who had never been angry at me, who was regarded at the international school as kindness itself, started screaming at me halfway through class: "Stop staring at me like that, you idiot!"

I saw drops of sweat on his forehead, and only then did I realize that he might be afraid that I had discovered his secret, that down there he, too, belonged to the race of the dwarfs.

If I have said that my baldness began with Mica, who approached me in a coffeehouse, then perhaps my baldness began much earlier, years before the first hairs abandoned me and I was forced to start wearing hats and caps and entering wig shops as though they were brothels where the filthiest sexual dreams came true.

Perhaps it all started with the discovery that, from my otherwise well-built body—as I have noted, there were many who took

me to be Brazilian—dangled the penis of a dwarf. A detail that
had entirely escaped my attention in all the previous months and
years, busy as I was trying to experience *l'amour fou*. I had been
too preoccupied with observing my mama's escapades to worry
about my own member, as though following those escapades would
bring me closer to her, until two girls from Luxembourg were
friendly and willing enough to draw my attention to my handicap. If you didn't know better, you would almost have thought they
felt sorry for me.

What is an obsession?

One could write whole volumes about it, one could lose one-
self in formulations and discussions about when a healthy interest
becomes an unhealthy interest, and about the misty zone in between;
when does the charming, infatuated young man become a trouble-
some, obsessed ghoul?

I myself have tried in the past to prove that all true interest is
unhealthy. One thing that is certain is that, on the day Milena and
Andrea walked into my life, the size of the male sex organ became
an obsession for me. Not only the size, but the organ itself, the thing
an sich.

Others, while still in their youth, say "enter and be welcome"
to sorrow, to melancholy, to the leaves that start falling in March,
or to something as banal as cancer or a congenital muscular
disorder.

I said "enter, be welcome, and dine" to my obsession.

An obsession that diminished in intensity slowly, very slowly,
but never went away completely, and, as is the way with obsessions,
never *will* go away completely.

The first few days after my discovery I felt as though my member had ended up on a strange body, a body that didn't belong to
it. As if someone had accidentally transplanted the transmission of
a Trabant into a Mercedes.

If I didn't hate the word "alienation" so much, I would say that I became alienated from my body, the way a man and wife can become alienated from each other after two years of marriage.

My body made all kinds of promises my sex organ couldn't keep.

Strangely enough, I blamed it more on my body than on my organ.

I began to fantasize about being a dwarf, even a half-misformed dwarf, one who tried to lure people into a sleazy nightclub by passing out flyers on the street and hoarsely extolling the virtues of the sleazy nightclub.

Another recurring fantasy was that I would marry a female dwarf, a woman I would have to carry on my shoulders when we went to the supermarket or department store, so that she could reach the shelves.

If I was a dwarf, my sex organ wouldn't be so unusual anymore. Maybe one day a woman would even say to me: "Wow, you've got a big one, for a dwarf."

In my fantasy I kept shrinking, until my body achieved harmony with my member. To my own amazement, scaling down my body seemed more realistic than scaling up my penis. And also much more desirable.

I began eating less, and instead of the French Surrealists I began immersing myself in the literature of sleaze.

I discovered that some people tossed naked dwarfs back and forth, as a kind of erotic game. Occasionally a dwarf lost his life during such play, which seemed to me a worthy demise. He who loses his life during an erotic game can exit the big top with his head held high.

From the day I met the girls from Luxembourg, I also saw my mama and my papa through different eyes.

One of my ancestors had had relations with a dwarf, and the dwarf's chromosome, his genetic material, had for reasons unknown latched onto my body, and not those of my brothers.

I don't come from a religious family, but if you didn't know better you would have suspected malice aforethought, a satanic fairy bending over my cradle.

Even during French, a class where I had always done my very best, if only because the teacher and I shared a love of the Surrealist, I could no longer concentrate.

All I saw were the gray woolen trousers of the teacher, Wolfgang Georgi, who had never entirely lost his Bavarian accent, not even when he spoke French. The whole discussion went right past me, because I was busy wondering whether he, too, belonged to the fraternity of covert dwarfs.

At the end of the lesson, Mr. Georgi said: "Marek van der Jagt, please remain seated. I'd like to talk to you after class."

Everyone else left the room.

The covert dwarf remained.

Mr. Georgi came and sat beside me.

His watery eyes looked at me amiably. I stared at the floor, convinced that he would now unmask me, that he would say: "I know Marek, I can see it, you don't even have to take off your clothes, you're a covert dwarf just like me."

But what he asked was: "What's wrong, Marek? You've changed. Is everything all right at home?"

"Everything's fine at home," I said.

Mr. Georgi nodded.

"And your mother? How is she doing?"

He was very fond of my mama, as were so many.

"Fine," I said. "Fine."

"Well," he said quietly, "it's probably just growing pains. I'm not really worried about you." Then he brought his mouth closer to my ear and whispered: "Your mother is the most beautiful woman in Vienna, Marek, even more beautiful than Romi Schneider."

I wanted to say that my mother bore absolutely no physical resemblance to Romi Schneider, but then I saw the giant lump in his pants, a Bavarian lump, a ski landscape, a three-dimensional map of Garmisch-Partenkirchen and surroundings, I saw the snake that rose up at his crotch, it seemed as though it would bite right through the wool, for Mr. Georgi had a fondness for expensive woolen trousers.

And I felt myself getting nauseous. I felt Peking duck in my gullet again, I saw the nakedness that caused pain, and I heard Andrea saying casually, as though talking about a can of peas: "At home I have a fuck cloth."

"Mr. Georgi," I said, my mouth dry, "my mother doesn't look at all like Romi Schneider."

He didn't say anything more. He just stared into space. Written on the board was the name of a suicide. Mr. Georgi liked us to read literature by suicides.

"Pardon me, please," I said. Then I left the classroom and didn't look back.

I ran home, people greeted me along the way, but I ran on, I didn't want to see anyone anymore.

At a traffic light, I stopped. I thought: I need to see a doctor.

I didn't mean the kind of doctor who examines your head or what I will refer to here, why not, as "the inner man." I was thinking along the lines of a cosmetic surgeon, an enlarger of breasts, lips, and the male member, a remover of wrinkles and potbellies. A body-stretcher, an aesthetic butcher. That was what I needed, and how.

Oh, entire volumes can be written about spiritual values and norms, entire lives can be spent doing nothing but that, but spiritual values and norms hobble along on crutches, their clubfeet in orthopedic shoes, behind the cosmetic.

13

Blitzkrieg

The day after my first kiss, I actually showed up—albeit reluctantly—for the meeting with the two girls from Luxembourg. What else was there to say? And to do?

The way a sick person is sometimes nothing more than his sickness, the way he sees in everyone and everything only the reflection of his own sickness, so too, in those days, was I little more than my handicap.

Pavel wanted me to go along for the sake of symmetry.

He said: "Two girls and a man, that's no good."

We did not discuss the discovery made by the girls from Luxembourg. Some families believed in the word and in communication, but we believed in silence. Silence was our regime.

Pavel had agreed to meet them at the sidewalk tables in front of Café Landtmann.

It was a lovely day, in my memory probably many times lovelier than it actually was.

There was a southerly wind. It was the warmest twenty-first of May in recent years, the radio said.

"Let's walk there," Pavel said.

We didn't live very far from Café Landtmann.

I usually walk out in front, with Pavel coming along behind, slower, more thoughtfully, with the air of a musician who sees reality

primarily as something that gets in the way of the beautiful com-
positions he would like to render.

Pavel hasn't changed much. These days he sees reality as something that gets in the way of the economic models he sets up, and
he's furious with reality at its failure to obey the World Bank and
his economic models, so furious that it has almost ruined his marriage. For even the teenybopper who is his wife does not, remark-
ably enough, obey the precepts of the World Bank.

But on that day Pavel walked out in front, like a victor, as though
he had personally turned the Turks from the city walls.

Perhaps he was walking like that because he realized that he
had triumphed over me once and for all, perhaps a mild infatuation had relieved him for a moment from the ever-advancing fear
that, in the long run, he would not be able to leave Yehudi Menuhin
in the dust.

Infatuation has a mellowing influence. Infatuation reconciles you
to your failures, maybe because infatuation itself is a kind of failure.
Losing yourself in someone else, doesn't that say enough? That must
be why Papa never lost himself in anyone, not even himself.

I walked behind Pavel, not as a brother, not as a footservant,
not as the vanquished, but as a dwarf in disguise.

If anyone thinks I'm exaggerating, then they have never experienced the power of an obsession.

Obsession relegates the world, reality, people to a corner, while
all that remains is a minor detail that is magnified a thousand, yea,
ten thousand times, and that minor detail rolls over the mind in a
Blitzkrieg, and fills that mind until that minor detail has become
the world.

For me, the world was the penis of a dwarf.

They were both lovelier and more full of life than they had
been the night before, even more happy-go-lucky, seemingly un-
touched by the great destroyer. Yet perhaps I saw that so clearly

only because I myself had suddenly become a dwarf, tenderly awakened with a kiss by the destroyer, the holy, the eternal, the only.

They were wearing the same clothes, but Milena didn't have her slippers on.

Pavel was the first to greet them with a kiss.

They seemed delighted to see us, but I when I gave Andrea a cautious little kiss I still couldn't help thinking about underpants with bears on them, and Pavel's hands.

"Three times," she said, "the way they do in France."

Maybe she'd forgotten that she'd already said that. Or maybe she said that all the time.

"How are you?" Milena asked.

"Fine," Pavel said, "excellent."

"A little sad," I said.

Andrea frowned.

"But why?" she said. "On a beautiful day like this? Do you like Abba?"

"Abba," I said. "Sometimes, but I have to be in the mood for it."

What is there to say about the rest of that afternoon? That we sat outside Café Landtmann for two hours and that Pavel coerced Andrea and Milena into eating a Wiener schnitzel? That Milena smoked a joint, and that Andrea and Pavel kept sticking to each other more tightly, like chewing gum on the bottom of a shoe? And need I say who was the chewing gum and who the shoe?

Or that I kept getting quieter, until Andrea said: "You're so quiet! And yesterday you talked so much!"?

That we walked through the city, Pavel and Andrea out in front, Milena and I hobbling along behind, and that I wasn't thinking about the warm day, about the balmy breeze, about Andrea's calves, or about Pavel's hands gliding over Andrea's thighs as though she was the newest addition to his collection of costly instruments, an instrument he would soon be playing as brilliantly as all her predecessors?

I was thinking about inches, about surface area, about specific gravity, about rulers, about the infinity of pi, about calculations that ultimately all had the same outcome, and about calculators and computers and satellites circling the Earth. All the equipment couldn't disguise that the sums all had the same outcome, and the outcome pointed to the same thing: to the covert dwarf living inside me. Happiness was a matter of inches lacking. Happiness is always a matter of something lacking, and later I heard Mama, in one of her more lucid moments, say almost precisely that. The doctor had asked her: "Is there anything you lack, Mrs. Van der Jagt?"

She looked at him, the way she always looked at men, and said: "Happiness is what I lack, doctor, but that's old news."

Milena was looking grumpier all the time.

She was lacking something, too.

I pointed to gables, parroted history books, presented myself in short as the hard-working guide, and when that didn't work I started telling stupid jokes.

We stopped so Milena could buy cigarettes, and I watched as Andrea and Pavel, in a fervent embrace, homed in on their own definition of *l'amour fou*.

As I slowly became nauseous, this time not because of the Peking duck crawling its way up, but because of the remains of the Wiener schnitzel Milena couldn't finish and which I had finally gobbled down simply in order to have something to do, I told myself that the dwarf in me had only been waiting for an occasion to break out. That it was pure coincidence that Milena and Andrea had been the ones to awaken the dwarf in me with a kiss, that it could have been anyone.

But I was suffering from mankind's old malady; I was looking for meaning. For me, coincidence was just a little too coincidental.

And I watched as Andrea's skirt was lifted up so far that I was almost able to make another pronouncement concerning her underpants of the day: animals or no animals, floral or plain. Who knows? After all, on the warmest twenty-first of May in the last century, perhaps there were no underpants at all, only the nakedness that causes pain.

With Wiener schnitzel on the rise, I stood and observed passion on the streets of the city.

I have observed passion, with binoculars, with a telescope, with the naked eye, from two inches, with double glazing in between. I can tell the children I will never have a bit about passion.

Milena came back with her pack of cigarettes, and I walked along with them a ways, telling a boring story about the Hapsburg dynasty, while the dwarf in me screamed.

As we were walking down the Zedlitzgasse, Milena said: "Andrea's pretty, don't you think?"

And then she whispered: "You know what you should try? A raw egg, every morning. That helps sometimes."

I couldn't take it anymore. I said: "I have to get home. Sorry, I'll see you later."

I didn't wait for a reaction. I raced off as though the devil was on my heels.

That evening Pavel didn't come home for dinner. His empty plate gaped at me.

Papa always had the table set for every member of the family, even if they didn't show up.

I stayed awake until Pavel came home. That was at six in the morning.

14

The Lonely God of Success

After a week of saying nothing, I discovered that my silence only increased my torment. I had to inform my family. I had to tell my mama that she had brought a handicapped child into the world. Of course, we were talking about a handicap that was easy to muffle away, as long as one refrained from sanitary relations with other people. But that didn't matter. It remained a handicap.

Besides, I didn't want to refrain from sanitary relations with other people.

I had tried eating a raw egg every morning, but it hadn't resulted in much more than a stomachache. That, and the maid saying: "Who's been stealing my eggs?"

At dinner, right before dessert—we were having *rote Grütze*, a dish of which Mama was extremely fond, Papa not so, but he had adjusted his expectations for dessert in a downward direction as well—right before the *rote Grütze* were put on the table, I said: "There's something I need to tell all of you."

No one spoke. It had been a long time since anything like this had happened, since the last time someone had wanted to say something. At the table.

Papa was the first to regain his composure. "What is it, Marek?"

Pavel was massaging his hands.

Daniel was rubbing his chin.

I believe Mama had completely missed the fact that I'd said anything at all; she was rummaging through her purse.

From the kitchen I heard the sound of plates clattering on the counter. The maid was in a bad mood.

"I'm handicapped," I said.

Pavel started laughing. It was more like a brief whinny, because Papa tossed him a punitive glance.

Daniel was still rubbing at his chin.

Never taking her eyes off her purse, Mama said: "Have any of you seen my gold lighter?"

And then, with a worried glance in the direction of the kitchen: "She wouldn't be stealing, would she?"

Papa slid the dessert ladle a fraction of an inch to the right.

"No one leaves the table," he said. "We're waiting for the *rote Grütze*, and Marek has something he wants to tell us."

As he spoke the words *rote Grütze*, he looked at Mama, but Mama had lost interest in the *rote Grütze*. She said: "Who's been using my gold lighter?"

"Marek," Papa said, "what is it you wanted to discuss?"

I saw Andrea's underpants with bears on them, I saw Pavel's hands, and I heard someone giggle, the way I would never hear it again. An intensely happy giggle, Andrea's giggle.

Since I'd met Andrea, I knew it for a fact. Happiness giggles.

I watched as a few flakes of skin came swirling down from Daniel's chin.

"I'm handicapped," I said again, and my voice cracked with tension, as though my handicap was a declaration of war directed at my family. In a certain sense, of course, it was, for a handicap did nothing to contribute to success. On the contrary. And the Van der Jagt family served the lonely god of success.

"Your son claims he's handicapped," Papa said to Mama. Apparently he had adopted the standpoint that handicaps and the handicapped were Mama's business.

At that, Mama looked up from her purse.

She looked at me for a few seconds. Then she shook her head slowly.

The *rote Grütze* was served.

"Bon appetit," Papa said. "This is Mama's favorite dish."

He always said that when we ate *rote Grütze*. As if he wanted to apologize for the fact that we had to eat it.

Mama slid her dessert away from her, Papa spooned around in the *Grütze*, Daniel picked at his chin, Pavel played with his spoon, and I waited for what was coming.

Papa finished his dessert first, and only then was the silence broken.

"Marek," he said, "where does it hurt?"

A strange question. As though handicapped people always hurt somewhere.

"Would anyone like my *rote Grütze*?" Daniel asked. "It's terrible."

"There's nothing wrong with the *rote Grütze*," Papa said.

"Would you all stop making so much noise?" Mama asked. "I'm trying to find something."

I said: "It doesn't hurt, Papa. I'm handicapped."

There was music, a waltz, coming from the kitchen.

Mama's favorite animal was the ladybug. Sometimes she found ladybugs out on the street, and then she'd take them home and put them on plants.

They never lasted long in our house; after all, ladybugs aren't pets.

Sometimes Mama even talked to the ladybugs.

On some days she thought her late father had come back as a ladybug. Her father's horse had run him into a tree. Killed him on the spot.

"Come take a look," Mama would say on days like that. "Your grandfather's on the hanging plant."

Then her children would have to look at a ladybug she thought was her late father.

Papa despised Mama's ideas about reincarnation. Sometimes he would say: "Your mother should have been born in the Middle Ages."

All these things I pondered, as I considered whether I should seize this moment to reveal the details of my handicap to my family, or wait a while.

Perhaps Mama would go running over to the hanging plant again and cry: "Come look at your grandfather!"

The maid came in, saw that we weren't finished yet, and withdrew.

"If you keep playing with your chin like that, Daniel," Papa said, "you won't have any chin left anymore."

"It's always so noisy here at the table," Mama whispered, "it's like a barracks."

Papa folded his hands, as though he were chairing an important meeting and was now about to cut the decisive knot.

"Marek," he said, "we can't help you if you don't tell us what's wrong. Where does it hurt?"

He spoke the last four words so loudly and clearly that it sounded like he was speaking to the deaf.

Where did it hurt? I'd already said it didn't hurt anywhere.

And if it did hurt, then it was the kind of pain you couldn't localize, pain without an address, the way Mama's lovers strolled into her life and were thrown out of it again, all without an address.

"This is about your son," Papa said to Mama. "Perhaps you could try paying a little attention?"

"I'm looking for my lighter," Mama whispered. "My gold lighter."

And Daniel said: "I don't know what she put in this, but it tastes like chemicals, like bleach. She's trying to poison us."

Papa nodded to me encouragingly. He seemed almost pleased, as though this made him finally feel like a father. For the second or third time in his life.

"Tell us, Marek," he said. "We're listening."

"I have the penis of a dwarf," I said.

Strangely enough, Papa's expression went blank not at the word "penis," but at the word "dwarf." Pavel began laughing hysterically, almost like a woman. Daniel fainted, and Mama said, rummaging absentmindedly through her purse: "Castrati sometimes have lovely singing voices."

"What do you mean?" Papa asked. "Pavel, pick Daniel up off the floor."

The maid came in, but Papa snarled: "No, not yet."

Pavel shouted: "I'm not picking him up anymore, I'm not going to pick him up, I've picked Daniel up too many times, now it's Marek's turn!"

"I'm handicapped!" I screamed.

The maid ran away, she wasn't accustomed to screaming and snarling. Successful people didn't snarl.

Might Papa also be a covert dwarf as well? I wondered. It seemed to me just like a dwarf's chromosomes to go skipping a few generations, but maybe I was wrong.

"I mean," I said, and I was amazed at how calm I was, "that my member would fit a dwarf very well. And I am not the only one who is of that opinion. Independent sources have confirmed my findings."

Pavel acted like he was choking. He giggled, but it sounded more like a muffled groan of desperation.

Daniel was still lying on the floor.

Might Daniel, I wondered, be a covert dwarf as well? How many covert dwarfs *were* there at this table?

"I don't want to hear you talk about castrati," Papa said to Mama. "This happens to be about your son. Maybe you could pay a little attention to your son for once. And would someone please pick up Daniel."

A high, piercing tone came from Mama's throat. Then she cried: "I can't take this noise anymore!"

Pavel was weeping with laughter.

Everyone seemed to have forgotten that I had the penis of a dwarf. Daniel had fainted, of course, but then that had nothing to do with me. He simply couldn't stand anyone else getting any attention; his favorite trick was to faint when Pavel was about to perform.

I got up.

They still weren't looking at me.

It was as though my words had never been spoken, as though they had dissolved right away into a thick, impenetrable mist.

And then I shouted: "You people gave me the penis of a dwarf, you're all a bunch of murderers!"

The maid came into the room, horrified.

The sound of the waltz from the kitchen grew even louder, Mama ran to the buffet to find a chafing dish she could throw up into, and I watched as Papa rose slowly from his chair, then boxed my ear harder than he ever had before. It made a sound like a gunshot.

Then all was still.

Papa sat down, I sat down, only Mama remained standing by the buffet with a dish in her hands, but she stood by the buffet so often with a dish in her hands that no one paid much attention to that anymore.

"So," Papa said, "now it's time for some coffee. Pavel, get Daniel off the floor."

The maid cleared away the *rote Grütze*. At Daniel's plate, she paused.

"Take that one too," Papa said. "Constance, Pavel, pick Daniel up."

Mama stood at the buffet, frozen, the dish still in her hands.

No one had to pick up Daniel anymore, he had risen on his own and was sitting in his chair. His eyes rolled—he had Mama's feeling for theatrics—and he lisped: "I need different medication."

Papa said: "Pavel, how's the music coming along? When can we expect another performance?"

The word "medication" alone made Papa feel ill.

Papa's question remained hanging in the air, because Pavel didn't reply. Suddenly, Mama said: "You shouldn't hit him in the face, Ferdinand."

Then she walked over to me, without even wiping her mouth, there was still something stuck to her lips, and she kneeled down before me and murmured: "Forgive me, Marek. Please, won't you forgive me?"

She was murmuring a whole litany there at my feet, and I found the praying worse than the penis of a dwarf, a thousand times worse.

"Mama, get up," I said. "Mama, please get up. You don't have to ask for forgiveness. You can't do anything about it."

"Pavel," Papa said, a little louder now, "when can we expect the next musical performance?"

But Pavel still wasn't answering.

The maid came in, helped Mama to her feet and then to her chair. She also dabbed at Mama's lips with a clean napkin.

It didn't happen very often, maybe twice a year at most, that Mama fell to her knees in front of a member of the family and began murmuring a prayer unintelligible to outsiders.

Mama's passion was like an avalanche in the spring, when the meltwater is running too high, and with her passion she could wipe entire villages off the face of the earth. Perhaps she would have been happy if she could have wiped away the whole world, if she could have turned the world into a black hole. But the whole world was too much, even for Mama.

These days I think that what we saw at the time as passion wasn't passion at all, but something very different; pain, for example, pain looking for a fixed abode, an address, a listing in the phone book.

Once the last remnants of vomit had been removed from Mama's chin, the maid said: "Shall I bring in the coffee?"

"Please," Papa said. "A cup of coffee would be very festive. And Pavel, when do you suppose we can once again enjoy one of your musical performances?"

"I have the penis of a dwarf!" I roared. They could ignore me, they could ignore *l'amour fou*, they could ignore everything, but I would ram the penis of a dwarf down their throats.

"Pavel?" Papa said.

Daniel was picking at his chin.

Mama desperately wanted to learn to fly and be able to cross the world in her own plane, because she hated stewardesses. Even when she flew first class, the stewardesses got on her nerves. She would have preferred to spend the whole flight in the cockpit with the pilot.

I looked at Mama and I thought about how often she'd asked for flying lessons. Papa and the doctors had seriously discouraged her from taking flying lessons.

Seeing as Pavel had left Papa's question unanswered, Papa answered it himself. When it came to questions and answers, he was a very practical person. "Your last performance, Pavel, with those cello concerts by Brahms, I thought that was wonderful. Didn't you, boys?"

"It wasn't Brahms," Daniel said. "And I need stronger medication."

More than three months before this, he had fallen on his chin. It still hadn't healed properly.

The telephone rang.

Everyone froze.

Pavel started to get up, but Papa said: "Sit down. We're not at home. The maid will answer it."

He got up, walked to the door and shouted: "Bettina, we're not home, no one's home."

Then he went to the CD player, put on Mozart's Violin Concerto No. 2, and sat back down at the head of the table, like a man extremely pleased with himself at having brought a difficult meeting to a good conclusion.

When I was little I always used to draw airplanes for Mama, because I knew how much she wanted a plane of her own. But Papa had told me that such drawings only made Mama confused.

Even the penis of a dwarf couldn't upset our family life for more than four minutes. They had probably already forgotten about it. Forgetting is prerequisite to going through life undisturbed. *L'amour fou* was wasted on my family.

The maid came in with coffee.

"Ah, fantastic," Papa said, inhaling through his nose exaggeratedly so we would know he was talking about the aroma of the coffee, and not anything else. As a matter of fact, Papa enjoyed sniffing deeply and regularly; in company where the conversation had lulled, he would begin bragging about his sense of smell.

"Would you please stop acting like a complete plebeian?" Mama said. "There are children present."

Mama hated it when Papa sniffed. Besides, she found it unbecoming when people showed that they thought something was lovely. For Mama, nothing in this world could be lovely enough. What was lovely came after death, she thought, or before birth, but not in between.

15

Criminal Dreams

Weeks passed.

The girls from Luxembourg sent a postcard from Luxembourg.

Pavel said: "You can keep it." His sentiment was not the kind that linked itself to postcards.

It didn't say much. "Greetings from Luxembourg and thanks for everything. Dancing Queen Andrea and Dancing Queen Milena."

But maybe that was enough.

I had tried, like Papa, to adjust my expectations downwards, but my expectations were like birds that had flown their cage and could no longer be caught.

I decided to hang the card on the wall, in case it ever came in handy. And I stopped staring at Mr. Keipe's crotch. With Mr. Georgi, as well, I exhibited my old behavior: attentive, interested, sympathetic, and friendly. If you hadn't known better, you'd have thought there was nothing wrong.

At home we no longer talked about the dwarf, or about my boxed ear.

About once every three days at dinner, Papa inquired after Pavel's upcoming musical performances, and when no reply was forthcoming he answered himself. Daniel kept picking at his chin, and Mama had trouble concentrating on what was on her plate. She regularly forgot that there was food in front of her, and sometimes we had to remind her to raise the fork to her lips. But to that, too, we had grown accustomed.

No one knew about my decision to become a dwarf, locked in the body of a medium-sized giant.

I worked on my collection *The Dwarf and Other Poems*. I'm not ashamed of that, but I'm glad no publisher was ever willing to touch it.

To discover how it felt to be a dwarf, I began walking around the house on my haunches.

Papa said: "Why's that boy walking around on his haunches all the time, is there something wrong with him?"

Mama said: "He's looking for something."

She was always looking for things herself, so she thought other people were too.

At first Papa tried saying: "Marek, straighten up and walk normally," but he gave up on that soon enough.

Before long I worked up the courage to walk on my haunches in public as well. Not for any great distance, I couldn't keep that up, but down certain alleys and along certain streets of Vienna I walked only at a squat. Bankgasse, for example, and Schenkenstrasse.

Some people stared as I went by, but after the first two or three times the shopkeepers became used to this new way of walking. A few of them even started rooting me on, shouting: "Fantastic, you're getting the hang of it!"

I have to admit, it's an incredibly tiring and strenuous way of walking. But with a lot of practice, it does get easier.

At Daniel's birthday party I walked around the room on my haunches, passing out drinks and hors d'oeuvres. "He should join the circus," said an older gentleman whose specialty was funeral insurance.

Papa dismissed the remark, and went on to hold a short but impassioned discourse concerning his own exemplary sense of smell.

When I started walking around the international school on my haunches with increasing frequency, it was once again Mr. Georgi who spoke to me about it first.

One day while I was standing at the coffee machine, he came up to me.

First he made some token remark about having the right change. Then he said: "I see you walking around on your haunches all the time lately. You were doing it on Wallnerstrasse too. Are you in training or something?"

I shook my head.

"Is it a fad?" he asked. "Something young people do these days?"

Again I shook my head.

"Well, what's the idea?"

I pulled my coffee cup out of the machine and said: "My legs are too long, Mr. Georgi."

Mr. Georgi took a step back, perused my legs the way someone might examine a cupboard they were thinking of buying, and after a few seconds said: "I don't think they're too long. They seem pretty much in proportion to me."

Proportion. He shouldn't have used that word.

"Oh, so you think they're in proportion, do you?" I said, trying to sound as sarcastic as possible. "What do you know about proportions anyway?"

Mr. Georgi tossed some money into the coffee machine.

"What's wrong with you lately, Marek?" he asked. "You've become so hostile. It's fine by me if you want to walk around in a squat, I was only wondering whether it had a purpose."

I walked off without saying goodbye.

That day I wrote a long letter to the girls from Luxembourg. I never received a reply.

Some people at the international school were scandalized by my walking around on my haunches. Others—like the gym teacher, a man with a questionable war record—hailed it as an innocent and healthy pastime, and a few others tried to imitate me. But no one kept it up for as long as I did.

Pavel began an affair with a Hungarian housewife, and gradually lost his interest in costly instruments. He also stopped rubbing ointment on his hands quite as often.

Whenever I saw a dwarf on the street, which didn't happen all that often, I thought "Ah, a colleague, but unbeknown."

I read a lot of books about people who were malformed.

Before class one day, a little less than a month later, Mr. Georgi whispered to me: "I want you to meet a good friend of mine this afternoon."

I didn't reply.

But when school was over, I found Mr. Georgi waiting for me at the coffee machine.

"Are you coming?" he said.

I shrugged. "If you insist."

"It's sort of far from here," Mr. Georgi said. "We'll have to take my car. How's your mother?"

I nodded, which was all the answer I deigned to give him.

"Is she in town at the moment?" Mr. Georgi asked, holding open the door of his Volkswagen.

"She's gone to Barcelona for a few days," I said.

"By herself?" Mr. Georgi asked. "I mean—"

"I know what you mean," I interrupted him. "No, not by herself. My mother can't be by herself, it drives her crazy."

I settled into the passenger seat.

Mr. Georgi started the car.

Mr. Georgi believed in the good in people; at least, he assumed the good in people.

The drive took us to a neighborhood across the river.

We didn't talk much. I had once let him read a few of my poems, and he had encouraged me to continue, but then he was an idealist who encouraged everyone to continue. He was so idealistic, he would have encouraged a suicide to continue slashing.

Each year, a few weeks before Christmas, he would have a Christmas tree brought into his classroom.

"So, kids," he'd say then, "we've got a Christmas tree now, and all interested parties are welcome to help me decorate."

It was a mystery to me how anyone could actually love the Surrealists and Christmas trees with almost equal passion. Sometimes Mr. Georgi decorated his Christmas tree all by himself. For want of interested parties.

We finally stopped in front of a villa.

"My friend Professor Hirschfeld lives here," he said.

"Oh," I replied.

Mr. Georgi rang the bell. He hadn't told me why he was bringing me here, but I hadn't asked either.

Professor Hirschfeld was of average length and almost bald, and he sported sideburns.

The living room he led us into was filled with old-fashioned furniture. Lots of dark wood, somber paintings, and a grandfather clock.

"Coffee?" Professor Hirschfeld asked.

Mr. Georgi said: "Yes, please, for both of us."

Maybe this Professor Hirschfeld is a publisher, I thought, maybe Georgi liked *The Dwarf and Other Poems* more than he'd let on.

He looked like a publisher to me: musty, a slightly neglected physique, a penetrating gaze, and a charming, almost coy sort of absentmindedness.

Professor Hirschfeld came back with porcelain cups, with horses on them.

Then he went back to the kitchen and returned with a pot of coffee and little bags of sugar that he'd apparently taken with him from the plane, because they had "Austrian Airlines" printed on them. Perhaps this meeting with Professor Hirschfeld would be the long-awaited turning point in my life.

Before me I saw a newspaper, bearing the headline: "AMAZING DEBUT BY STUDENT (15). THE RIMBAUD OF VIENNA HAS ARISEN."

"Well," Professor Hirschfeld said, "how are you?"

"Wonderful," I said, "and you?"

Reich-Ranicki on TV, waving *The Dwarf and Other Poems* and growling: "This is the best thing I've read in the last twenty years! This breathes new life into German-language poetry as a whole!"

After slurping at his coffee, Professor Hirschfeld said: "I'm sorry I don't have any cookies to go with it."

Mr. Georgi coughed nervously. "Never mind."

Professor Hirschfeld put his cup on the table, wiped his mouth, sneezed quite loudly, then said: "Mr. Georgi has told me a bit about your interesting hobby."

Hobby? I didn't consider my poetry to be a hobby.

"It's not a hobby," I said.

"Well, what is it?" Professor Hirschfeld asked.

What was it? What could you call it without making a fool of yourself?

"It's very important," I said, and I thought about the time I had heard Papa say: "I took my hobby and made it my profession; I'm a satisfied man."

"Do you do it frequently?"

I looked at Mr. Georgi, but he avoided my eyes.

"Regularly," I said.

"And what do your parents have to say about that?"

"Nothing."

"Nothing? Don't they ask you about it?"

"His mother does a great deal of traveling," Mr. Georgi said, and again he avoided my gaze.

"A businesswoman?"

"You might call it that," I said.

I looked at the curtains. The curtains were gray.

Mama didn't like curtains. Mama needed fresh air.

"Could you show me how you do it?" Professor Hirschfeld asked.

"Now?" I asked. "Right here?" But even as I uttered the question, I realized that all this time he had not been talking about *The Dwarf and Other Poems*.

It was as if they'd hit me on the forehead with a soup ladle, hard, that's how it felt—and not just once, no, a few times in a row. Like my forehead was a steak that needed tenderizing, and now that it was tender enough they were going to fricassee and fry me.

"Show us, just once, would you?" Professor Hirschfeld asked.

"Marek, remember, the way you were walking that time I ran into you in Wallnerstrasse?"

Mr. Georgi got up and began walking around Professor Hirschfeld's living room on his haunches.

"Like this, remember?" he said. "And last Wednesday, in the chemistry lab. You remember, don't you?"

A terrible foreboding came over me.

Perhaps Mr. Georgi had finally lost his senses. Perhaps the bottle had once again become the most important thing in his life.

He lived alone with his collection of tropical fish, and long ago, long before I ever attended the international school, he had been admitted to a clinic. The official version was that he'd had back problems, but the initiated, which was everyone at our school, knew that the bottle had turned his world into a delirium without exit, and that he had been sent to a mountain clinic where they had slowly showed him the way out.

Professor Hirschfeld pointed at Mr. Georgi, who was still squatting on the floor, and said: "So you often walk down the street like that?"

"Well, often. Sometimes," I said. "Often is another matter."

"There's no need to be afraid," Professor Hirschfeld said, "I only want to see exactly how you walk."

He got up and began walking around the living room on his haunches too. Along with Mr. Georgi.

"Come, join us," he said.

I slid down out of my chair. It can't do any real harm, I thought, and if it makes them happy . . .

I walked around on my haunches with them.

They were lousy at it. But they hadn't practiced.

At first your thighs start hurting after a few steps, and you have to build it up slowly. Every day another couple of yards.

"You two aren't doing it right," I said. "But you have to build it up gradually; when you start taking piano lessons, you can't expect to play Mozart right away."

"And you built it up gradually?" Professor Hirschfeld asked.

He was still squatting on the floor.

"Yes," I said. "When I really want something, I keep at it."

Professor Hirschfeld was the first to stand up.

Then Mr. Georgi got up as well.

I was the last to stand up and go back to my chair.

"Why are you so interested in this way of walking?" I asked.

"I've never seen anything like it before," Professor Hirschfeld said. "Never."

"Professor Hirschfeld is a scientist," Mr. Georgi said.

The word "scientist" remained hanging in the air, it was an important word for Mr. Georgi, something he would have liked to be himself. But the bottle got in the way of that, and all that remained was the international school in Vienna.

"And what kind of science do you practice?" I asked.

"The interpretation of dreams," Professor Hirschfeld said. "For almost forty years I have been living my life amid the dreams of others."

Some life returned to his old body. His eyes began to gleam.

"Professor Hirschfeld has studied the dreams of criminals," Mr. Georgi said, "and he is currently writing a wonderful book about that."

Professor Hirschfeld nodded in deep satisfaction, and again I had the funny feeling that I was in the room with two men who were gradually losing their senses.

"That's fascinating," I said. "Have you studied a lot of criminals?"

Professor Hirschfeld wagged his finger at me.

"Not just criminals," he brayed into the living room, as though addressing a full auditorium. "Only those who have committed violent crimes. Exclusively violent crimes."

"No purse-snatchers, in other words," Mr. Georgi said, pouring us all some more coffee.

"No purse-snatchers need apply," Professor Hirschfeld cried. "Let them take their business elsewhere. I have studied almost five hundred cases. And not just in Europe. I have been to Japan, to New Zealand, to Chile. And I have compared the dreams of criminals with those of people who are not considered criminals."

He was rocking back and forth excitedly in his chair.

This man apparently loved the perpetrators of violent crimes the way some people loved Brahms or Mozart. "And what is it you expect from me?" I asked.

I was suddenly reminded of Milena, and of Algeria, where she said no culture was to be found, and of her father the Viking, and the postcard she and Andrea had sent me, and of the fact that I would never take the night train to Luxembourg.

"I believe Professor Hirschfeld can help you," Mr. Georgi said.

"Why?" I asked.

"Because Kurt, Professor Hirschfeld, is a friend of mine."

"But why do I need help?"

They know everything, it suddenly occurred to me. They have always known all about it.

Professor Hirschfeld put on his reading glasses, looked at a notepad, took off his glasses again and asked: "What exactly do you feel when you walk around Vienna like this?"

"I concentrate," I said.

"On what?"

"On my thigh muscles. But I don't understand. What's the connection with your specialty?"

"There is none," Professor Hirschfeld said.

Atop a cupboard was a carafe with a dark red fluid in it, probably port.

"I'd like to help you," Professor Hirschfeld said.

"With what?"

I knew my own poems by heart, back then, and I suddenly felt the overpowering urge to stand up and start reciting my poems.

I wanted to recite my poems on every street corner in Vienna; poetry wasn't about getting rich, insurance made you rich, this was about getting my poems out to the people, like hepatitis C, like a virus that has to spread vast.

Maybe it wasn't actually port on top of the cupboard, maybe it was armagnac, or pistachio liqueur.

"Do you feel different from other people?" Professor Hirschfeld asked. "Do you have the feeling that you say things they don't understand, and that they say things you don't understand?"

"I've never thought about it."

Papa had been clear: silence is the highest form of communication, and what was there to understand about silence? Silence was like the blank screen before the movie starts, there was nothing to understand. Silence wasn't some criminal's dream that had to be interpreted.

"So why don't you read my poems?" I suggested.

"Do you write poems?"

Professor Hirschfeld looked at Mr. Georgi, and Mr. Georgi said: "Oh yes, Marek is very gifted. You wrote 'The Leprechaun,' didn't you?"

"The dwarf," I shouted, "not the leprechaun, the dwarf. A leprechaun isn't a dwarf, Mr. Georgi. You tell everyone, 'Yes, go on, I'm listening,' but it doesn't mean a thing. You didn't even read those poems."

And then I stood up and started reciting my poems.

I waved my arms. During some stanzas I stomped on the floor, and at the stanza where the dwarf attacks a window-cleaner I spit huge globs of saliva on the floor, because the dwarf in the poem spits too, and when I had completely finished the longest poem of all—four pages' worth—a remarkable calm settled over me.

"Very interesting," Professor Hirschfeld said, "and compelling. I believe I can help you."

It was then that I had the first huge fit of rage in my life; it was as though fifteen years of rage were pouring out right there in Professor Hirschfeld's living room. Many fits of rage would follow, and in the end my life would resemble one long fit of rage that could end only in a coronary, in two collapsed lungs, or in the electric chair.

"You two say you want to help me," I screamed, "but you're the ones who need help. You're blind to the beauty of my words because you're already dead, they've just forgotten to bury you, but there's grass growing above your heads already, only you can't see it because you're always looking down your noses. But I am the dwarf, not the leprechaun, Mr. Georgi, and I look up and see the grass growing over your heads and I see the grass growing out your ears and your noses and your mouths, and so far I've kept my mouth shut out of courtesy, but I won't keep my mouth shut any longer. The two of you are like a couple of fish that have been hanging on some hook since the Battle of Waterloo. Deader than Vienna, even deader than life insurance. All I have to do is look at you and you fall apart, there's nothing left, nothing, absolutely nothing."

I walked over to the cupboard and grabbed the carafe. I pulled out the stopper and lifted the carafe to my lips, but had to spit it out right away, because it was too strong for my untrained gullet.

"I don't want your help," I shouted, "I want to help you, I want to mow the grass above your heads, I am the divine lawnmower. That's right, listen to me, you stiffs, I'm the divine lawnmower."

Then I recited the second poem from *The Dwarf and Other Poems*, and it made me feel like I was coming down from the mountain carrying tablets of stone.

When I was finished I sat down again and crossed my legs.

Professor Hirschfeld plucked at his sideburns. Mr. Georgi was examining the gray curtains.

All that was left of *l'amour fou* at that moment was revenge. Revenge on my own sex organ, revenge on the people who confused leprechauns with dwarfs, revenge on my mama's lovers who thought to please her with cheap imitation jewelry, revenge on the gym teacher, revenge on the city of Luxembourg and the train trip I would never take, revenge on the Surrealists who had lured me with music that was no longer performed on this earth, revenge on the French teacher who had taught me about those Surrealists, revenge on life insurance, revenge on the money I exuded, revenge on the ballet dancer I'd never become, revenge on the poet I would never become, revenge on Rimbaud, revenge on a civilization in which I put no stock, revenge on the people who thought civilization stopped at the edge of Vienna, revenge on the concept of genius, all of which was ultimately one and the same revenge, revenge on life itself. People say that love generates passion, but the God of Vengeance is stronger than all the love put together.

Out on the street someone was trying to start a car, but it wasn't working.

Finally, Professor Hirschfeld broke the silence. "We could all stand a little *schnapps*, don't you think?"

"No, no," Mr. Georgi said, "that only makes me importune," and he laughed politely at his own joke.

Professor Hirschfeld poured a drink for himself and for me, but not from the carafe I had tried. It was from a bottle he brought in from the kitchen.

"This is the clear McCoy," he said, "it doesn't come any better than this." And suddenly I pictured him saying the same thing to all his criminals, I imagined him drinking *schnapps* with them before buckling down to yet another dream.

"What has actually happened to those criminals?" I asked. "The ones you've studied?"

Professor Hirschfeld knocked back his drink and said: "Most of them are in prison, some of them are in a mental hospital, others are dead, one of them has returned to normal society and is now a professor of biochemistry."

"Weren't you ever afraid?"

"I had no time to be afraid."

Professor Hirschfeld tore a page out of his notepad and wrote something on it.

"Here's my number," he said. "Use it. It doesn't matter when, it doesn't matter what you want to talk about."

I put the number in my pocket.

"Are you still studying criminals?"

"No," Professor Hirschfeld said. "Now I'm studying the results of my study. I don't actually know which is harder to interpret: dreams, or my own research."

He stood up from his chair. "You will have to excuse me now."

"Yes," Mr. Georgi said promptly. He stood up too, grabbed Professor Hirschfeld's hand and said: "Kurt."

"My pleasure," Professor Hirschfeld said. "Pleased to be of assistance."

Then he shook my hand. Out on the street someone was still trying to start a car.

"If you want, you can also bring your mother with you."

"If I come, I'll come alone."

"You can also come by to recite poems," Professor Hirschfeld said. "I don't know much about poetry, but I like the sound of the human voice, even when that voice sprays saliva all over the place."

I said nothing.

Professor Hirschfeld remained standing in the doorway, and when we got to Mr. Georgi's car I turned around again.

Professor Hirschfeld waved.

His vest flapped in the wind, and once again I thought of criminals who had sat in the same chair as me.

"What an extraordinary man," I said.

"Yes," Mr. Georgi said.

He dropped me off close to my house.

"See you tomorrow," he said. "And I'm sorry about mixing up leprechauns and dwarfs."

"It doesn't matter," I said, "it really doesn't matter."

I went to my room, read the postcard from the girls from Luxembourg for the umpteenth time, and opened the window.

16

Miss Oertel

Summer came.

Daniel fainted more often than ever. He said: "It's all drawing to an end," but no one paid any attention.

Great and important things were on their way.

I didn't know what kind of things, only that they would be great and important.

My hunch was right, but just as Professor Hirschfeld could not interpret the results of his research, so I could not interpret my hunch.

It was there, but what it was saying was unintelligible to me.

My attempts to go through life as a dwarf became less fervent.

I walked around less often on my haunches, and when I did, I did it for shorter periods of time. And one day I stopped doing it altogether, but I don't think anyone noticed.

Papa, Mama, and my two brothers had resigned themselves to the fact that I wanted to go through life at a squat, and when I traded in that desire for another they resigned themselves to it with the same ease.

Mr. Georgi inquired about my poems about once every three weeks, just to be polite. "Are you going to give me something to read again?" he asked.

"Yes, of course," I said. "It's coming." But I never gave him anything else to read. People who didn't know the difference between leprechauns and dwarfs did not deserve my poetry. One day he also said: "Photography is creative too, isn't it, Marek?"

Mama began getting headaches, Papa was in the midst of a merger, Pavel had given up music, and I was trying once again to bring *l'amour fou* into practice.

A bit less hopefully than the first time. Everywhere I saw candidates, in department stores, in streetcars and subway trains, in theaters, in pharmacies and in parks, but now I knew that the candidates might very well not regard *l'amour fou* as the chief end of man. Yes, there were even some who might say: "I'd rather wake up with the flu than with *l'amour fou*."

She smelled of roasted chestnuts. To lure me once and for all into fighting in his army, the God of Vengeance had sought out a drawing teacher who smelled like roasted chestnuts. And in view of the fact that chestnuts were roasted throughout the city every winter, and Viennese winters are long, I am reminded each year from October through March that the God of Vengeance had lured me in, just as *l'amour fou* had once lured me in.

I met her in the library. The library where I collected books in order to find out more about *l'amour fou*.

She spoke to me, and I spoke back, unaware of any danger whatsoever.

She was fifteen years older than me, and she invited me to her house for a cup of tea.

She lived with her mother, and a few years earlier she had traded in nursing for the art academy, then began teaching crafts courses herself. She taught at a night school. Arts and crafts for adults. And because the night school did not pay generously, she also gave private lessons.

Her name was Miss Oertel.

When I came to her home—we first had to climb three sets of stairs, because the elevator was out of order—she closed the sliding doors behind us and said: "There, then we won't bother my mother."

"Don't go to any trouble," I said, but Miss Oertel said: "A cup of herbal tea is done in a jiffy."

I heard her talking to her mother in the kitchen.

Miss Oertel had very short hair that stood straight up on her head. I preferred long hair that could blow in the wind, that could fall down in front of eyes and nose and be pinned up at the back, but I had reached the conclusion that what I preferred made no difference at all.

I sat down in an easy chair that swallowed me immediately, I was pulled into it like a mouse into a trap.

I looked around, and Miss Oertel's voice grew louder and louder, it sounded like they were having a difference of opinion in the kitchen.

She was the one who had spoken to me. "What do you do here?" she'd asked. "I see you in the library all the time."

We were standing in line to bring back our books. I was overdue.

"I look up things about *l'amour fou*," I said. "*L'amour fou* is my life's work."

That's how we made contact.

After we had both brought back our books and I had paid my fine, we continued our conversation.

I walked along behind her. Miss Oertel went to the Braille section. "Is it for you?" I asked.

Miss Oertel did not seem blind, not even nearsighted.

"No, no," she said, "it's for a friend."

Miss Oertel told me that she taught drawing and was a great fan of Thomas Bernhard.

I said: "I'm not really, he gives Austria more attention than the country deserves."

I admit, I had stolen that sentence straight from the mouth of my Germanic languages teacher, but isn't *l'amour fou* worth a little concession here and there?

Besides, when you think about it, we all go through life with borrowed opinions, opinions which, in many cases, we have also misunderstood.

Strangely enough, I didn't feel a bit of what they call the force of attraction, and nothing at all of what I felt when I saw Andrea. Here was no nakedness that could cause pain.

But I thought: contact is contact. Onward.

Miss Oertel was very large, and also had a number of other characteristics more typical of the male of our species.

She came back from the kitchen.

"Well," she said.

And then she cried: "Oh God, I forgot the tea strainer."

She stormed off and came back with a strainer.

Our conversation was pleasant, insofar as conversation can be pleasant between two people who don't have much to say to each other and whose communication skills are not particularly well developed.

She told me a long story about the island of Sylt, where she had met the love of her life, a Turk, married of course, but that was not the worst of it, she said. What the worst of it was, she didn't tell me. Instead, she suddenly stopped and said: "Anyway, I still know how to apply a sterile field."

"Excuse me, Miss Oertel," I said, "but what's a sterile field?"

"I haven't forgotten a thing," she said, "not a thing. I know how to insert a catheter into a man's bladder, I know how to take body temperature, I know how to put someone under narcosis, how to deliver bad news, and I also know how to inject someone with Phenol. I still remember all that, as if it were only yesterday. And, not to forget: how to introduce a gastric tube. When we did our exam on the gastric tube, I was the best in the class."

She poured a little more herbal tea and looked at me with a gaze so eager that there could be no doubt but she would have liked to insert a catheter into my bladder right there on the spot. And then apply a sterile field, although I still had no idea what I was to imagine by a sterile field.

Something about her reminded me of Papa, although I didn't know what.

"Do you perhaps regret having left nursing for the art academy?"

She shook her head slowly. "Oh no," she said, "but it was a very thorough education, and I haven't forgotten any of it."

According to Mr. Georgi, people in this city all lived in the past. I always thought he said that because he lived in the past himself, the past from back before his stay at the mountain clinic where they robbed him of his last hallucinations. Like so many people, he probably saw himself as the measure of all things, but maybe he was right, maybe Vienna really was the town for people who'd rather not get started on the future.

"I've been observing you for a while," Miss Oertel said, "the way you sit there. In the library. I like to observe people."

"And that girlfriend of yours is blind?" I asked.

"That's right," she said, "my best friend is blind. That's why I go to the library all the time, to borrow audiobooks for her. She especially likes listening to Isabel Allende."

Then the sliding doors were pushed aside; between them, like a general surveying the field of battle, stood a commanding figure in a blue dress.

Mrs. Oertel had been a baker's wife, or at least that's what her daughter had told me, there in the Braille section of the library.

Her arms were fat and white. Mrs. Oertel exuded a vague menace.

"Mama," Miss Oertel said, "this is Mark van der Jagt."

"Marek," I said. "Marek with an 'e' in between."

Mrs. Oertel came towards me. If I hadn't known better I would have thought she was going to give me a resounding box on the ear. It was important for me to repress thoughts like that, so I struggled up out of my uncomfortable easy chair. She was two heads taller than me. She shook my hand vigorously.

"Are you here for drawing lessons?" Mrs. Oertel asked.

"No," I said.

"Clay?"

I looked at her daughter, I didn't know what reply I was expected to give.

"He's here for a nice talk," said Miss Oertel. Compared to her mother, she was petite and feminine.

"Oh," said Mrs. Oertel. From the sound of it, she only barely approved of nice talks.

"I can't stay long, though," I said, but Miss Oertel said: "No, no, don't go. There's still plenty of tea."

Mrs. Oertel sat down in an easy chair exactly like the one I was in. For people of average stature, the easy chairs exuded the same kind of menace Mrs. Oertel did.

No one said anything anymore.

Perhaps I brought out the silent side in people.

I coughed a few times, holding my handkerchief over my mouth.

"It's been ten months now," Miss Oertel's mother said, lighting a cigarette.

I looked at the smoke. Hadn't I read somewhere that *l'amour fou* could manifest itself in the strangest situations and at the most unexpected moments, and that even the elderly, the dying, the malformed, the reprobate, bore within themselves the seed of *l'amour fou*?

Could it be that the *amour fou* I had been searching for so long had manifested itself in a baker's wife and her daughter?

"Ten months," Mrs. Oertel said, and inhaled so deeply that she seemed to be sucking the last dregs of life out of her cigarette. "But it feels like only yesterday. Did she tell you about it?"

I looked at Miss Oertel. From somewhere came the smell of fried egg.

"I don't like talking about it," said Miss Oertel.

"My husband went to the bakery that morning, happy as a lark. That afternoon they called me. Gone, from one moment to the next. He was helping a customer. Gone."

"I'm sorry," I said. The smell of fried egg was becoming more penetrating. "Could it be that something's still on the stove?" I asked.

Miss Oertel got up and stomped off to the kitchen, leaving me alone with her mother.

"You have a very nice home," I said.

"Nice," Mrs. Oertel said. "You call this nice?" And she ground out her cigarette.

"I sold the business right away," Mrs. Oertel said. "The girl didn't want it anyway."

The girl, that was Miss Oertel.

Somehow I could imagine her not wanting to take over her parents' bakery, but it's always a bad idea to burden others with unsolicited advice and opinions.

"We should really have sold it a long time ago," Mrs. Oertel said. "The neighborhood was going downhill. Those people don't know good bread when they see it."

"No, of course not," I said.

"My husband had bad knees. His knees were completely worn out. He walked with a cane. The doctor told him: 'New knees, but then you'll be flat on your back for a year.' He dreaded that. He didn't want to let the business go to pot for a couple of new knees. Sometimes I think he didn't want new knees, that that's why he didn't try to fight it, that he figured: just let me slip away like this, me and my old knees. Like a piece of candy?"

From a cupboard she took a dish of lemon drops wrapped in cellophane.

"No thank you," I said.

Miss Oertel came back. She was getting prettier all the time, but maybe that was only my own resolve to find beauty in places where it was scarce.

"You left the gas on," Miss Oertel said. "It burned onto the pan."

"I'd better be going," I said.

"Would you like a fried egg?" Mrs. Oertel asked.

"My mother always cooks for my drawing students," Miss Oertel said. "I tell them: you can have private lessons, but that includes a meal."

Old Mrs. Oertel laughed. "Look at him, he's all skin and bones."

Mrs. Oertel may have hated nice talks, but she seemed determined to fatten me up.

I recalled all kinds of fairy tales, my overactive fantasy was playing up again, I saw myself disappearing into a kettle being stirred with a huge ladle by Mrs. Oertel, while Miss Oertel shouted from the next room: "Don't let it stick to the pan, Mom!"

Reason, as I understand it after four years of studying the summaries of famous philosophers, is something you can believe in like a god or a whorish nun, but nothing more than that.

Just as Professor Hirschfeld's search had brought him to the dreams of criminals, so my search for *l'amour fou* had brought me to Miss Oertel and her mother. Let no one claim that the God of Vengeance doesn't have a sense of irony.

There in Mrs. Oertel's living room I still believed that it was reason that made me suppress my overactive imagination, the way civilized people suppress horniness when it rears its head at the wrong moment.

"He's always at the library," Miss Oertel said.

Mrs. Oertel lit another cigarette.

"I was just telling him about Dad's knees," Mrs. Oertel said.

"That's right, they were completely worn out," her daughter said.

Mrs. Oertel inhaled contentedly. "The war, shrapnel, they never bothered to remove it carefully after the war. No, of course not, they had other things on their mind. I can spoon out a tomato better than they spooned out his knees. Am I right?"

"Yes, Mom."

"I'd better be going," I said.

"First I'm going to fry you a few eggs," Mrs. Oertel said. "Can't have you fainting on us. Empty the ashtray, would you?"

Her daughter got up and emptied the ashtray.

"At first I was heartbroken, but now it's actually a relief, being your own boss around the house after fifty years."

"Fifty years, that's a long time," I said.

"And we'd been hesitating about his knees for the last five. Should he have an operation or shouldn't he? Or maybe only operate on the one knee. And the girl didn't want to take over the business. We begged her, but she wouldn't hear of it. Looking back on it, it was a good thing, because the bakery would have gone down the tubes within three months with her behind the counter. Am I right?"

"Yes, Mom," Miss Oertel said. "Don't ever put me behind a counter." And she laughed, fast and shrill.

Mrs. Oertel went to the kitchen to fry some eggs that didn't burn onto the pan this time, and her daughter said: "Why don't we sit on the couch?"

"Yes," I said, "that's a good idea."

We sat on the couch together and looked at a little painting of a waterfall.

"My uncle painted that," Miss Oertel said. "That takes talent, too."

"Nice," I said.

The smell of fried bacon spread through the house.

"You're special," she said. "Do you know that?"

I smiled. My famous smile.

"Tell us a bit about the island of Sylt. How did that go, with the love of your life?"

"Oh," she said, and slid away from me a bit, "not well at all."

I could tell that Miss Oertel was growing sad.

Her lips began to quiver.

That was always a bad sign.

"He gave me to his brother," she whispered, and slid a little closer.

"The Turk?"

"Yes," she said, "and his brother gave me to his cousin, and that cousin gave me to his best friend."

I bit my lip.

How does one adopt a pose? Smile, bite your lip, ask a friendly question, wipe a little dust off your coat. You have to be predictable in order to be recognized, whether that's recognition as a person, as a writer, or as a bicycle repairman. And when people talk about originality, they actually mean predictability in new gift-wrap, or old gift-wrap that's at least been ironed neatly. It is a mistake to go any further than the moderately unexpected. I wanted my *amour fou* to be recognized so badly, even if it was only by one person, even if only by Miss Oertel.

"That's terrible," I said.

The house started smelling of fried potatoes too. What was Mrs. Oertel cooking up in her kitchen?

Miss Oertel's lips were now quivering more than ever.

"Were you molested?"

The question was out of my mouth before I could think about it.

"No," she said, "I did what was asked of me. After all, I loved him. I was passed from hand to hand on the island of Sylt."

The little painting of the waterfall seemed to grow increasingly insinuative.

"And I was still so young," Miss Oertel said. "He abused a young girl. Now he disgusts me."

But when I looked into her eyes, I saw disgust mingled with a large dose of desire. It seemed unwise to pursue my questioning.

"And during nurse's training you learned how to tell people bad news?"

"Oh yes," Miss Oertel said, "I received a ten for that exam, I was the best, it's a real art to tell people bad news in a way that makes it acceptable for the recipient."

I realized how cold it was in the room. But it isn't every day that you run into someone who'd been passed from hand to hand on the island of Sylt. And besides, I had a fried egg coming.

I nodded. "Your mother is really cooking up a storm," I said.

There was no reply.

She had put her arm around me, and I thought I heard a muffled sob.

"After that, were you passed from hand to hand very often?"

"No," she said, "only on the island of Sylt."

Someone screamed. It was old Mrs. Oertel, but it sounded like an old man in mortal agony.

"I believe your mother's calling," I said.

Miss Oertel wiped the tears from her eyes. Fortunately she didn't wear makeup. At least not today.

We went to the kitchen.

Three places had been set at a little table.

A fried egg lay glistening on a slice of bread, along with an unidentifiable piece of sausage and a slice of hard-fried bacon.

I was overpowered by intense nausea.

"Eat," Mrs. Oertel said, "it will do you good."

I sat down.

"They're free-range eggs," Mrs. Oertel said. "I gathered them myself this morning."

"The neighbor has chickens," her daughter explained.

"How idyllic," I murmured.

Then it was quiet, only a faucet dripped on. I closed my eyes and took a bite.

There was no more *amour fou*, there was only Mrs. Oertel and the neighbor's free-range eggs and the island of Sylt, where one was passed from hand to hand.

After our meal of fried eggs sunnyside up, unidentifiable sausage, and a pudding yellow of hue and with hard black things in it that turned out to be raisins, Miss Oertel put on some perfume and we went back to the couch, across from the little painting of the waterfall.

I had been knocked for a loop. I had no idea how I would ever get away from there, but that didn't seem to be of paramount importance. Keeping my food down was priority number one. I was starting to feel like Mama, but then she never bothered to keep down her food.

"Have you ever been passed from hand to hand?" Miss Oertel asked.

I thought about Milena, standing by the door in Pavel's room.

"Never," I said.

Miss Oertel's hair was standing up straighter than ever, and heavy perfume mingled with fried bacon to form an odor which was undefinable, but which fortunately no longer spoke of roasted chestnuts. That, however, was pretty much all you could say for it.

Crockery clattered in the kitchen. Mrs. Oertel had said: "I'll wash the dishes, you two go and have fun."

"Did you enjoy it?" Miss Oertel asked.

I nodded.

Gagging is something one should do in private.

The strange thing was, the more I felt like gagging, the more I was convinced that what was taking place between me and Miss Oertel, and what was still to take place, was actually *l'amour fou*.

174

Hadn't some obscure Surrealist once written that one had to wade through a sea of mud and an ocean of pus before finally catching a glimpse of the ultimate *amour fou*?

The glimpse I caught was of Miss Oertel.

"I want to show you some of my drawings," she said. "Come with me."

We walked up some stairs and came to a little room containing a large, rather old-fashioned bed with a yellow bedspread.

"It's handmade," Miss Oertel said.

I rubbed the bedspread between my fingertips.

"My grandma made it, unbelievable, isn't it?"

"Unbelievable," I said.

"She died ten years ago," Miss Oertel said.

From a closet she pulled out a folder full of drawings.

Then she sat down beside me and showed me her works of art.

I looked and said nothing. Occasionally I whispered an inaudible compliment.

A stuffed elephant slept beside her pillow. I also saw a folded handkerchief. And a pair of pajamas.

After Miss Oertel had shown me all her drawings, I applauded. She nodded gratefully and put the folder back in the closet.

"Four years of my life," she said, "but it was worth it."

She sat down beside me on the bed and asked how I liked her room.

"Very nice," I said.

"Shall I show you something?"

"If you like."

"I've had this ever since I was four," she said, pointing at the elephant.

I complimented her on the elephant. I'd already complimented her on the rest, right down to the dust on the floor.

"I've been watching you for a long time, did you know that?"

"No," I said.

A married Turk on the island of Sylt appeared in my mind. Maybe it wasn't even his fault, maybe she'd seduced him in a cutaway bathing suit.

"You have such a lovely way of walking," Miss Oertel said. "So concentrated, so proud."

Proud, I'd never heard that one before.

I remembered a discussion at the international school about whether a skill could be considered knowledge, whether the skill we called walking indicated that the person in question also possessed knowledge concerning the act of walking.

Those were the kinds of discussions we had at the international school, and they aroused in me the idea that life itself was a skill some people possessed and others didn't.

"You have a lovely walk, too," I said.

She beamed, but maybe that was only my imagination.

"But not proud," she said, "not like you."

Miss Oertel grabbed my hand. Miss Oertel caressed that hand and said: "Soft, like a baby's."

I recalled that Miss Oertel knew how to apply a sterile field, and that she knew how to deliver bad news, and it seemed to me that within the not-too-distant future she would do both. And it wouldn't remain at one sterile field, just as her mother had not fried only one egg.

I wondered whether the Turk on Sylt had also had the skin of a baby.

Suddenly, with my hand still in hers, she asked: "Do you like my blouse?"

I looked at her blouse, which I hadn't noticed before. All my attention had been focused on her haircut and her occasionally quivering lips.

"It's silk. Do you like silk?"

"Yes," I said. "Very much."

"But it's lousy silk, when you hold it up to the light you see that it's full of little holes."

"I don't see any holes," I said.

"They cheated me."

Miss Oertel's lip began quivering again, and I prayed to the nonexistent God to never again expose me to quivering female lips.

"I don't see any holes," I repeated. "Really I don't."

"You have to hold it up to the light," Miss Oertel said, and started unbuttoning her blouse.

She wasn't wearing a bra.

"They cheated me," she said. "It's cheap Chinese junk."

"They also make a lot of nice things in China," I said.

But before I could say any more Miss Oertel tossed her blouse on the bed and pressed one of her breasts against my face so forcefully that it seemed she was planning to shut me up once and for all.

I sat there, stock-still. Perhaps *l'amour fou* was about to begin at last.

We sat there like that for at least two minutes. On the bed.

Then Miss Oertel took her breast away from my mouth, picked her blouse up off the bed, held it to the light, and said: "Look."

I looked, and had to admit that her blouse was full of little holes.

"Did moths get to it?"

"No," she said, "it's cheap Chinese junk."

If the word "proud" applied to anything, then it was to Miss Oertel's breasts. They didn't sag, there were no varicose veins meandering over them, and they weren't a scary brown, not from the beach or a solarium, because I don't like that.

Miss Oertel saw me looking, and said: "My name is Sabine, but the people who really know me call me Bine."

"Do you want me to call you Bine?"

"Yes," she said, "call me Bine."

Then she began yanking on my sweater.

"Wait a minute," I said.

Together we yanked at my sweater until we'd succeeded in pulling it over my head.

With the eye of an expert nurse, Bine Oertel examined my stomach and chest. Then she seized one of my nipples between thumb and forefinger and began rolling that nipple back and forth like it was a clove of garlic she wanted to grind to a pulp.

My imagination got in the way of reality again, for in my mind's eye I saw old Mrs. Oertel coming up the stairs with a big ladle in one hand and a huge kettle in the other.

I pulled myself together. What's a little pain in the nipple? He who refuses to suffer a little pain is not deserving of *l'amour fou*.

I pressed my mouth to Bine's mouth, and tried to turn off all my thoughts. Unfortunately, that only worked a little.

In literature for certain ladies and gentlemen, one would say: "Our tongues played a fiery game." Well, our tongues didn't play any game at all, they had no time for that, our tongues were two lobsters that were being boiled but couldn't believe it yet.

Suddenly Miss Oertel pulled away.

She took a step backwards and stuck two fingers in her mouth.

She pulled a long brown hair out of her mouth. One of my hairs.

"I'm sorry," I said, "they fall out."

"It doesn't matter."

She held the hair in her hand like it was a worm.

She said: "I like it when you look at my breasts."

"Me too," I said, "I like looking at them."

Then, from downstairs, came the sound of old Mrs. Oertel's voice. Strangely enough, that voice didn't break the spell; on the contrary, it only made it more charming.

I took one of Bine Oertel's nipples between thumb and forefinger and did to it what she had done to mine.

"I'm going downstairs," Bine said, "to see what my mother wants."

She put her blouse back on and ran down the stairs.

I sat on the bed and toyed with the idea of spending the night at Miss Oertel's house, if old Mrs. Oertel approved, of course.

I felt a certain degree of apprehension, but apprehension was there to be overcome.

Apprehension was really nothing more than one's imagination acting up.

Is passion compatible with self-control?

In the case of Bine Oertel, the answer must be negative.

She came rushing up the stairs like a madwoman, slammed her bedroom door, and said: "My mother's going to watch TV now."

"Is there anything good on?" I inquired.

"A detective program," Miss Oertel said, and started unbuttoning her blouse again. "My mother loves detective programs."

I still felt a vague irritation in my left nipple.

Mama often said you could get cancer from being pinched. Mama was even more afraid of cancer than of being alone.

My lips were chapped, I needed to rub something on them. My lips were often chapped, but I was too lazy to rub salve on them. One person in the family preoccupied with oils and salves was more than enough.

Bine Oertel kneeled down in front of me and started taking off my shoes.

She had the dexterity of an older, solicitous nurse, one who knew what she was doing.

I had to surrender to her as to a surgeon. Then she took off my socks as well, and stuck my big toe in her mouth. I laughed quietly, more out of embarrassment than anything else, because my big toe couldn't smell all that good, or taste all that nice.

Papa had a little machine he used every Sunday morning to scrape the calluses off the soles of his feet.

Pavel used that machine too sometimes; I didn't, because I didn't have any calluses yet.

"Do you still love him?" I asked.

Miss Oertel took my toe out of her mouth.

Now that the saliva on my toe was cooling off, I noticed for the first time just how cold it was in Miss Oertel's little room.

I heard the crackly sound of a television being turned on downstairs, and it occurred to me that people are actually jamming stations, wandering antennae who try to knock other stations off the air.

I wanted to love Miss Oertel, to throw myself at her feet and tell her everything I knew, everything I thought, everything I had hidden from other people because my own thoughts scared me. "I am the dwarf," I wanted to say, "the dwarf who's going to change your life, the dwarf you've been waiting for forever, maybe even without knowing it."

But there were too many jamming stations on the air, the love for Miss Oertel wasn't coming through, it was ending up as static, crackling, sighs, heavy breathing, squeaks, as if we were all hooked up to a heart monitor.

"Who?" Bine asked.

"The Turk. Do you still love him?"

"I've waited for him for six years," she said, my foot still in her hand. "That's long enough, isn't it?"

"More than enough."

There was music coming from the TV downstairs.

Bine put one hand on my knee and started tugging at my belt. It had once belonged to Daniel, but he gave it to me when he grew tired of it.

Like so many people in our family, Daniel was a snob. But for him it was his life's fulfillment, a religion with countless false gods who occasionally overplayed their hand and fell from the mountaintop.

"You have such a great body," she said.

"You think so?" I asked.

She nodded. When was she going to deliver the bad news, and how would she do it?

"Half-child, half-man," she said.

She took off my belt.

Half-child, half-man, that was a pretty measly compliment.

If she'd said that to the Turk, no wonder he'd gone back to his wife.

That day I was wearing my corduroy trousers, and she unbuttoned them. On my stomach I felt a hand.

A cold hand.

Somehow the picture of myself as a radio tower just wouldn't go away.

Then she pushed me onto my back. Still wearing her pants and shoes, she straddled me and started playing with my Adam's apple.

"I didn't shave," I said. "Sorry."

"What's to shave?" Miss Oertel said, and laughed.

There was no apparent reason why Miss Oertel would want to strangle me, but then those were appearances. A person bent on killing will always find a motive. Blood lust requires no motive.

But Bine Oertel didn't strangle me, Bine Oertel petted my cheek and said: "My god, you're so beautiful."

There's no use denying it, I can't plead that there are gaps in my memory; however many gaps my memory may have, the day I met Miss Oertel is gap-free.

It's essential for a writer to have a good memory. I read that once in an interview with a writer who had forgotten a few things that turned out to be crucial.

But is there such a thing as a memory that is *too* good, or, better yet, a mnemonic process gone haywire?

Whatever the case, I will try to describe the events systematically and chronologically, and if I feel any emotion at the description of what I heard or of the circulation being cut off to a particular body part, I will suppress that emotion.

I'm not sure I'll feel any emotion at all. Professor Hirschfeld said that I'm frozen.

Downstairs, Mrs. Oertel was enjoying an installment of "Inspector Morris."

At least I assume she enjoyed it, because she was in a much better mood when I saw her again in her kitchen later that evening.

Bine Oertel undressed me like a baby in need of a clean diaper.

She did everything, I didn't have to do a thing.

I let her go; I figured, *l'amour fou* has begun, surrender to it, follow the slimy trail of the slug known as passion.

Bine Oertel licked the nipple she had first bruised, then the other, and then my navel, and she left a four-lane highway of saliva on my belly and chest.

If man could see himself through other eyes, I thought, he would see that he lived in a remote corner of the universe, in a building wrecked by earthquakes and never repaired, abandoned by architects and contractors, a place where passersby would shake their heads and say: "How can anyone live in a place like that?"

"You taste so salty, I love it," Bine Oertel said.

"Yeah," I said, "you too."

I hadn't done much yet, but that would come.

Everything would still come. Everything was still to begin.

How long can one live with the idea that everything has still to begin? Can you die with that idea as well, or might that make you awfully neurotic at the end there?

"I used to give my horse big pieces of salt too, they love that."

"Did you have a horse?"

"A pony," she said.

Then she unbuttoned my pants. A hand ruffled through my pubic hair.

"Abandoned by God and our fellow man," I said.

I couldn't stop thinking about that building destroyed by the earthquake.

Miss Oertel was taking off my pants.

I lifted my butt up off the bed a little to make it easier.

Then she took off my underpants as well.

The same mouth that had just tasted my big toe now tasted my member; in terms of form and substance, there wasn't much difference. Except my big toe had a toenail.

Miss Oertel sighed.

In any case, I interpreted her moans as a sigh.

And that sigh I interpreted as a lamentation, the old, eternal lamentation that has lost none of its relevance: "Why me, God? Were there no better candidates?"

I pushed her head away and jumped off the bed.

"What's wrong?" Bine Oertel asked.

"I want you to be honest with me," I said.

"I am honest."

"You have to tell me everything."

"I'll tell you everything."

"I'd rather hear the truth than a polite lie."

"I don't tell polite lies."

"I can't take any more polite lies."

Miss Oertel, undressed only from the waist up, climbed off the bed now too and came over to me. "What's wrong, Marek?" she asked. "I've been honest with you. I've spent more than six years waiting for that Turk, that's the way I am. I've been faithful to that bastard for almost seven years."

Her lip was quivering again.

But first you were passed from hand to hand on the island of Sylt, I thought.

"Listen," I said, "it's not about the Turk or how long you've waited for him. It's about this, this is what's wrong, and I want to know the truth."

I pointed to the toe-without-toenail between my legs.

Miss Oertel looked at me in amazement.

"But you're beautiful," she said.

My tutoring in philosophy and in other subjects has these days grown to become almost a full-blown industry.

I never graduated from the university, and perhaps I never will, but the tutoring is flourishing like never before.

I go to people's homes. Big homes, little homes, big desk, dusty couch; nothing fazes the tutor.

I am a patient tutor who, if he has any opinions, does not air them. I am a bearer of facts and figures, and in conversations with parents I emphasize repeatedly that the problem student may have those facts and figures at his disposal, but that he does not know how to apply them.

When I say that I smile amiably but full of confidence, like a presidential candidate.

"And what I am going to do is to teach your child to apply those facts and figures," I say then, after a moment's pause.

I am a tutor devoid of ideals, which is what makes me so effective.

I don't want to convey a love of the subject, in fact I don't even want to let the student apply what he knows, for that would only needlessly complicate things.

Personal contact with the student is something I avoid.

Sometimes I'll go out for a beer with the student, but that is not personal contact. That is business.

When I flew into my second major fit of rage, there in front of Miss Oertel, what did I know at that moment? What facts and figures was I applying?

In what did I believe? Is rage something you have to believe in?

If there is anything I've believed in, anything in which I still believe, then it's rage and the words that give form to that rage, that convey that rage from one radio tower to the next.

I'm too much a determinist to suppose that I could have decided to believe, not in rage, but in something very different; motherhood, for example.

Miss Oertel said: "You're beautiful."

Miss Oertel said: "You're fine just the way you are."

And I ranted: "I'll never forgive you for these lies, Bine. You're lying to me, you're lying the way everyone lies, you're no better than the rest. You're even worse."

Miss Oertel took off the rest of her clothes and said: "You've got a nice cock."

I shouted: "You're a hunk of meat, you don't know your ass from a hole in the ground."

Miss Oertel giggled.

I recited poems from *The Dwarf and Other Poems*, with mistakes and all, because there were some strophes I couldn't remember anymore by heart. My poems didn't seem to make much of an impression, because all Miss Oertel did was kneel down naked before me and take the member, that so resembled a big toe, in her mouth.

"I will purify the temples," I shouted, "I will drive out the moneychangers and the false priests with the lash. I will drive your mother out of the temple, for her bread is bad bread, her bacon is bad bacon, her eggs are filthy eggs, and I will spoon the shrapnel out of your father's dead body, for I will tolerate no more lies."

Miss Oertel went on putting my accursed member in her mouth, and taking it out again and putting it in again, as though my tirade were no more than the six o'clock news. As though this was all daily fare.

When Miss Oertel stood up at last the erection was a fact, but the whole thing still looked more or less like my big toe.

Miss Oertel looked at me expectantly. I spit in her face.

If she didn't react to my tirades, if she didn't care about me wanting to purify the temples, then maybe she would react to my spit.

There was no slap in the face.

My eyes were not scratched out.

The folder with the drawings in it was not broken over my head.

Here is what happened. Miss Oertel said: "You're a strange boy, Marek."

And she took me to bed.

She didn't even bother to wipe the spit off her face.

While Miss Oertel was deflowering me, I felt like an antenna, a jamming station. But the only station on the air.

As far as I could tell, Miss Oertel didn't feel like a jamming station.

She felt like a person, and I cannot rule out that she felt pleasure.

To the extent that a jamming station can feel pleasure, I enjoyed it too.

When she climbed off me, she said: "Good thing I started taking the pill again three months ago. It was in the air. This was in the air."

"Listen," I said, getting up from the bed, "to what just occurred to me. People are, in fact, jamming stations."

Miss Oertel looked at me. She opened her mouth, but she didn't say anything. She shook her head, as though I'd said something very strange.

"Don't you have any respect for me at all?" she asked then, and boxed my ear.

That was the second time in the last few months.

Her mouth began quivering again in that peculiar way of hers. "I'm sorry," she said, "I'm sorry, I didn't mean to do that."

"Never mind," I said, "I'm getting used to it."

"How did you like it, anyway?"

"What?"

"With me. How did you like it?"

"Very nice," I said, "but I wouldn't want you to misunderstand that business about the jamming station. I just thought it was important. Because if people were jamming stations, that would explain a lot."

I saw tears, lots of tears, and Miss Oertel said: "Doesn't this mean anything to you?"

"A great deal," I said. "Much more than I can say."

She wiped her eyes with the back of her hand. "On Sylt I was passed from hand to hand, but after that I waited almost seven years, Marek. I waited for you."

"Yes," I said, "I think that's very nice."

There was a knock on the door.

We both froze.

Mrs. Oertel shouted: "The apple pie is almost ready, kids."

I hid in Miss Oertel's closet. It was the first thing I could think of. When I was little I used to hide in Mama's closet all the time, because it smelled so wonderful.

"Mama, don't come in!" Miss Oertel yelled.

We heard rumbling. Unidentifiable cracking noises. What was Mrs. Oertel up to? Why wouldn't she leave us alone? Bine Oertel was of age. Bine Oertel taught at a night school for adults. Arts and crafts. Bine Oertel was not a child anymore.

"I wasn't even planning to come in," old Mrs. Oertel shouted. "But now I want to see what's going on in my own house."

She opened the door. No, it wasn't like opening it, not the way normal people open doors. Mrs. Oertel threw her full weight against the door. And there she was, standing in the room.

Old Mrs. Oertel wore men's bedroom slippers. I could see that through the crack in the closet door: big blue bedroom slippers with tassels on them.

Miss Oertel and her mother didn't say a word.

I was still standing behind the closet door, and I could see Bine Oertel's knees. They seemed filled with some strange fluid.

The way those two women stood there without a word was gradually becoming too much for me.

I had to do something. This was my responsibility. I couldn't stay in the closet forever.

Besides, Mrs. Oertel wasn't crazy, she knew perfectly well that I hadn't flown out the window. Which meant there were only two possibilities. Either I was under the bed, or I was in the closet. Old Mrs. Oertel struck me as the kind of person who wouldn't stop until she'd found me, even if it meant tearing down the house.

Then, before I could even think about it, before I could weigh the pros and cons, I stepped out of the closet and began to speak: "The temples have been defiled, Mrs. Oertel. The uninvited have hunkered down in the front pews and transferred treasures to their own sheds, goats and cows are walking around, even though the sacrificial altar closed long ago, all that is to be heard is the sound of babbling, the temples are defiled, Mrs. Oertel, but I have a dream. I shall purify the temples, and I shall do it with the lash, and with the broom, I will turn my vacuum cleaner on every corner of the temple, not slapdash, a dustcloth here, a rag mop there, no, I shall purify it to the nubbin, that is what I will do. I am the jamming station and you two are the silence, I rattle the gates of your family tomb, I wake the dead with my lash."

I spoke calmly and collectedly. "This isn't too bad, this stuff I'm spouting," I began thinking, "I should do this more often." Oertels young and old were staring at me, they seemed interested.

It was as though I were peddling homeopathic cures door-to-door and they were in need of my panaceas, or were in any case inclined to acquire some of my wares at a reasonable price.

But halfway through my monologue Mrs. Oertel turned and walked out, closing the door quietly behind her.

Close to the bottom of the stairs, I heard her call out: "The apple pie is almost ready, kids."

Miss Oertel and I got dressed without a word.

Less than ten minutes later, the three of us were sitting on the couch across from the painting of the waterfall, drinking coffee and eating apple pie. Hot apple pie with whipped cream.

Eggs and bacon may not have been her strong suit, but Mrs. Oertel could bake apple pie like there was no tomorrow.

"It was exciting today," she said. "'Inspector Morris,' I mean, real exciting."

"Oh, that's nice, Mama," Bine Oertel said.

She was eating greedily.

I thought about Dancing-Queen Andrea who was now somewhere in Luxembourg, maybe busy with her fuck-cloth. Nothing could be ruled out.

At best, I would later be qualified to teach courses in *l'amour fou* to prisoners who had gone off the straight and narrow, but who desperately wanted to get back on it again.

The real *amour fou*, the living, breathing one that took place in real life and not in books, would remain beyond my reach.

After her comment about the exciting TV program, Mrs. Oertel ate on in silence. But once she had gulped down the lion's share of her apple pie, she gave me a penetrating look and said: "So you want to purify the temples, do you?"

I wiped my mouth.

"Yes," I said.

"Well it's about time," she said, and poured a little more cream in her coffee. I saw Bine Oertel looking at me in alarm, as though she thought maybe purifying the temples wasn't such a great idea.

"Mother, I wish you'd stop walking around in Papa's bedroom slippers."

Her mother set her plate down on the table with a bang.

"I don't need you telling me what not to do, Bine Oertel. It would be a crying shame to leave these slippers unused, they were almost brand new, I gave them to him less than three weeks before he passed away."

What seemed to bother Mrs. Oertel most was that death had made no allowance for the bedroom slippers she had just bought for her husband.

"They remind me so much of Papa," Bine whined, "please, Mother, I'm begging you, don't wear them anymore. When I look at you, it's like seeing Papa."

Mrs. Oertel's expression hardened, a series of curses popped from her lips like little burps. Then she caught herself and said: "Bine, if you don't find yourself a man real soon, you'll die an old maid."

Bine's lips quivered fiercely. Just as our house was the house of silence, this house was the house of tears.

"Another piece of pie?" Mrs. Oertel asked.

"No thank you, I really must be going now," I said. "Tomorrow I have to get up early."

I had told Professor Hirschfeld that my imagination was stronger than reality, that I actually didn't see people, only my own figments. Can you miss your own figments?

"A little more coffee then?" Mrs. Oertel asked.

I suddenly found old Mrs. Oertel much nicer than her daugh-

ter, even if she did look a lot like her husband, even if she enter-
tained rather outspoken opinions about food and the way in which
people should consume it.

"Half a cup," I said, "but then I really must be going."

Bine said: "Tomorrow I've got a class again."

And Mrs. Oertel said: "That modeling clay is what gets on my
nerves."

A little giggle escaped Bine's lips.

"Some of them don't want to just draw," Mrs. Oertel said, "they
want to work with that clay too. That gets on my nerves. Because
guess who gets to clean it up?"

It was clear enough to me who got to clean it up.

I downed my half a cup and stood up.

"Thank you for everything," I said, "it was a wonderful evening."

"Come back soon," Mrs. Oertel said. "My best girlfriend hasn't
come by for a week, because of that damn elevator."

Old Mrs. Oertel squeezed my hand.

"I don't mind," I said, "climbing a few flights of stairs."

Then I pulled my hand away and stepped over to Bine Oertel,
unsure whether I should shake her hand or whether it would be
better to kiss her goodbye.

"Thanks for everything," I said. "It was wonderful."

"I'll see you at the library again, won't I?"

"Oh yes, of course," I said.

"I'll walk you to the door."

"Good luck," Mrs. Oertel shouted after me.

The smell of fried bacon still hung in the stairwell.

Out on the street I gave Bine Oertel a quick kiss, before she
could deliver the bad news.

"Adieu," I said, "my sweetest."

And those three words moved me more than the naked Bine
Oertel herself.

"Adieu," Bine said, "sweetest," and pushed a lock of hair back from my forehead.

Then she went inside.

At home, in my room, I listened to "Dancing Queen." But Abba didn't help either.

For a few weeks I avoided the library, then decided to join a different one altogether, something I blamed myself for deeply afterwards.

I never saw Bine Oertel or her mother again.

Which is not to say that they had disappeared from my life.

17

The Sex Organ Is a Multifunctional Thing

During the third year of *l'amour fou*, Papa developed problems with a valve in his heart, but the doctors said he could easily live to reach a hundred and ten. My brother made sacrifices to the god of our hearth, and his social status gradually increased.

Mama lived in a flush of infatuation that consumed so much of her energy and emotions that on some days she no longer knew exactly how many children she had borne. There was no longer any keeping track of who the object of her infatuation might be.

I visited Paris and the Rimbaud Museum, on my own. I wandered through the museum and through Paris with my head full of theories about *l'amour fou*, I had gradually become something of an expert, yet the actual practice remained beyond reach. About once every six weeks I paid a visit to Professor Hirschfeld.

We would talk about his work and the progress he'd made, or better yet, the lack of it. Professor Hirschfeld was not afraid of dying, but all the more of the possibility that he might die before his research was complete. A few times he had asked me up to the room where he kept his archives. "Here," he said then, pointing at dozens, no hundreds, of numbered files that looked as though he were preparing a federal case against some Mafia don, "here I have compared the dreams of five hundred criminals with those of five hundred non-criminals. The proof is in there somewhere, it's already there, but I still haven't found it yet."

The fear of dying before his research was complete had taken such hold on Professor Hirschfeld that he was slowly becoming an alcoholic.

I wanted to ask whether he ever analyzed his own dreams, but I didn't dare. It was my last year at the international school.

Two weeks before Christmas, Mr. Georgi had a Christmas tree installed in his classroom, then decorated on his own and, in the first week of January, burned it on his own as well.

His mildness was a dogma that tolerated no doubt.

And me?

I had stopped writing poems about dwarfs, although I still lived at odds with reality, with the big toe some higher power had stuck between my legs without so much as a how-do-you-do. The fear of blood and physical pain had stifled my fantasies about separating that toe from the rest of my body with a potato peeler. But the war raged on.

"Achtung baby," Pavel said one day when we happened to arrive home at the same time. "You still handicapped?" He patted his crotch.

If he had not said "Achtung baby," then I might never have gone to see Dr. Ahorn, and had he said it only one time, then I might still have abandoned the whole idea. But Pavel stopped calling me Marek, only "baby." "Achtung baby," to be precise. And whenever he got the chance, he would pat his crotch after saying it.

I had to win this war. I was no Achtung Baby, I was Marek van der Jagt.

Finally I sought contact with a cosmetic surgeon. Now that I had abandoned all hope that my condition would prove an inexhaustible source of creative energy, cosmetic surgery was the only thing left. I could not settle for sublimation, I would have to remove the noxious weed, root and all, and plant in its stead a blossoming bower. One of my mother's former lovers put me in touch with Dr. Ahorn, the most famous plastic surgeon in all of Switzerland and Austria put together, with offices in Vienna and Geneva. I told the lover that it was for the friend of a girlfriend. He asked no further questions.

I visited Dr. Ahorn the way others rob a bank for the first time.

In a nearby *Konditorei*, I screwed up my courage with sickly sweet liqueur. They didn't sell anything else. Then I walked six times around the block, put up the hood of my jacket, put on my sunglasses, and rang the doorbell.

A secretary or nurse opened the door, I pushed her aside and closed the door behind me, before she could do it. Then I took off my sunglasses and said: "I have an appointment with Dr. Ahorn; the name is van der Jagt."

Only later did I realize that she must have thought me awfully rude, some boor who pushes aside friendly doctor's assistants.

She looked me over from head to toe, and said somewhat high-handedly: "Come with me, we'll fill out the papers."

I took a seat on a leather couch in the clean white waiting room. On the walls were photographs of women who had been set aright. There was also a greeting card pinned to the wall that said: "Thank you, Dr. Ahorn. You have changed my life." I saw more fan mail as well. Dr. Ahorn must have been a happy man.

The assistant wanted to know all about me.

"Can't you," I asked, "just work with a number and a code name, like a Swiss bank?"

"We're not a bank," she said.

"I realize that, but maybe a number and a code name would be enough."

"We are extremely careful with all personal information."

"Of course, I understand that, but I'd really prefer just a number and a code name."

But she would not be moved.

Finally, I told her everything. Except for the most painful details.

She even wanted to know my shoe size.

I then waited for almost an hour and a half, until another assistant, this time one who was a little more friendly, showed me into Dr. Ahorn's office.

Dr. Ahorn was a big man. Too big for Mama even, she didn't like anything over five foot ten. I'd become good at viewing men through Mama's eyes.

He shook my hand warmly, then rattled on for twenty minutes about the latest developments in cosmetic surgery, and about the opposition he'd had to overcome in his early years as a cosmetic surgeon.

He said: "I have no qualms about claiming that cosmetic surgery has made more people happy than open-heart surgery."

Having said that, he leaned back in his chair, and I saw how much satisfaction he drew from the thought of having made so many people happy. It was hard to blame him for that. Even a cosmetic surgeon occasionally goes off in search of deeper meaning.

"Of course, you can die on the operating table," he said, "but driving a car is riskier."

He pulled an elegant fountain pen from his inside pocket and wrote my name on a blank sheet of paper.

"I have had people of all ages here," Ahorn said.

Then he wrote my date of birth beside my name.

"We are the way we appear," Ahorn said. "Aesthetics is no excessive luxury."

I took off my raincoat, which Mama had gone with me to buy.

I had never imagined that cosmetic surgeons would look like Dr. Ahorn. But then, why should a cosmetic surgeon necessarily be a paragon of beauty himself?

"From those with less financial leeway, I do accept payment on installment; I believe that everyone has as much right to cosmetic surgery as they do to a car."

He smiled.

Did he have any idea why I was here? I hadn't said anything about it on the phone, and I had been intentionally vague with his assistant concerning the reason for my visit.

"What part of the face is it?" she'd asked.

"It's not the face, it's the body," I replied.

"And what part of the body?" she asked, her fingers with their neatly painted nails resting on the keyboard. How many miserable souls had she already entered into Dr. Ahorn's computer? I found myself wondering.

"A couple of parts," I said, "too many to list at this moment."

Ahorn folded his hands. I saw a wedding band. "So what can I do for you, Marek?"

I looked around. Everything was so clean, so new.

For a moment there I considered standing up and taking off my clothes, so that Ahorn could see for himself what he could do for me. But I lacked the courage. Even there.

The banality of the words I had to speak made them stick in my throat.

This was about a disgrace, and a disgrace was no laughing matter, even if it was between your legs.

I leaned forward.

"It's about a disgrace."

For a moment, the tic under his left eye became worse.

Maybe he thought he was dealing with a madman, or that I was threatening him indirectly. But this time I was not about to bring up the temples, nor would I mention my desire to purify them. Professor Hirschfeld had once said: "I have met people who act crazy, to avoid having to live. They take the bus to the clinic every morning, so they don't have to participate in life. An interesting concept, don't you think? Or might simulation itself be the symptom of a disorder?" Professor Hirschfeld had looked at me expectantly. But no answer came, the answer remained in me, the way those other answers would always remain in Professor Hirschfeld's archives. Archives that perhaps no one would ever look at after he died. I hadn't told Professor Hirschfeld about my plan to visit Dr. Ahorn. Professor Hirschfeld was to cosmetic surgery as the book is to the fire.

The doctor coughed. Again I was struck by his wedding band. It was an awfully big one.

How can you tell of a defeat, a defeat that actually consists of nothing but being seen? The other's look was my defeat.

My brother was not a disgrace, nor was my father. Mama could have been one, but she considered life itself to be a disgrace.

"What do you mean?" Ahorn asked.

I took a deep breath.

"There are major and minor disgraces, doctor," I said. "Below my navel, at this moment, is a major disgrace."

Ahorn scratched his cheek. His tic seemed to be acting up again.

"I'm not entirely sure what you mean," he said.

"I can show you," I said.

I had to push on now.

"No, no, tell me about it first," Dr. Ahorn said.

It was obvious that he didn't know much about disgraces, that he hadn't run into very many of them in his life.

This visit was a mistake.

Instead of performing cosmetic surgery on me, Ahorn wanted to differ with my definition of a word. Or was he simply afraid of seeing me naked?

"My disgrace starts with being seen," I said.

Ahorn looked at me worriedly.

"I agree with you that pleasing others is an important task in this life, and that cosmetic surgery can help us to better fulfill that task, but I am not eager to see the term disgrace associated with what we do here."

He had spoken slowly, choosing his words deliberately, as though he was on the witness stand. As he listened to me, he occasionally bit his lower lip. For someone so full of the aesthetics of the body, I thought that was rather strange.

I felt rage rising up. Rage at his lack of understanding, rage at his tic, rage at the humiliation, rage at the way he dressed, rage at his wedding band, rage at myself, the way I was sitting there.

"I can be brief. I am a dwarf down below."

Ahorn jotted something down, but I couldn't see what it was.

"Right," he said. "Down below." He coughed nervously.

As though you could possibly be a dwarf up above.

He looked at the sheet of paper on which he'd scribbled my name, my date of birth and an unintelligible comment, and then said: "Let's go to the other room, I'll examine you there. Take off your clothes," he shouted after me, as if I hadn't thought of that myself.

I went to the other room and undressed slowly.

I heard him talking to someone, I even heard him laugh.

When I was almost naked, I only had my sweater on—after all, this wasn't about my breasts—the doctor came in.

"Take off your sweater too," he said.

He put on a pair of gloves.

I had once seen a movie in which a police inspector put on a glove to pull cocaine out of a suspect's anus.

"Do you want me to lie down?"

"No," he said, "remain standing."

He squatted down.

I felt a gloved hand gently seize my thigh.

I stared straight ahead, at the door. That door could open any moment and one of the many female assistants could come walking in with the announcement "Dr. Ahorn, it's urgent."

Then she'd see me, and maybe she would start screaming, loud and shrill.

The door didn't open, and the cosmetic surgeon gently squeezed my testicles.

This was what life boiled down to. If someone would ask me: "Describe life to us in a few words, Marek van der Jagt," I would tell them about Dr. Ahorn and a gloved hand squeezing my testicles. "The rest is irrelevant," I would say. "The rest is decoration, the rest was a chain of streamers that my mama had hung up and that the others tore down off the ceiling."

Ahorn had a coughing fit and turned his head away, but remained squatting in front of me.

"Excuse me," he said when he was finished coughing. "The air in here is rather dry."

"Yes," I said.

"In planes, too. I do a lot of flying."

"Yes," I said.

"I tried putting a bowl of water on the radiator, but it didn't really help."

All I could do was nod.

Then Ahorn lifted my sex organ and looked at it from the bottom.

I heard him cough again.

A whole procession came traipsing through my mind: Andrea, Milena, Miss Oertel, Mama, Pavel, and they were all coughing.

Ahorn stood up.

"You can get dressed," he said. "I'll wait for you in the other room."

The doctor left the room and I picked up my underpants from a chair.

The sex organ seemed smaller than ever. The sex organ was getting ready to disappear.

Before long it wouldn't be there at all. Then I would finally be the sexless one.

Dr. Ahorn was at his desk. He was writing.

Someone had put a cup of coffee on the desk for me.

I sat down, and couldn't help but be reminded of Socrates and his cup of hemlock.

Ahorn looked up, went on writing, then put down his pen and smiled.

I took a sip.

"Marek," Ahorn said.

He coughed.

"Does this dry air bother you too?"

"No," I said.

What was this? Had I come here for the dry air?

Again, he coughed.

"As you know, you have bigger and smaller sex organs."

He rested his chin in his hand, as though he didn't know what else to say.

Somewhere in the building I heard a dog bark.

"The way you have big and little ears," Ahorn suddenly went on, "and big and little noses, and big and little mouths and big and little feet. You have people with a size 7 and people with a size 12. You've got . . ."

He leafed through a file.

"You've got size 9."

"That's right," I said.

I wasn't here for my feet, there was nothing wrong with my feet.

"I have size 10," Ahorn said.

"Nice," I said.

Ahorn rested his chin in his hand again.

He seemed to be deep in thought. A cosmetic surgeon who raved on about shoe sizes and dry air and who squeezed my testicles gently with his gloved hand. Yes, this was life, there was no escaping it and I could not permit myself, did not want to permit myself, to turn a blind eye to the beauty of it all. There was even beauty to be discovered in Dr. Ahorn, all I had to do was try a little harder.

"Marek," he said, "I'm going to be straight with you. Your sex organ definitely falls under the smaller sex organs. But as a cosmetic surgeon, I have to ask myself: Is it really small enough to warrant an operation? Is it so small that we should even consider an operation? Do you understand what I'm saying?"

"Yes," I said.

There was a knock at the door.

"Yes," Ahorn said.

One of his assistants came in.

"Mrs. Pepplau is going home, Doctor," she said.

Ahorn nodded.

She closed the door behind her.

"Where was I?" he asked.

"The operation," I said.

"Oh yeah." He coughed. "Listen, Marek: take a breast enlargement, for example. One of our most popular procedures, although lately I've noted a remarkable rise in the number of breast reductions. A procedure like that, a breast enlargement, is much easier than the procedure needed to deal with your problem. As a physician I have to ask myself: Is it responsible to perform such a procedure? Is it so small that we need to operate? In your case, I can already provide a clear answer to that question. It is definitely small, but not so small that I would wish to even consider an operation. Certainly not when you realize that such a procedure is not without attendant risks. What we might win is in no proportion to what we stand to lose."

I heard barking again.

What we might win is in no proportion to what we stand to lose. What was he talking about losing? My sex organ was starting to disappear anyway, he might not know that, but I could see it happening, I was on top of it. I could see it with the naked eye.

"That's the way it is, Marek," the cosmetic surgeon said. "That's my opinion. As a physician."

"No operation?" I said.

"No operation," he said.

"So what then? Pills?"

Ahorn leaned back. He looked around his office with a friendly smile, as though he was seeing it for the first time.

No answer came.

He leaned forward, then leaned back again, but no answer came.

Only after a few minutes did I hear him whisper: "Then live, go on living," but maybe that was my imagination.

"I have the feeling that it's slowly disappearing," I said. "Every day a little more. When I looked just now, there was already less of it than there was yesterday."

"That what's disappearing?" Ahorn asked.

"The sex organ," I murmured.

Ahorn drummed his fingers on his desk.

He whistled a little tune.

Maybe he was pondering it, maybe he'd been overcome by melancholy at the thought of the sex organ disappearing. Everything that disappears can produce melancholy, even the disappearance of a sex organ that is not your own.

Then Ahorn seemed to have whistled every tune he knew.

"All things human," Ahorn said, "have a beginning and an end, said Judge Falcone, who was brave enough to combat the Mafia and paid for it with his own life."

What did the Mafia have to do with this?

"I just read a wonderful book about Judge Falcone, but that's another thing," Ahorn said, and he smiled as though he was proud of the fact that, although he operated on the human exterior and made it more beautiful, he was still not entirely unread.

I nodded gravely.

"You disappear," Dr. Ahorn said, "and your sex organ disappears with you, but the chance that your sex organ disappears before you do is very slight. Of course, the sex organ can start malfunctioning, like a stiff leg or a partially blind eye. The sex organ is a multifunctional thing, I don't need to tell you that, you're a bright young man, and I can even tell you a little secret: trouble with peeing, especially among men, is something that's a lot more common than that other problem. But why worry? You have time, Marek, you're still young."

Young. He shouldn't have said that.

"If I knew it would help, I'd pay you with my life. I'd pay anything."

The doctor drummed on his desk again.

He was almost becoming likable.

"A hero," he said, "is someone who is prepared to die for his ideals. Judge Falcone died for an ideal. Not all ideals are worth dying for. I suspect that you're better off not dying for most ideals."

Then Ahorn stood up.

"Good luck, Marek," he said, then whispered: "If you'd rather not receive the bill at home, you can pay at the desk on your way out."

In the waiting room was a lady with a little dog on her lap.

The assistant had the bill all ready for me.

"Is there a cash dispenser close by?" I asked.

I walked home. "Out of the way!" is what I felt like shouting at people. "The sexless one is approaching."

My ideal was not worth dying for.

My ideal was not even worth an operation.

It was good to know that.

L'amour fou was a worthless ideal, in no way comparable to freedom, socialism, or justice, even if that only applied to a select few.

I had to admit: Mama, Papa, and the others were right. Life was a worthless invention.

18

The Pig

A few weeks after my visit to Dr. Ahorn, the physicians discovered that Mama had a minor tumor in her head.

They said it was benign, that it had been there for years, and that it could remain there for years as well.

For a couple of days Papa was particularly nice to Mama. Which made everyone in the house uncomfortable, as if Mama was already dead; from everything Papa said, you could tell that the dead had more right to love than the living.

"Take the children, go on a trip," Papa said one evening. "Get a little rest in the mountains."

Papa liked to rest in the mountains, which is why he always told other people to do the same.

Mama thought she was dying. Every evening at dinner she would say at least once: "This is probably my last meal."

Having adopted a position of irreconcilability with life for most of my growing-up years, she now became irreconcilable with death, which she had come to consider retroactively as even more malignant than life itself.

Lovers who called up were told: "Don't come to see me, I'm dying."

Most of the lovers who heard that a few times gave up, only

the truly resolute wanted to make love to my mother even while she lay dying.

Some people, when they think death is approaching, feel the need to reconcile themselves with their fellow man. My mother was above all forms of reconciliation, and that went double for reconciliation with her fellow man.

In fact, the idea that she was going to die made her more harsh.

"Whenever I see your father," she said one evening, "I lose all desire to eat."

Papa took his plate to the kitchen, because that tumor really was getting to him. Besides, he preferred to keep the peace.

Another time she said: "You're my children, but you're all rejects. I can't do anything about it. That's just the way it is."

She began playing the piano again, as though her heart were breaking, with tears running down her cheeks, because Mama remained sensitive to music until the very end.

No matter what the doctors did to persuade her, she remained convinced that her life was coming to a close, that it was more a matter of days than of weeks. Buoyed up by that thought, she threw out the great majority of her lovers.

"I'm not going to mince words," she said. As though she ever had.

"You were never much good in bed," I heard her say one day on the phone. "And not out of bed either."

Even Szlapka, the florist, who had always been willing to put up with a great deal in the hope of filling a lost hour with my mama, threw in the towel.

"She's changed," he said, when I ran into him on the street. "She's not the same anymore."

"It's only temporary," I said. But I knew better.

Rolf Szlapka looked at me. He nodded.

We both loved the same woman, albeit in different ways, and we both knew it wasn't temporary.

Mama, who had always been a bit disgusted by people, now started becoming awfully disgusted by people.

She said: "You know how hygienic I am; when I touch someone, I have to wash my hands right away. That's why I'd rather not touch them. I can't keep washing my hands all day, can I?"

The maid had to walk out in front of her with a dustcloth, to wipe down the doorknobs, and extreme measures were taken to keep Mama from encountering the filth people spread around.

The most bullheaded among her lovers had flowers delivered, or delivered the flowers themselves, but got no further than the front door. The flowers almost never survived more than a couple of hours.

When Mama saw flowers she didn't like, they ended up in the trash. Her aggression was no longer limited to humans and animals, her wrath now embraced the vegetable kingdom as well.

At the same time, however, I am compelled to note that Mama never kicked or struck a person or an animal. On a few occasions, I even saw her stand up for a horse.

In Vienna, there are horse-drawn carriages that drive around for the tourists.

Sometimes Mama would get emotional over some badly neglected horse that had to drag a bunch of tourists around Vienna. In her opinion, the tourists should drag themselves around Vienna.

One afternoon, when I was twelve, she saw someone kicking a horse. With tears trickling down her cheeks, she said: "Marek, go see how much he wants for that horse."

I walked over to the coachman and asked how much he wanted for the horse.

The coachman started laughing, but as soon as he saw Mama he named a price.

Mama opened her purse and wrote out a check.

The horse was unhitched and we took it home. At first the horse put up a struggle, as though it was fond of the coach. Neither Mama nor I had much experience with horses, although it seems that as a girl she had done a good deal of riding. But, she said: "I've forgotten how. And I'm a bit too old to start a stable."

We tied up the horse in front of the house and it took Papa a whole week to find a buyer for it. He missed two very important meetings because of that horse, especially after the police got into the act.

Two policemen came by the very first day, even before Papa got home.

"The public road is not a stable, Mrs. Van der Jagt," the one policeman said. He had a long gray beard.

I was standing next to Mama, and from the way she squeezed my hand I could tell that her ideas about the public road did not completely coincide with those of the policeman. She didn't like beards, either.

"Not a stable?" she asked. "But what is it then? If the public road isn't a stable, officer, then what *is* the public road?"

Mama was not fond of the long arm of the law, and the only reason why she never tried to twist that arm out of its socket was, I believe, because the law did not interest her enough.

Things would definitely have gotten out of hand with the horse and the policemen if one of Papa's business contacts, Mr. Kopacek, hadn't come by and sent the policemen home with vague promises and a shot of schnapps. Mr. Kopacek bought and sold retail property.

He was always talking about his storefronts. He would say: "Well, I'd better get back to my storefronts."

He's still one of my father's business contacts, and recently he said to me: "Isn't that something for you, storefronts? Marek, isn't that something for you?"

The point I'm making is that Mama was never cruel to animals, and one time she even bought a horse to save its life.

But when Papa started trying to convince Mama once, sometimes even twice a day, at breakfast and then again at dinner, to go to the mountains and clear her mind, she wasn't worrying about horses. She didn't worry about animals at all, in fact, not about people either. What she almost certainly was worrying about was that someday soon she wouldn't be around anymore, because that was almost all she talked about in those days.

The atmosphere in our house became even more depressing, insofar as that was even possible.

My concerns about becoming the sexless one suddenly seemed futile to me. What was a sex organ, after all, when you stopped to think about it? If you had one, fine, but if you didn't have one that was okay too. People never noticed the difference anyway.

Mama said: "When I look in the mirror, I don't feel like laughing: I feel like crying."

"But you're looking radiant," Papa said.

It *was* true that Mama looked radiant in those days. But it was also true that Mama had started spending more time than ever examining herself in the mirror, as though dying were a pimple, or a wrinkle that could no longer be plastered up.

She gave away a lot of money, to foundations, but also to people who in her view were unable to put together a decent income for themselves.

During those last few weeks before her death, she discovered worthy causes everywhere, except in her own home.

A few of her distant relatives called, but she told them: "You haven't called me once in the last twenty years, so don't bother calling me now."

Finally Papa took the bull by the horns.

"I've found a wonderful hotel for you, way up in the mountains," he said. "In Bavaria. You'll get plenty of peace and quiet there."

Papa was very fond of Bavaria. Maybe it was because his insurance company had its head offices in Munich, and he went there often, or maybe he admired the Bavarian character. I don't know. Papa liked to go to Bavaria.

That evening we ate venison, with a stewed pear.

Papa not only loved Bavaria, he loved to eat game as well. Papa liked manly things, even though he didn't do much in the way of sports. In the winter he would occasionally ski down a slope, and once a month he gave his children a sound thumping, but that was pretty much it for sports.

I have a picture of him in which he's standing on his head, but everyone occasionally does something that's out of character.

Papa slid a brochure across the table, in the direction of Mama's plate.

"The ArabellaSheraton Alps Hotel," he said triumphantly, as though pronouncing the name was enough to make him happy. "Kopacek's been there, he says it's fantastic: lovely rooms, a wonderful view, good service."

He knew how much importance Mama attached to good service. Death or no death, the service had to be nonstop.

Mama looked at the brochure without opening it.

"It's on a lake," Papa said, "high in the mountains. Fresh air. Not far from Schliersee. I went there one time, as a boy." He smiled.

Papa didn't particularly like dredging up his youth. Apparently, his memory of Schliersee was a particularly fine one.

I wondered whether he extolled the virtues of his insurance policies the same way he did those of the ArabellaSheraton Alps Hotel, until I remembered that he hired people to do that for him.

"Maybe Marek could go with you," he suggested.

He knew very well that Daniel and Pavel would never go along.

Mama shrugged.

She took off one of her earrings and toyed with it.

The table was cleared.

"What am I supposed to do there?" Mama asked. She pointed at the brochure. The cover had a picture of a hotel, on a lake, with mountains in the background.

Mama's voice could shut everyone up. Even when she thought she was dying, that voice of hers still shut everyone up.

When Papa didn't answer, she asked again: "What am I supposed to do there?"

"Take walks," Papa said quietly. "Relax a bit, in the sun."

"It's November," she said mockingly.

"That's different," Papa said, "in the mountains, the sun there is very intense."

I looked at Mama, the way she was sitting there, I looked at her straight back, her carefully coiffured hair, and how she always had one of her bags within arm's reach.

A lot of people thought she was beautiful, and I have to admit, when she thought she was dying she was more beautiful than ever before.

"The mountains," Mama mumbled. "You're just trying to get rid of me, I'm not even allowed to die in my own house."

Papa winced.

"Die wherever you want," Daniel shouted, "but stop dawdling."

Papa winced more.

Not even death's approach could keep Mama from buying a whole new spring wardrobe. That included a lot of hotpants, because her predilection for hotpants was something over which death had no dominion.

"If you ever take a wife," she suddenly said to me, "pay attention to her hips. Broad hips are important for childbearing."

"Yes, Mama," I said.

"Broad hips," Daniel said. He shook his head.

Pavel laughed exaggeratedly. Even laughing was something he did exaggeratedly. Fortunately, when he went to work for the World Bank, he stopped laughing altogether.

Not so very long ago, I asked Pavel whether he remembered Mama saying that about the importance of broad hips, but he'd forgotten all about it. His memory's like an expired promissory note; it's still there, but you can't do anything with it.

"Constance," Papa said, "I want you to go to the mountains. You need to get this idee-fixe of yours about dying out of your head."

The maid opened the door. "Ma'am," she said, "there's someone at the door. He says it's urgent."

Mama got up. She didn't say a thing.

We remained at the table. I was thinking about broad hips, and about the unlikely places where wisdom was to be found.

Then we heard Mama shriek.

"Go away," she shouted.

Papa started getting up, but sank back down again. It was none of his business. Mama had screamed at lovers before. When there was no getting around it.

We heard her screaming, loud and clear: "You pig!"

Daniel coughed.

Someone ran up the stairs.

"The mountains," Papa said. He folded his napkin. "The mountains are magnificent. The mountains are . . ."

Papa waved his hands in the air. He was searching for the right word, but we didn't help him; in fact, we couldn't help him.

Someone came running down the stairs.

Again we heard Mama scream, and then a piteous man's voice that I didn't quite recognize.

Mama burst into the dining room. She had a pistol in her hand.

At first Papa said nothing, just looked at her. Then he said: "Constance."

"The pig," Mama said.

The butt of the pistol was made of ivory. Mama had told me that, I believe the butt interested her more than the pistol itself. I clearly remembered stopping with Mama on numerous occasions in front of the display window of the gun shop on Dorotheer Gasse. "Look at that," she'd say then. "Look at the butt of that pistol, would you, Marek?"

"Yes, Mama," I'd say then, "I see it." I didn't see much though, pistol butts did not particularly interest me.

Mama pointed the pistol at the chandelier and fired.

Even a little pistol like that makes more noise than I'd imagined.

Daniel started screaming.

Papa put his hands over his ears.

The chandelier did not crash to the floor, and Mama just stood there with the gun in her hand, as if it were something she did all the time, as if she were used to taking a shot at a chandelier every ten days or so.

"Keep eating, boys," Papa said. "Don't look."

I didn't want to keep eating. After all, there were limits. If Mama shot at the chandelier, you couldn't expect us to go on eating. But Papa was a person who refused to be daunted by anything, not even by bullets.

I decided to leave the dining room. I had no desire to be in on this anymore.

In the vestibule I saw Mr. Hobmeier's son, hat in hand, his face shiny with sweat. I didn't recognize him at first. He had changed, put on weight, grown flabbier.

"Marek," he said, and held out his hand.

Just then another shot rang out.

The dining-room door flew open. Papa came out, carrying his plate. Daniel and Pavel were right behind him.

Papa closed the door to the dining room and turned the key in the lock.

"She's shooting at the furniture," he said. "That woman has gone off her rocker."

Then he caught sight of Mr. Hobmeier's son.

"Mr. Van der Jagt," said Mr. Hobmeier, Jr., "good evening. I hope I'm not disturbing you?"

Papa quietly showed Hobmeier, Jr. the door, then said: "Everyone loses control from time to time."

Mama must have stayed locked up in the dining room for at least half an hour. When the doctor arrived, the syringe full of tranquilizer lying ready in his bag, she was still standing there with the pistol in her hand. "The pig," she said. "The pig."

"Take it easy," the doctor said, "easy now," and took the gun away from her. We brought her to her room, and long after the doctor had gone I was still sitting beside her bed.

19

To Schliersee

Less than a week after the incident with the pistol, Mama and I left for Bavaria. School had given me a few days off, and Papa was delighted enough that anyone in the family would go with Mama to the ArabellaSheraton Alps Hotel.

He said: "I'd love to go myself, but I can't leave now. We're right in the middle of a merger."

The whole family knew he would rather die than go off with Mama to the ArabellaSheraton Alps Hotel. Lies of convenience, Papa felt, were not really lies.

Edwin, Papa's chauffeur, drove us there. "If we leave early in the morning," he said, "I can be back in Vienna that same night."

Mama bought three pairs of hiking boots the day before we left, because the doctor had said that walking would do her good. Papa had even typed out a letter for us at the office, with instructions on how to get by in the mountains.

"Ensure a gradual buildup," he wrote, "every day a mile or so more." And, later in the note: "Don't do too much climbing at first."

Maybe love was a matter of habituation, maybe after all those years Papa had become habituated to Mama and was now afraid of how quiet the house would be once she was no longer there.

Mama took a lot of luggage with her. She said: "I can't show up to dinner in the same dress I had lunch in."

She had always liked to change clothes at least three times a day, but now that death was breathing down her neck she changed even more often than that.

Papa's chauffeur didn't like Mama much; he was a man of principle, and had an even harder time tolerating adultery than he did criminals from Africa. Adultery on the part of others, that is: his own adultery was a different matter.

During the drive he didn't say much. Nor did Mama. Twice he asked us: "Is the music bothering you?"

Mama stared out the window. It had been raining in Vienna, but just before Kufstein it stopped, and the clouds began to break.

The mountains looked dismal.

I have never liked mountains much.

Every once in a while Mama pointed at something, without me knowing what she was pointing at, and one time she asked whether the earrings she had on weren't too big for her ears.

I said they were not.

"I don't like big earrings," Mama said emphatically.

We became stuck in traffic, and the chauffeur said a few times: "These people can't drive."

He had attended special classes to become a chauffeur; in his eyes, most of the other people on the road were cretins.

Mama sucked on a lemon drop, and I thought about how peculiar it was to go through life with a mother you knew nothing about. That seemed less peculiar, however, when you realized that that mother barely knew a thing about you, either.

I've never had much of a desire to ask questions. Every question could cause pain. Or, to put it more accurately, every question could provoke an answer you didn't want to hear.

A person doesn't need to know everything. We know too much as it is.

Past Kufstein, just before the German border, the chauffeur suggested we stop in at a roadside restaurant for a drink.

I ordered coffee with a piece of *Käsekuche*, Mama asked for mineral water.

"With a slice of lemon," she said, "I'd like a slice of lemon."

But this was a roadside restaurant where they'd never heard of lemons.

"Maybe we'd better be going then," said the chauffeur, who was afraid of a scene.

A fear that was not entirely ungrounded.

Papa had once asked Mama: "Why do you always have to make a scene? Why can't you go anywhere without having to draw all the attention to yourself?" She had looked at him the way Mama could look at people; her gaze alone could make people feel like inferior beings.

"I will continue making scenes until I draw my last breath, and that's the only thing I'll promise you," she told him.

Papa had folded his hands in silence, as if he knew that this was one promise Mama planned to keep, then went upstairs to scrape the calluses off his feet. Because, as I mentioned earlier, that was what he did on Sunday. Sunday was callus day.

"If there's no lemon, I don't want the water," Mama said to the waiter. "Take it back to the kitchen."

"But the bottle is already open," the waiter said in a high voice.

"Take the water away, or I'll scream," Mama said.

"I have to go to the toilet," I said.

In the men's room, I looked at myself in the mirror. Dancing Queen Andrea and *l'amour fou* were still out there somewhere, but in my life they had been banished to the periphery.

I moved my face up closer to the mirror.

Hemingway had a beard. There were also Surrealists who'd had beards, although their beards were less famous than Hemingway's.

I would never have a beard. Maybe a moustache, at most.

I had stopped peeing in urinals, I always went into the booth. Even when they stank.

Other people's gazes kept my urine from flowing freely.

The ArabellaSheraton Alps Hotel consisted of a main building and an annex. On a lake.

Other than that, there wasn't much along that lake.

A couple of houses, a cafeteria, a bus stop, a little stand where they sold souvenirs.

The chauffeur carried the luggage up to the desk.

Mama looked around and said: "I won't be able to stand this for very long."

She buttoned up her winter coat. The sun was shining and shedding a bit of warmth, but the wintry wind was stronger.

"Go take a look," she said, "at when the buses leave."

I walked down to the bus stop and looked at the timetable.

"There are five buses a day," I said when I got back.

"If I were a painter, this would be a nice place to paint."

"Yes," I said.

"But I'm not a painter."

She was wearing a hat. A fur hat.

Daniel, who cared about animals, sometimes said to her: "Why don't you wear fake fur?"

Mama cared about animals too, but she didn't like things that were fake.

The chauffeur said: "They're waiting for you at the desk, Mrs. Van der Jagt."

The receptionist was a friendly girl in a reddish-brown uniform.

"Everything's been arranged, all you have to do is sign here," she said.

Mama looked at me. "You see?" she said. "They think I can't do anything anymore."

"The sauna is closed for remodeling," the receptionist said.

"I don't like saunas," Mama said. "I find them unhygienic."

The girl smiled and went on imperturbably: "But the swimming pool is open, every day until ten."

When she mentioned the swimming pool, I was suddenly reminded of my gradually disappearing member. In connection with that gradual disappearance, I had given up swimming. Not that I had ever been much of a swimmer, but still.

The receptionist handed us two keys. "Room 109 and Room 110," she said. "Have a nice stay."

"I won't be able to stand this very long," Mama said. "I know that much already."

"If there's anything we can do to make your stay more pleasant," the girl said, "just let us know."

The receptionist's voice sounded less confident than it had at first.

While we were waiting for the elevator to arrive, our luggage came up on the service elevator.

The chauffeur would wait for us downstairs.

"Well," said the man who had been assigned to show us our rooms, "after you."

In a book I once read that some people ate coffee beans to freshen their breath.

Since then I've always chewed on coffee beans.

At home we ground our own coffee. Papa didn't like having other people grind his coffee for him. Every morning the maid ground coffee beans. By hand.

Thinking back on those days, that may very well be what I miss most, the sound of coffee beans being ground, the smell of freshly ground coffee, and Papa walking around the house, sniffing like a hash-hound that figures it's finally on the trail.

Mama found it a disgusting habit. Putting coffee beans in your mouth.

She never chewed gum either. Sometimes she sprayed something into her mouth, and she went to the dentist once every two weeks, just to be sure.

In the elevator Mama said: "Take that bean out of your mouth, Marek. That's worse than chewing tobacco."

"Well," the man from the hotel said, "did you have a nice journey?"

"Take that bean out of your mouth, Marek," Mama repeated.

One of Mama's greatest talents was ignoring people. Sometimes, though, I've wondered whether she actually ignored them or simply didn't see them, because she was so absorbed in, so obsessed by, a detail, an earring, a matchbox, a coffee bean.

"The journey was very pleasant," I said.

Papa had arranged the rooms. Mama didn't bother with rooms. At most, she declared them unfit.

Room 109 was opened for us.

Mama walked into the room, and then straight on through to the balcony.

"I want to be higher," she said.

"Excuse me, ma'am?"

"Higher," she said, "higher," and she pointed at the ceiling.

"The hotel has five floors. How high would you like to be?"

"As high as possible," Mama said.

"I can offer you 312," the man said, "but then I'm afraid you can't have adjoining rooms."

"People can change rooms," Mama said. "That's not too much to ask, is it?"

The man cocked his head.

"I can't offer you adjoining rooms on the fourth floor," the man said. "But the third floor would be a possibility."

"No, that's too low for me," Mama said. "I need air."

Then she walked over to the bed and sat on it, to see if the springs were all right.

"Marek," she said, "take that bean out of your mouth." And, without pause: "You can consider yourself lucky if you leave this place without a bad back."

"We have a physiotherapist in the hotel," the man said, who had perhaps misunderstood her or only picked up on the phrase "bad back."

"No, thank you," Mama said. "We'll be needing two adjoining rooms on the top floor. I am doing poorly." This last phrase she pronounced emphatically, almost threateningly.

The man from the hotel took a step back, looking worried. Apparently the hotel preferred not to receive guests who were doing poorly.

"Ah, I see," he said.

I remembered Mr. Georgi from the international school saying that dying people smelled of death long before they actually died, and then I thought about how Mama used to predict the future, back when I was still in elementary school. I couldn't recall exactly what kind of future she had predicted for me, only that she had once said that I would be a very famous ballet dancer, that my body would give comfort to older women, and that after they had seen me dance those older women would be able to reconcile themselves to death's approach.

"Do you need a doctor?" the man asked.

"Not a doctor," she said, "peace and quiet."

"If you move onto the third floor today, then we can move you to the fourth tomorrow."

Mama laid down on the bed, opened her purse, and pulled out a bracelet.

"Help me with this, would you, Marek?" she said.

She wanted me to close the latch on the bracelet.

"This once belonged to Grandma," she said.

The man from the hotel had withdrawn discreetly to the vestibule, as if the latching of a bracelet was a deed he preferred not to see.

Mama got up, walked to the vestibule, and said: "We'll take a look at that other room now."

The last time Mama had taken a trip with anyone in our family was, I believe, when I was nine.

After that she only went on vacation with her lovers. The flush of infatuation could lend even insufferableness the sheen of romance.

We took the elevator to the third floor.

As the elevator went up, the man from the hotel kept making a clicking noise with his tongue, probably trying to keep his nerves under control.

Fortunately, Mama was too preoccupied to notice the clicking noises.

The man held open the door to the room on the third, and Mama went marching in.

She sat down in an easy chair by the window and surveyed the room.

The man from the ArabellaSheraton Alps Hotel rubbed his hands together.

"Tomorrow," he said, "I'll have two rooms ready for you on the fourth. Next to each other."

"Tomorrow might be too late," Mama said.

The man looked around the room as if searching for something he could spruce up. When he didn't find it, he just opened the curtains a little further and said: "You have a very lovely view here as well. Look."

"Yes, very lovely," Mama said.

"Early tomorrow morning you can move up a floor," the man said, "this is really only for one night."

"Let's take this one," I said.

"You can also have breakfast brought up to your room," the man said.

"I don't eat breakfast," Mama said, "I only drink grapefruit juice."

"So you'll take the room?" the man asked. He was speaking almost in a whisper. "It's really only for one night."

Around Mama, everyone became docile sooner or later.

"This is worse than a nursing home," Mama said.

I also received a room on the third floor. For one night. Mama had resigned herself to it. Once she would have screamed bloody murder; in some ways, she had mellowed a great deal.

The chauffeur brought up the last of Mama's suitcases. He looked around for a moment, then wished me luck and left to drive back to Vienna.

Mama said: "I'm going to lie down for a bit."

I was looking out over the lake they called the Spitzingsee. Here I was, with Mama on a lake in the Bavarian Alps. The ballet dancer I should have become, the ballet dancer who would have reconciled older women to life with his gracious movements, that ballet dancer sat hunched up in a chair in his hotel room and looked out across the Spitzingsee. I remembered clearly the way Mama had looked at me in horror when it turned out that I had almost no talent for ballet. When the lady from the ballet academy told her: "But you can see it as a hobby, something he does in his spare time," Mama took me off ballet right away.

There are many ways to fail, but to fail in the eyes of the person who brought you into the world is one of the bitterest ways I know.

Papa called, to ask how the trip had gone and whether we had already seen the Schliersee.

"Everything went fine," I said, "but we still haven't seen the Schliersee."

At around five-thirty—I was lying on my bed with my clothes on, it was pitch dark already—a female hotel employee called to say that my mother was sitting by the swimming pool and was refusing to talk to anyone.

I said: "My mother meditates sometimes."

"Oh, I see," said the woman's voice at the other end. "Still, she seems to be doing poorly."

"I'll come down and take a look," I said.

The corridors I walked through were identical to the corridors in all hotels like this. All over the world, hotel corridors like this look the same, as do the rooms. Even the people who work in those hotels all look the same.

I came past the gym, then past a door with "massage" written on it.

Mama had herself massaged sometimes, but most masseurs didn't stick it out long with her.

"Please: no street shoes beyond this point," a sign said. "Pool reserved exclusively for guests of the ArabellaSheraton Alps Hotel."

I took off my shoes.

There were two people in the swimming pool. It was hard to tell what sex they were.

Mama was sitting in a lounge chair, wearing red gloves.

There was a newspaper in her lap; on the chair beside hers was her coat, neatly folded.

"Are you all right?" I asked.

One of the swimmers crawled out of the pool.

It was a man. He took off his bathing cap.

"Are you all right, Mama?" I asked.

She pointed at the pool, opened her mouth, but no sound came out.

"Is something wrong?"

"Stop treating me as though I'm sick," she said.

I looked at her red wool gloves, which I'd never seen before. Mama's consumption was so conspicuous that she no longer knew what she had, and therefore could never find anything, so that new purchases had to be made again and again.

The maid had once said to her: "Let me organize your wardrobe for you." But Mama didn't like organization, especially not in her wardrobe.

Luxury is a form of melancholy. The luxury in which Mama wallowed did not add to her happiness, was not even intended to add to it; that luxury was a state of mind in which her love seemed to thrive best.

The male swimmer was busy drying himself.

It was clear at a glance: what this man had in his trunks was unbelievable. It looked like a pound of sirloin.

Mama's luxury was a form of sorrow that seemed to need no reason to exist, and that could therefore never be helped.

Apparently he wasn't finished swimming yet, for he lay down on one of the lounge chairs.

The other swimmer just kept on swimming.

The scent of chlorine tickled my nostrils.

"What's happening here, anyway?" Mama asked.

The newspaper slid to the ground. A *Herald Tribune*, a few days old.

"People are swimming laps," I said cheerfully. "They say it's good for you."

"Yes, I can see that," Mama said. "I've been sitting here watching them for almost two hours."

She probably hadn't been able to sleep.

"But you could have called me, Mama?"

She shrugged. "And there's nothing in the paper either," she said.

"I would have loaned you a book."

"Shall we see if we can arrange that?"

"Arrange what?" I asked.

She moved her fingers up and down like she was playing the piano.

The gloves were really very charming.

"No," I said, "let's not try to arrange that."

A bath superintendent in a white uniform entered the pool area.

He was wearing gym shoes that made weird noises on the tiles.

He walked around the pool. The last swimmer was doing bend-and-stretch exercises in the water.

Mama asked: "How are you doing, anyway?"

The water splashed over the edge.

"The pool will be closing in half an hour," the bath superintendent announced in a loud voice.

"Why don't you take off the gloves?" I said. "It's far too warm in here for gloves."

Mama glanced at her gloves, and if you had looked only at her hands in those gloves you might have thought she was a little girl who had gotten something new and was so happy with it that she had to wear it to bed.

The bath superintendent left the pool area.

"Well," Mama said, "at last we're *entre nous*."

I grabbed her hand so I could pull off her gloves. The gloves were attracting attention. The bath superintendent had already looked at them dubiously a few times. "Let's go eat," I said.

Mama had little hands, and through the gloves you could feel how warm they were.

"I can't go to the dining room like this," Mama said. "What am I going to wear? I haven't brought a thing."

The last swimmer now climbed out of the pool. It turned out to be a portly woman.

"You packed lots of things," I said. "I'm sure there's something in there that will look lovely on you."

She shook her head, and suddenly I couldn't imagine how she'd ever come to bear children.

"Let's go," I said, "the pool is closing."

"Have you spoken to your father?" she asked suddenly.

"Yes," I said. "The merger is keeping him awfully busy. He sends his regards."

She picked the newspaper up off the ground.

The male swimmer walked past.

"Are hereditary illnesses common in our family?" I asked.

Mama looked at me.

She shook her head.

"Most of them just died," she said.

I asked: "Were they all able to reproduce, or were there some of them who couldn't?"

"They didn't all reproduce," Mama said, "fortunately enough."

"But were they unable to, or was it that they just didn't want to?"

"I don't know," Mama said, "is there a difference? What difference does it make?"

Mama looked around as though she was telling me things not meant for other people's ears.

"Hereditary illness," Mama whispered. "You ask such peculiar questions, Marek. Your grandfather had a riding accident. A branch decapitated him."

"I thought he was just splattered against a tree."

"No, he was decapitated," Mama said. "The head was in the coffin, but separate."

"We should be going," I said.

"I looked in the coffin," Mama said almost tonelessly. "I was a very inquisitive child, I looked in almost all the coffins."

I took Mama to her room. All her suitcases were open. The contents of a few of them were scattered on the bed.

"There's not enough closet space," she said.

I opened the closets. Not so awfully long ago I had hidden in a closet in Miss Oertel's room. Four people could have hid themselves in this closet. I stepped into the closet.

There are people who think that all these details added up mean something; in fact, that all these details added up actually say something: a walk-in closet you walk into, Dancing Queen Andrea, Miss Oertel's mother, Professor Hirschfeld studying the results of his research, and then there's me, selling facts and figures to the handicapped. I don't even sell them, I just pretend to. And all those things added up are supposed to mean something. In the best of cases, what it means is that your life ends in a fit of rage.

Mama finally chose a black dress with flowers on it.

She wanted to move to a room with more closet space, and if they didn't have one, then to another hotel. And she needed a big safe for that suitcase half-filled with diamonds. I convinced her to eat something first.

We wandered through the corridors of the ArabellaSheraton Alps Hotel. Every once in a while she paused in front of a door. "Do you think maybe," she said then, "this one has more closet space?"

"No, Mama," I said, "all the rooms here are exactly the same."

Fifteen minutes later, when we finally got to the dining room, Mama said: "We could also have called room service."

From vacations long ago, back when we still went with the whole family, I remembered us eating in hotel rooms. Because with Mama, you never knew when something would go wrong.

"What did you mean, actually, when you said that you looked in almost all the coffins?" I asked.

We were walking through the dining room, and Mama squeezed my hand.

"I was an impossible child," she whispered.

The dining room overlooked the lake, but it was dark out. You couldn't even see the water.

The tables had salmon pink tablecloths.

There was also a waiter with a red beard walking around. He showed us to a table by the window, and lit a candle for us.

The Alps Hotel dining room was not particularly crowded.

The bearded waiter was Slovenian. He brought us a cocktail which he said we didn't have to pay for. Mama told him she wanted to pay for everything.

"The bath superintendent," Mama said, once the cocktails were in front of us.

"What about him?"

"Did you see how he looked at me?"

She opened the wine list, then closed it again.

"You pick out a bottle," she said.

"Maybe we should just order a glass?"

Cheerful Christmas music was playing in the background, but Christmas was still four weeks away.

"I made my parents' life a living hell," she said, sounding deeply content. "And then my father was beheaded by a branch."

I thought about Dancing Queen Andrea, about a pair of panties with bears on them. The absence of meaning is every bit as hard to comprehend as infinity. Then I suddenly thought of Miss Oertel, and especially of Miss Oertel's mother, particularly her arms.

"Have you already made a choice?" the man from Slovenia asked.

"Not yet," Mama said, and she stared out the window behind which there was nothing to see.

"Did it affect you deeply, when your father was killed?" I asked.

Mama whispered: "They don't have anything here."

"What do you mean?"

"The menu. There's nothing on it. It's all disgusting meat."

"They have salmon," I said, pointing to the right side of the menu with "Fish Platters" on it. Most of the fish platters had been crossed out, but not the salmon.

Then she said: "Yes, it was terrible, his accident. After that I was never allowed to go riding again."

20

Mama Was a Star

We didn't do much of anything, the first day at the ArabellaSheraton Alps Hotel. Mama slept until two, and by the time she was all dressed up it was time for dinner again.

That evening we were waited on by the Slovene again, who was even friendlier than the night before.

Mama told him: "I need more closet space."

The Slovene promised to take care of it. And indeed, that same evening we received access to a single room. It was vacant anyway. The management said it was no problem at all if Mama wanted to use the closets in that room as well. So we were taking up three rooms. I hoped it would remain at that.

The second day was the day of the bath superintendent.

"He's looking at me," she said.

"But Mama," I said, "everyone looks at you."

On the third day she wanted to go hiking.

We got up early. Mama plugged in the little radio she always took with her and listened to Bach, with intense pleasure. She couldn't decide which hiking shoes to wear. She had already tried on three pairs and taken them off again.

The day was clear but cold.

She put on some lipstick. After all, you never knew who you might run into in the mountains.

She had already bought all the hiking maps they had at the desk. And a panoramic map as well.

"I want to go to the Brecherspitz," she'd said.

"Why there?"

"It looks good," she said. "When I go hiking, I want to do some real hiking. We didn't come up here to the mountains just to laze around. If I'd wanted to stroll over hillsides, I might just as well have stayed in Vienna."

"We could also hike over to Schliersee, that's not as far. It's nicer to walk to a village than to a mountaintop, isn't it?"

Mama shook her head decisively. Today she wanted to go to the top, just as she had wanted to go to the top all her life. On the other hand though, she had once told us at dinner, after she'd hooked up with a famous French painter: "Fame to me doesn't have quite enough sex appeal."

I zipped up my shoes. Hiking boots were a bit too-too for me, I did my hiking in normal shoes.

"Your grandfather loved hiking too," Mama said.

"Shall we pack some food and water to take with us?" I suggested.

"No," Mama said, "we're not going to drag all that along, we'll find something along the way."

"I'm pretty sure there won't be a restaurant on top of the Brecherspitz," I said, but Mama refused to drag food along. Finally, all I could do was give in.

We left the hotel at 9 A.M. As we went out the door, the receptionist called out: "Have a nice walk."

Mama was wearing her red gloves and a knitted cap; the cap was red as well.

She was in much better shape than I'd expected.

Mama hiked as though she was training for the world championship racewalking, as though she was on her way to a lover she didn't want to keep waiting. I had never seen Mama hurry like that before, or maybe only on rare occasions when there was a lover she wasn't sure of yet. Most of her lovers she was sure of within half an hour.

We walked along the Spitzingsee to the Spitzingsattel. Mama kept asking to see the map.

"Where are we?" she asked.

Each time I pointed it out again. "God, this is taking a long time," she'd say then. "The bath superintendent told me there's a fantastic view from the Brecherspitz."

"Did the bath superintendent say that?" I asked.

If life is something that can be denied, then writing is definitely a denial, one of life's sneakiest and most subtle denials. But that, of course, is not why I stopped writing poetry, or why my book *The Dwarf and Other Poems* wasn't even destroyed, but simply got lost. Lost somewhere amid old newspapers and magazines that will probably never be read again, but which I'd decided to keep anyway.

I had arrived at the timely insight that I was mediocre. But, then again, what is timely? Professor Hirschfeld postulated that it was perhaps better to never become convinced of your own mediocrity, that it was better to go on living in the belief that a masterpiece was on its way.

Mediocre as a ballet dancer, mediocre as a poet, mediocre as a philosopher, absolutely inferior as a lover, and of course mediocre as a writer. That I decided to tell the story of my baldness did not spring from some secret hope that someone would detect in me a bit of talent or, God help me, of genius, it was not to rise up above my mediocrity, the way the Brecherspitz that day seemed to rise up from the Spitzingsee. It was because vanity proved stronger than everything I knew about my own shortcomings.

I entertain little hope, that is a promise I have made, for hope leads to pain and only prolongs suffering unnecessarily.

Professor Hirschfeld was wrong. You should not live as though a masterpiece is on its way.

Everyone has the right, at least once in his life, to file a complaint against himself. I have no intention of surrendering that right.

Long ago, in one of my poems, I was overconfident enough to write: "Oh you hypocritical lackeys, you who serve mediocrity in an abandoned palace."

Mr. Georgi read it and placed an exclamation mark beside that line. "An exclamation mark," he said, "means I like it."

An exclamation mark, ha! Beside a line like that! It's laughable. It's a scream. And that overconfidence stuck in my craw like a fishbone. I myself am a hypocritical lackey, and if I once thought that my king, my lord and master, was called *l'amour fou*, then I have since looked reality straight in the eye, in the bright, merciless light of an indoor swimming pool. I am a tutor, my lord and master is called the passing grade, I kneel before it in the dust, for it I run and hunt, for it I dab a little aftershave behind my ears.

It was already past noon by the time we reached the Untere Firstalm, at 4,324 feet. I was exhausted, but Mama was radiant, although she'd complained a few times about her fear of heights. "I can't look down, Marek," she'd said.

"Then don't," I said. "You were the one who wanted to go mountain climbing."

There weren't many other hikers, we saw a couple of people with dogs at first, but the further we got from the Spitzingsee the fewer people we saw, and after a certain point we saw no one at all.

"Shall we go back?" I suggested. "Untere Firstalm seems good enough to me."

"I want to go to the Brecherspitz," Mama said. "The bath superintendent says the view there is superb."

I was hungry and thirsty.

We drank ice-cold water from a mountain stream.

"Everything here is still pure," Mama said; what I noticed was how red the cold water made our hands.

One more time I said: "Let's go back to the hotel, Mama," but she just kept walking.

She was bound and determined to reach the Brecherspitz.

Ten minutes later we'd arrived at the Obere Firstalm, half an hour later at the Freudenreichsattel. "We're almost there," Mama said.

She leaned against a tree. She was panting a bit herself now.

"Your grandfather," she said, "was the stingiest man on earth. He gave the servants moldy cheese on their bread."

"Didn't you ever say anything about it?"

"I didn't know any better," she said, and off she went again, as if in one day she had to make up for all those days when she'd only lain in bed or sat in chairs.

"What about your mother?" I asked.

"She was even stingier. When your grandfather died, the servants didn't even get moldy cheese on their bread anymore."

"So you come from a very stingy family?"

"That's right," she said. "I suppose that's why I married a stingy man, but then that was a mistake."

Mama scampered up the mountain like a goat, and I trudged along behind her.

The path kept getting smaller. To the left was the mountain, to the right the valley, and somewhere far off in the distance you could hear a mountain stream.

"Why are you asking me all these questions?"

"Well," I said, "if we're here anyway, we might as well talk."

We couldn't walk beside each other anymore.

"You go up in front," she said.

I started worrying that we wouldn't make it back before dark.

"Aren't you hungry?" I asked.

"No," Mama said, "physically, I feel fine." But I saw how she had started sticking to the left of the path, and how she had started clutching at branches more often. The fact that we hadn't seen another hiker for the last three hours also seemed like a bad sign.

"Where are we?" Mama asked.

I stopped and pulled out the map for the umpteenth time.

"Here," I said, "somewhere around here, but I'm not exactly sure where. What time is it?"

Mama looked at her watch. "Almost two o'clock."

The path kept getting steeper, and the chasm to our right kept getting steeper too. Everything seemed to be getting steeper.

"If we go down on the other side of the Brecherspitz," I said, "we won't be too far from Schliersee. We can take a taxi back, or catch a bus."

"All right," Mama said.

At every bend I thought: now we'll see the summit, but all I saw was more of the same. Trees and a path that slowly wound upward. The sound of the stream grew quieter, until at a certain point it disappeared completely.

"Watch your step, Mama," I said. "It's slippery here."

I looked back. She smiled. I saw brownish-green spots on her gloves, from moss and from the branches she had grabbed.

It had grown cloudy. The clouds reminded me of snow.

"Quite a hike, isn't it?" I said, trying to sound cheerful, and I was reminded of my decision to walk around Vienna on my haunches, and of the dwarf I had never become.

We came to a sign. "Brecherspitz 500 yds."

"We're going to make it," I said. "Five hundred yards, that's nothing."

"Let's take a break," Mama said.

She took off her gloves and blew her nose.

"Not for too long," I said. "We have to be in Schliersee before dark, or at least at the main road."

"Sure," she said, as if I'd said something ridiculous. "The silence here is incredible."

"Yes," I said.

"Your father used to enjoy walking in the mountains too." She looked thoughtful.

"Marek," she said, "when I die."

"Don't, Mama. You're not going to die, the doctors all say that. You're not going to die."

I was talking louder, I could hear my own echo.

"Marek," she said, "when I die."

"Quit it," I shouted. "I don't want to hear about it. You're morbid, you've been brooding over dying for weeks, but I don't want to hear about it. Either die or don't, but stop talking about it all the time."

My echo was louder now. Like an echoing well.

She put her gloves back on. "Marek," she said. "I want you to promise me that you'll never try to find out who your father is."

Her voice didn't have an echo. She was speaking too softly, her voice was too delicate for an echo.

"What do you mean?" I asked.

"Nothing," she replied. "Just what I said. Let's go."

"What do you mean by that?" I asked, a little louder now.

"Marek," she said, "don't act like you've never suspected. Everyone knew it, it was all over Vienna, don't play dumb."

There were brownish-green spots on her red gloves. That will never come out, I thought. A crying sin.

"What do you mean, don't play dumb?" I shouted. "I've never played dumb. If anyone played dumb, it was you. You. Not me. Stop ruining my life."

Mama walked on.

I yanked on her coat. She turned around.

"I thought we were in a hurry," she said.

"What do you mean?" I screamed.

Never again have I heard an echo like that one, there at 500 yards beneath the summit of the Brecherspitz.

"It's getting dark," she said. "We have to go."

She tried to turn around, but I pulled on her coat again.

"Stop ruining my life," I shouted. "Stop it, once and for all, just stop it."

I had hold of her coat and I shook her. The cloth tore, and I kept shaking.

Professor Hirschfeld says I should delve deep into my memory.

I have delved deep into my memory. I have seen myself as an eight-year-old at ballet, I have seen Milena and Andrea, and old Mrs. Oertel staring at me as I announced my desire to purify the temples, I have seen Max and his mother. I have delved ever so deeply into my memory, and still Professor Hirschfeld wasn't satisfied.

If I were to draw a map of my memory, it would be the map of a city with a very clear center. That center is a big square, and all the little streets run into that square. That square is located five hundred yards from the summit of the Brecherspitz. A little more than six miles from the Austrian border.

The time has come to speak of details now, of the fuzzy area between slipping and pushing. Where does pushing end and slipping begin? But then again, the net result of slipping and pushing is the same: falling.

I should start with Mama's laughter.

Mama laughed. As loudly, as cheerfully, as exuberantly as I had rarely seen her laugh.

She repeated: "It was all over Vienna, everyone in Vienna talked about it. Don't act like you didn't know. I've told you about it so often, ever since you were little, I told you."

That was a lie. And Mama laughed. As though she had just heard a good joke, as though this was all something to laugh about.

Her laugh did have an echo, her laugh was not as delicate as her voice, and through that echo it seemed as though everyone was laughing, as if the mountains were laughing, and the clouds that looked like snow and the bare trees and the leaves on the ground, as though everything and everyone was laughing.

I couldn't laugh. At a crucial moment, five hundred yards from the Brecherspitz, my sense of humor deserted me.

I couldn't see the joke; it was there, but I couldn't see it.

Humor is apparently not universal by definition: what can give one person reason to laugh, is reason for another person to push.

Yes, that's how it was. Mama laughed and I pushed. Maybe I picked her up, like a ballet dancer, while Mama laughed, she laughed at everything and everyone. The God of Vengeance was splitting his sides.

My mama kept her distance from life and the living, only for one brief moment there, close to the Brecherspitz, she wasn't able to. Or was she still at a remove from life when she fell? Maybe she laughed because she knew what was coming, maybe she wanted me to push her, hoped that I would push her, but Professor Hirschfeld is having none of that.

The official version went by the name *slipped*.

I am the only living eyewitness, and my version says *pushed*. Laughed and pushed. With all the strength I had in me, I pushed her away. Because she laughed. At a moment when I myself could not laugh.

If we had turned back at the Untere Firstalm, if Mama had not laughed five hundred yards below the Brecherspitz, if I had not been so hungry, if I had laughed too, if she had told me about it before, or never, but above all: if she hadn't laughed.

And then?

Then I grew very calm, because I couldn't hear Mama's laughter anymore. Or screaming. Or yelling. It grew quiet all around me.

I looked down and saw nothing. Oh yes, the bare trees, the leaves, the bushes, I saw all of that.

Professor Hirschfeld wants to know what I was thinking, but I wasn't thinking anything.

I thought: I need to look at the map, and that's what I did.

After that I started running, insofar as you could run on that path.

First I ran the last five hundred yards to the top and then back down, I ran, I fell, and I ran. Without growing tired, without feeling any pain in my side, and without thinking. I ran.

All I was was a running body. Maybe I was actually happy, running down the Brecherspitz. I fell and ran on, I didn't even notice that I'd torn my pants, that I had cut myself. I noticed nothing. I ran.

Until I reached Neuhaus, a village close to Schliersee.

I ran through the streets of Neuhaus, it was growing dark. I waved my arms and shouted "Emergency!," the way I had once yelled that in Mr. Hobmeier's shop.

And I kept that up until people finally started listening to me. "Mama," I said, "she fell."

I wasn't completely crazy. I didn't say "Mama's been pushed, Mama was thrown." I said: "Mama fell." Whether we stick to the official version or the version of the eyewitness, the net result is the same: falling.

The rest of that day is a dream.

I had to point to where it had happened on the map.

I said: "Around here."

Everyone was nice to me, and admired me for staying so calm and being able to read the map so well. In my condition.

They took me to the foot of the mountain in a van. I had to wait there, with a policeman who said: "You two should never have gone to the Brecherspitz at this time of year. But let's just hope for the best."

Mama was a star, but one without a real profession. There weren't many people who saw her shine, and even fewer who knew that she regarded eliciting desire to be her profession.

That's a dangerous profession, more dangerous than singing opera or writing. But still, when I think about how Mama walked into Rolf Szlapka's flower shop, and how her presence alone could make men freeze, I wonder whether perhaps the world shouldn't have shown more appreciation for her art. An art that consisted of promises, half-truths, intrigues, a game that ended up again and again in the desire to be loved by my mama, and even more than that, in the desire to save her from the isolation and unhappiness that clung to her. She lived to elicit desire, the way other people live for their children or to become a millionaire, but that desire was as far as it was allowed to go.

It took them a little while to find Mama, they had to go on even after dark, and it took even longer before I saw her. But long before that, they had already let me know that Mama would never again laugh as raucously as she had done there, five hundred yards below the Brecherspitz.

They fed me some cognac, and a police van brought me back to the ArabellaSheraton Alps Hotel, where the staff had been informed of the situation. There I was given a sleeping pill, that's how nice everyone was to me. And on my pillow lay a pink marshmallow duckling.

I had pushed my mama into the abyss, and the ArabellaSheraton Alps Hotel had put a pink marshmallow duckling on my pillow.

Meaning, I challenge thee. Come down, give it your best shot, make your bid for immortality, one try is as good as the next.

The next day they asked me why Mama's coat was torn. I said that I had tried to catch her, but that she had slipped away from me, the coat slipped from between my cold, wet fingers. And that sounded so plausible, so probable, so very understandable, that no one asked me another question.

Later that same day my whole family came up from Vienna, including the maid.

Everyone felt sorry for me. I was the center of attention. Again and again I had to tell them how it had happened. How Mama had been bound and determined to go to the Brecherspitz, yes, they even asked the bath superintendent whether he had praised the view. "Yes," he said, "I did, but I also said that you should go in the summer, or in the spring."

And everyone in my family said: "Just like Mama."

Everything I said tallied with the facts, everything I said was true, there were only a few little measly details to which I gave a twist until I no longer knew that I was twisting them, until my version of reality had become reality itself.

My version was the version of the rest of the world. My intimate little lie became other people's truth.

Our family doctor in Vienna said: "No wonder he has nightmares, anyone would have nightmares who saw what he's seen."

21

The Story of My Baldness

This manuscript conceals itself behind the innocent little word "novel."

This manuscript will change nothing in the official version, primarily because changing that official version would serve no one's interests. It would benefit no one. Not my brothers, not Papa, and the authorities definitely have better things to do.

Those who read this will, at best, accuse me of having a wild imagination; at worst, of having a sick mind. Those who go looking for me will have to look under the "F" of fiction, and there different laws and rules apply, no official version exists there, at most only paper on which the author has penciled in a few changes in the margins.

How does it feel when your lie becomes the truth to the rest of the world, a truth that has even made the papers? It doesn't feel at all.

At first it feels uncomfortable, but that discomfort doesn't last long.

If my lie has become other people's truth, a truth they feel, see, hear, a truth that makes them weep, then what about what I saw, felt, and heard, and what was the status of my tears?

Discomfort is easier to dispose of than a tame field mouse.

My immortality now lies in the hands of Professor Hirschfeld and his study. Who could fail to see in that the hand of the God of Vengeance? The punishment for the untalented, the criminal dream research of Professor Hirschfeld. If he lived long enough, maybe he would collect the dreams of all the untalented people, only to arrive at the startling conclusion that all lack of talent is criminal.

Which brings me back to Mica and my baldness. At last. That was how this all started in the first place. But inessentials have a way of becoming essentials, and vice versa. Mica, who was kind enough to wait for me at The Four Roses cocktail lounge, even though I was more than an hour late, because I didn't dare to cancel my appointment with Max.

Mica who simply stared at me when we met, so that I had to wait for her to start talking and tell me what to do with that suitcase full of Mama's clothes. What could I tell her that she didn't already know?

During our third meeting, Mica played the accordion and drank vodka, although without her wig this time, and I was reminded of how Mama had fired her elegant little pistol at the chandelier and how Papa had said: "Keep eating, boys, don't look."

Mama's hands shook, the way mine do now, but her hands didn't shake when she shot at the chandelier. She was an elegant woman who enjoyed elegant weapons, and that evening I sat at her bedside. The curtains were closed. "Marek," she said, "those pills make you shoot weird."

"What pills?" I asked.

"The pills to keep your emotions under control. The only thing I notice is that I'm all shivery inside now. My kidneys shiver, my lungs shiver, my liver shivers, my uterus shivers, everything shivers. Is that noticeable, how everything shivers?"

"No," I said.

"Mica," I said, "what is it you want from me?" I recalled being asked something similar once, long ago, by a Dancing Queen from Luxembourg.

"I've been waiting for you for an hour," she said.

"I'm a tutor," I said, "I couldn't cancel my lesson."

"I don't want anything from you," she said, and she seemed to be choosing her words carefully. "I was curious, that's all."

"What am I supposed to do with the suitcase?"

She moistened her lips with her tongue. It wasn't a provocative gesture, apparently it was just something she did when she was thinking.

"Otto owns a dry cleaner, and he had some of your mother's clothes."

"He waited a long time to give them back."

"Otto is a sentimental fellow," Mica said.

The woman with flies in her ears was behind the bar, just like last time.

"What about you?" I asked.

"Not me," she said, "my sentiments don't bother me anymore."

"Just after the war," she told me, "Otto started a laundry in a cellar, and he went on to make a fortune in dry-cleaning. Can you imagine that, Marek? You didn't know him when he was eighteen, but it's a miracle he ever made it so far. When he arrived in Vienna, he could only speak two words of German."

"There's always a need for clean clothes," I said.

She told me all this as we sat in The Four Roses cocktail lounge, and I looked at her accordion and her face, and above all I listened to her. Her voice had something soothing about it, she had a voice that made you feel like falling asleep beside her, with your head in her lap. It didn't matter what she said, as long as she kept talking.

"Where did you meet Otto?" I asked.

"I'm his sister," she said. "We came here together from Odessa. I started the laundry with him, but at a certain point I sold my share. I was bored with dry-cleaning. That's when I started playing the accordion and drinking schnapps." She laughed, as though it was a great joke. A brilliant move. As though she'd outsmarted everyone by taking up the accordion and drinking schnapps.

"Any further questions?"

I shook my head.

I didn't want to know any more. I knew too much already.

A little later, Otto came in. Maybe he came in all the time, to see Mica perform.

He looked no different than he had the day before. A little man, hung with jewels, who walked with a stoop. He sat down beside Mica.

I was struck again by his brooch, a little airplane with diamonds at the tail.

"She's quite a woman," he said, when Mica went off to the ladies' room. "But it's a good thing she never had children, they wouldn't have survived."

The lady with flies in her ears brought Otto a drink.

"It came to me too late in life," he said, "my statues, the things I can do with clay. I think I'm in the midst of what they call a second career, or a third one, if you consider renting rooms a career." He laughed.

He took a piece of paper from his inside pocket. "Here," he said, "an invitation to the opening of my exhibition. Come have a look."

"Thanks," I said, and put the invitation in my pocket.

"Someone should write a book about Mica," he said. "But I can't write, I can only make statues. That woman is one of the seven wonders of the world. Good thing she never had children, though."

He choked on his drink and started coughing. Mica came back and asked: "Is he claiming that I'm one of the wonders of the world again?"

"And what about you?" I asked him. "Do you have children?"

He emptied his glass and smacked it down on the table.

He looked at Mica, but Mica was busy with her accordion.

Then he stood up.

"Come to my opening, there'll be music and drinks."

He laid his hand on my back for a moment, said something to Mica I didn't understand, and walked out of The Four Roses.

"A sentimental man," Mica said after he'd left. "But he doesn't like to show it. When he has to cry, he locks himself up in the toilet. He really wanted to see you, even if it was only once. He was curious."

I looked at Mica. "Does he make nice statues?" I asked.

She shrugged.

The word blood-tie doesn't necessarily mean anything either, no more and no less than a pink marshmallow duckling on your pillow at the ArabellaSheraton Alps Hotel.

You can change anything: your passport, the color of your hair, your clothes, your name, your religion, your job, even the color of your eyes. But how do you rid yourself of your memory?

"Two weeks from now, you'll be happy," Mica said, flagging down the lady with the flies.

Who doesn't want to be happy in two weeks? That's the reason why I didn't ask her "How can you be so sure?" Or: "Why two weeks?" Happiness, in my eyes, was a boa constrictor, but even I wanted to be choked for once by the boa constrictor of delight. Papa hadn't recognized the boa constrictor in time, that's why he thought it was Mama's beauty that plunged others into unhappiness.

The strange thing is that Mica was right. Although I only realized that once happiness had already long come and gone. Maybe Mama had been right too, maybe happiness really is incompatible with the present.

That night, when The Four Roses seemed about to close, Mica

took me home with her. She had a nice house, a leftover from the days of Viennese dry-cleaning. She was a little tipsy, or at least she fell against me every now and then, and she said: "Ask me more questions. I love your questions."

We talked about Otto and about Mama, and why it was that so many men had loved Mama, or thought they loved her. Mica thought that Mama's long suit had been her total lack of attention, and that people ultimately loved that inattention as well, that it was precisely that lack of attention that made her irresistible.

Mama couldn't break a promise, because she couldn't remember what she'd promised.

But those are theories, meant perhaps only to soothe old wounds, as theories are so often meant to do.

Later that night, as I stood in front of Mica in only my knee socks and underpants and realized the irony of standing half-naked before a woman with a stiff leg, a woman who had made her money in dry cleaning, it suddenly seemed better to tell her everything. I couldn't really start in about purifying the temples again.

"Mica," I said.

"Yes," she said.

"Before we go any further," I said, and I searched for the right words.

She drank vodka at home too. I suddenly remembered Mr. Georgi saying to me: "What grows between a woman's legs is a rose you must pluck." And he had looked earnest as he spoke those words. Mr. Georgi had a way of looking earnest.

Mica was sitting on the couch. In her nightie. She had asked me: "Do you mind if I go ahead and put on my nightie? It's easier to talk that way."

I took off my socks. That looked better. No socks.

"There was a woman," I said, "a young woman, a Dancing Queen. When I met her I had just started looking for *l'amour fou*, I thought that *l'amour fou* was the chief end of man, that it was the only thing really worth pursuing. Do you understand?"

Mica nodded. If you drink enough vodka you understand everything, but maybe she really did understand. "*L'amour fou*," she mumbled, "of course, what else is there?"

My blue knee socks were on the couch beside her.

"Where was I?" I asked.

"You were telling me about the Dancing Queen."

"The Dancing Queen. Yes," I said. "I thought she was *l'amour fou* incarnate, and maybe she was, but the point is: she drew my attention to a handicap I was not aware of before that time."

Mica's eyes grew bigger.

"A handicap?" she said. "Oh no, has it been. . . ?" And she made a clipping motion with her fingers.

"No," I said, "not that, it's fully functional. But the end result is, how shall I put it, the end result is minimal. Half a pinky."

"Half a pinky," Mica said. "Jesus Christ."

"Three-quarters of a pinky, when viewed charitably and with an open mind."

Then she started laughing. She was bent over double. "Three-quarters of a pinky," she giggled.

That was the reason why I had decided to go through life as a dwarf, I told her, because I had thought I was a dwarf who had ended up in the wrong body, and that I had walked on my haunches through the streets of Vienna in order to become the dwarf I was supposed to be.

Now Mica was laughing even harder. "That's rich," she said, "I'll have to tell Otto about this, he loves this kind of thing."

I told her everything, from beginning to end, even about my visit to Dr. Ahorn, and finally I stood naked before Mica.

She ran her fingers through my hair and said: "I have something for you. Homeopathic remedies. They're not cheap, but they work like a charm."

There, right there on the spot, Mica freed me of my past; Mica said I didn't have to be afraid of a lack of talent or half a pinky, and I believed her, because she made me happy.

Since then, that innocent little word "novel" has been glued to my past. It's no longer real, it's no longer mine alone; it's public, the way my mama once was, and every bit as inattentive.

Mica also freed me of my hair, although that was perhaps less of a deliverance.

The almighty God of Vengeance played his final hand.

The homeopathic remedies Mica had sold me for a considerable sum of money, which were intended to greatly increase the size of my machine, never made that machine grow a single millimeter. But that was not the problem. To be honest, I had long given up all hope of a bigger machine, just as I had given up hope of becoming a great poet. I had resigned myself to the inevitable: no *Büchnerpreis*, and a minimal dwarf's machine.

But, I figured, I'll try anything once, you never know. The same way I never gave up all hope of someday experiencing *l'amour fou* in my daily life.

Mica's medicines, however, had contraindications. Contraindications that were not mentioned on the box, or in the information leaflet. Mica swore afterwards that she had not known about those side effects, that she knew other men who had taken the same medicine and had grown like all get-out down below, without experiencing any side effects.

The remedies, which of course were not homeopathic, freed me of my hair.

First my scalp started itching. An itch that kept getting worse. Before long I was walking around in a blizzard of dandruff. I was forced to start wearing a hat.

I didn't see the connection with the pills I'd bought from Mica and was taking three times a day. I had just switched to a new shampoo, and I blamed it on the shampoo.

Then my hair began falling out. I immediately stopped taking the homeopathic remedies, but by then it was too late. The hair loss continued, and no other cures could help.

Laboratory study has shown that it was almost certainly Mica's tablets that wreaked such havoc on my scalp. The factory where the tablets were made has been closed down, and lawyers have assured me that there is no use filing for damages. "A waste of money, Mr. van der Jagt," they all say. "Believe me, a waste of money."

But what's a little baldness when one has known happiness? Even if that happiness was only brief, and I only recognized it once it was already gone.

It's like hair on your head: it's great when you have it, but when you don't there's always *Himbeergeist* and other schnapps.

The more I loved Mica, the more my hair deserted me.

Even if Mica's body was a ruin, which many said it was—Eleonore actually referred to her as a "bombed-out town"—then it was a ruin in which I could wander around for days, for weeks, a ruin I never wanted to leave, a ruin where I wished to be buried.

That is how I grew addicted to Mica, until I had nothing left.

My scalp, too, refused to stay with me any longer. It fell from my head in huge flakes. As though the boa constrictor of happiness wasn't content with simply strangling me, but was also devouring the lid off my brains.

Love is a war on many fronts, and one of those fronts was my scalp.

"Two weeks from now you'll be happy," Mica had said. How could I doubt her words?

22

No Encores

The Story of My Baldness could just as easily have been called *The Story of Wasted Talent* or *The Story of No Talent*. *The Story of My Mediocrity* would have been an option too, but then what was it Mama said again? When you're standing in a darkened corner of the room, you can't expect to draw a map of the city.

Of everything that is lacking, my hair is the least, and that is why that delightful word "baldness" seemed best to me.

That Mica finally brought *l'amour fou* into my life and took me closer to *l'amour fou* than I had ever dared to hope is not something I see as a reward for my efforts, or as a form of justice. *L'amour fou* was no Dancing Queen from Luxembourg, but an older woman who palmed homeopathic remedies off on me to enlarge the fish bone between my legs.

It is a mistake to think that happiness is the chief end of man. It is a somewhat less grave mistake to think that *l'amour fou* is the chief end of man. But the gravest mistake of all is to think that *l'amour fou* leads to happiness. And still, I hasten to add, that should not be seen as a renunciation of *l'amour fou*. Apparently there is a form of love that does not lead to happiness, that wants to have nothing to do with happiness, yet which is perhaps worthwhile nonetheless. I would not rule out that Mama renounced happiness because it scared her, or because she simply considered it a dreary business. Mama once said of a ballet dancer: "He dances like a raspberry pudding. What a catastrophe that no one sees that." Maybe that was what happiness meant to Mama: a dancer who danced like a raspberry pudding, a catastrophe, like a Sunday-afternoon barbecue, a trip to the mountains, a four-course meal served by the maid, and three successful children.

Of course I will never know what made Mama tick, but I suspect that for her happiness was accompanied by much more deception than beauty, and that that was what people really meant when they said that Mama's beauty plunged people into unhappiness.

The destruction she caused was not the product of evil or indifference. Only of a deep-rooted desire for something which I have called *l'amour fou*.

These are not excuses, I do not wish to excuse her, or myself. Professor Hirschfeld says: "Science has nothing to do with excuses; science makes reliable predictions."

One afternoon, six weeks after Mica first saw my machine, I went to visit Professor Hirschfeld. Just before I left, he told me he was giving up his quest for truth. From now on, he planned to sleep late in the morning.

Not long afterwards, I ran into him one evening close to the Westbahnhof. He was in the company of a woman who looked bad, even by Westbahnhof standards.

"Marek," he said, "what a surprise! How are you? Allow me to introduce you: this is Irina."

I shook her hand. It was sticky.

Professor Hirschfeld pulled a bar of chocolate from his inside pocket and broke it in two. "Please, have some," he said.

I didn't dare refuse.

We talked about the university, the ring binders with the glosses of famous philosophers, the students, but it was clear that he was more interested in the Westbahnhof itself.

"What are you doing down here?" I asked.

"This," he said, looking around, "is my dominion."

I was afraid to ask about his research.

"So what now?" I asked, like a schoolboy visiting his idol for the first time. "What are you going to do now? What do you expect?"

"From what?"

I hesitated.

"From life."

He looked around. Irina took Hirschfeld's hand, and they stood there like that, as though they were actually standing on a playground.

"That it goes on for awhile," he said, "and then stops. What about you?"

"Me too," I said. Then I turned and walked away.

"No encores," Professor Hirschfeld called out to me, "it's been wonderful, but please, no encores."

Not long after my last encounter with Professor Hirschfeld, I asked Papa whether he actually knew who my father was. Quite calmly, during dinner. Eleonore was on tour in Africa. There too, older women wanted to know how to get rich.

Papa had by then resigned himself to my bald pate, the way he had resigned himself earlier to the fact that I wanted to go through life on my haunches.

He looked at me, he looked at me for a long time, as though I had finally succeeded in surprising him. Or did he look at me that way because I had broken some unwritten law? I'm still not sure whether what he hissed at me then was "rotten kid," or "rotten yid."

Yet these are details.

Who knows, and who decides, where pushing stops and slipping begins? And who knows where the rotten kid stops and the rotten yid begins?

And what difference does it make, if the net result turns out the same?

Otherwise everything remains the same. And everything will always remain the same.

I am a tutor. Not Max's tutor anymore. A tutor to others. I am sought after. As a tutor, that is.

I have learned to live with my own absence. In actual practice, what it comes down to is that I say to myself: "Marek, two weeks from now you'll be happy." Then I start counting the days till those two weeks are over. And then I say to myself again: "Marek, two weeks from now you'll be happy, in two weeks the boa constrictor of happiness will be curled around your neck." This lends structure to my life.

I often think of Mama still, and of her attempts to avoid living, which is perhaps also a form of beauty.

Writers, writers who are writers by profession, know that they will be read. Even if it is only by a couple of people, even if only—should worst come to worst—by their own editor.

I could not and would not count on a readership. Not another *amour fou*. Yet still, I tried to imagine one reader; without being able to imagine a single reader, it becomes an awfully lonely business. At first I had thought of Mica, but she ditched me, perhaps the combination of baldness and half a pinky was a bit too much for her. Then I thought of Otto, but he had already heard most of the stories from Mica. Finally I thought of Professor Hirschfeld, and after that I thought only of Professor Hirschfeld. Maybe his quest for knowledge was also an *amour fou*, even if that quest finally ended up at the Westbahnhof.

Total absence may have won at last, the absence of Mama, of Mica, the absence of talent on my part, the absence of my hair; but if I could lay the pile of paper at Professor Hirschfeld's feet, whether he read it or not, then I could look up at the God of Vengeance and say: "So there!"

There is one more thing left for me to tell.

Max finally ate everything in the medicine cabinet. With my help.

The first fatality is a bit of a shock, but after that it gets easier.

At the funeral I was introduced to everyone as "Max's tutor," and Mrs. Blumenthal gave me a big hug, so big I thought she was never going to let go.

"The truth is," she said, "what I really feel like doing is jumping in after him. But who can guarantee me that there's life underground?"

I turned away.

If you haven't found anything to live for, you should at least find something to die for. But I will find it.

Before summer arrives, I will go back to Schliersee. On my own. To go hiking. I plan to take the train to Bayrischzell. Close to the station there is a pizzeria where they make very fine pizzas indeed. Bayrischzell is the end of the world; after that there is nothing, mountains and more mountains, and finally, Austria.